CORRUPTED BY A
BILLIONAIRE

LOVECHILDE SAGA BOOK 4

J. J. SOREL

AUTHOR'S NOTE: There are elements of self-harm, violence, and adult themes relating to the selling of sex, however, I don't go into graphic detail.

CHAPTER 1

Manon

THE GIRL LOOKED UNDER sixteen, and she wasn't the first, which played with my head. While I believed we had a right to decide what we did with our bodies, if I could relive my life at fifteen, I wouldn't have shacked up with Peyton. As far as I was concerned, I wasn't put on this earth to be a man's plaything, contrary to my dear mother trying to convince me otherwise.

With the benefit of hindsight, I wished I'd dropped my V-card on my terms and not my mother's. As I studied Sapphire, with those wide, innocent blue eyes switching from hope to fear with every blink, I felt like telling her to run away before her life became a tangle of poor decisions threatening to mess with her head and future. But she practically pleaded with me to allow her to auction.

"Do you have any proof of age?"

"I just turned sixteen. Promise." She licked her finger and held it in the air.

And I was meant to buy that cute gesture as proof?

I opened my hand. "ID." Though checking girls' ages wasn't required, I did anyhow. It wasn't just to protect myself should the police come calling, but because my conscience demanded to know.

She fumbled in her bag and passed me her card.

We were in the dressing room at My Cherry—my name for Ma Chérie.

It was early evening and my time to pep talk the nervous ones. Like convincing them that selling their virginity would buy them a head start in life, even though most didn't need convincing, as they had come to me via website inquiries.

With my grandmother's blessing, I operated from Merivale. She'd even suggested a sitting room at the back as my new office. As much as she hated the Cherry bar, I figured she liked that I had some kind of focus. And after all the shit that had gone down at the Pond after I fucked up, well okay, more like fucked the boss—not Uncle Ethan, of course, I'm not that twisted—I needed something to stay out of trouble.

Earning money also meant I didn't have to beg my mother for cash, which always descended into her raving about how I needed to step up my efforts to rope Rey into marrying me.

Mm, well, I had news for her. Like never.

Sapphire kept chewing her already destroyed nails. Another red flag. She was too nervous for this scene. And I was sick of having to convince unwilling girls. I'd done that in the beginning, mainly to keep Rey off my back.

When I'd reminded my mother that Rey wouldn't want me because of all the sex I'd already had, she'd said, "He doesn't need to know that. Just prick your finger to make sure there's blood on the sheet."

I had no intention of ever fucking Rey, but I'd gone along with it anyway to avoid listening to her rattle on about the advantages of being with a rich man. Been there, done that with Peyton. Designer jeans and dresses, nice dinners, and even a Hermes bag for my sixteenth birthday didn't bring me that much joy in the end because the bigger my tits grew, the more he couldn't keep it up.

In any case, I planned to make my own money and go for someone who made my skin tingle with just a glance, like Drake.

Sapphire was beautiful, and I could see her fetching a good price, but that thought made my stomach curl because she was way too sensitive. One needed to be tough to sell themselves to anyone.

Giving girls a kick start in life was the only positive about My Cherry, and at least most of the men were filthy rich and generally well-behaved. The aggressive ones were gotten rid of quick smart. Rey wasn't stupid. The last thing he needed was the law to come crashing down on his sleazy paradise.

"Are they all old?" Sapphire bit her lip.

I should have taken her to an ice cream parlor rather than a dressing room filled with lingerie.

"No. Some are even in their late twenties. Not many, though. There is one youngish guy who recently joined."

Her eyes sparked. "Really? Is he hot?"

I had to squeeze my lips to stymie a condescending smile because that could have been me once. And Peyton was hot. My mother chose well there. Most of the clients at My Cherry weren't, however. The good-looking ones were often cocky and even heavy-handed and got quickly tossed out.

"No. Most of the clients are just filthy rich men who like the idea of being your first."

Her long, lustrous golden hair fell over her face as she stared down at her turned-in feet.

"Look, Sapphire, maybe try something else."

"No. I need to do this."

I sighed. "Fine. Let me get you fitted."

Sapphire followed me into a room that smelt like a department store perfume counter.

Stroking the hanging lace and silky items, she looked amazed. "There's not much fabric, is there?"

"That's the idea." I selected a baby-blue corset and a lacy thong and held it against her. "This should fit."

Biting her lip again, she took the corset from my hand. "It's kind of tiny, isn't it?"

"What size feet?"

"I'm a six."

I found a pair of spiky heels, and from a drawer, I selected white fishnet stockings. "These will work." I handed them to her.

She fumbled about then froze.

"Why are you doing this?" I asked.

Biting her lip again, she played with her fingers. "I need the money."

"That's why everyone comes here, but is there a reason you need the money?"

"For my dad."

"Is he sick or something?"

"Kinda. He lost his job, and we're about to be kicked out of our flat." Her eyes glistened with the makings of tears.

Yep, life sucked.

"So, how do you know about this place?"

"A few girls from college knew of someone who did it. She got like half a million pounds for a week with a guy. He took her to Mallorca. She got a whole new wardrobe too. I think she might have even married him." She smiled as though she were talking about what happened when someone completed a college degree and not them having sex with someone old enough to be their grandfather.

"There aren't too many marriages from this. That's a rare experience here." I refused to gloss over the reality of what took place after the girls landed themselves a buyer.

At first, I had. Rey made me fill the girls with hype about how their lives would change for the better. I'd become more direct and even brutally honest. I'd taken a few too many calls from girls following their experience at My Cherry.

Some were even in therapy. That left a shit taste in my mouth. One had to be tough to do this kind of thing, and Sapphire was way too fragile for my liking.

"How much do you think I could make?" she asked.

Sapphire was skinny and didn't boast the curves some guys preferred, but then, they had all kinds of tastes. Some preferred flat chests. Those were borderline pedos, like Peyton, who got rid of me when my tits grew too large. That was why I'd become a stickler for proof of age. I would not stand by and let underage girls slip in on my watch.

There were also those vanloads of girls. Some couldn't speak English. I no longer saw those and even wondered if they were still happening on my nights off. I supposed I'd asked too many questions about the girls that looked underage.

"Bidding normally starts at around ten thousand pounds."

She knitted her fingers. "That would help, I guess."

"Have you kissed a boy or had one touch you?"

I had a sudden urge to protect her. My mother had recently accused me of becoming soft after I'd given a beggar money. She'd lectured me on how he only had himself to blame. I had tried telling her that maybe, through no fault of his own, he'd lost his way. She grumbled something about me becoming weak, and that people would take advantage of me.

Maybe she had a point because suddenly, I wanted to write a cheque and hand it over to Sapphire so she could live a normal life and help her dad.

"I've had a few boys kiss me. But..." She shrugged. "I'm not that interested in sex." She looked ashamed, as though it were only natural that girls were horny and ready to fuck whoever, whenever.

Until Drake, I hadn't felt like fucking anyone.

"How will you feel when an older man runs his hands all over you?"

At least honesty would avoid one big, shitty mess where she bolted out crying. I'd had a few of those, calling and telling me how horrible their experience had been or complaining that the man hadn't become their sugar daddy or even boyfriend. Whenever I caught a glimmer of doubt in their eyes, I just opened the back door and gestured for them to leave.

Rey didn't have to know that, of course. He still thought I was a virgin. What a laugh.

I no longer needed to have him close, thanks to my grandmother's generosity, even if my mother believed that once Grandmother Caroline learned about how bad I was, she would toss me out on my arse.

Wagging her finger, my mother loved to remind me how I would have to fend for myself because she wouldn't be there to dish out cash.

Thanks, Mum.

"Look, I'm sensing that this is too much for you. Why don't you come along tonight as my guest? Some girls watch from the sidelines and decide whether it's something they want to do."

"No. I want to do it. I have to. Maybe a few drinks. Maybe a drug?" She shrugged.

"A drug?" I frowned. "You don't do drugs, do you?"

"No. But I thought it might help me relax."

Some girls did that, and I turned a blind eye. What they did to their bodies was their business.

"I booked you for tonight's showing. Do you still want to go ahead?" I looked at my watch. It was seven.

"I'll do it." She gulped.

I handed her the lingerie. "Then put this on, and I'll take some photos and upload them on our members-only page. That way, clients get to see who's on."

"Do we have to dance or something?" she asked, sounding cute.

"Some of the more confident girls gyrate a bit. They get the best prices. But normally, you just walk around on the stage with other girls."

"Do I have to strip naked? Or open my legs?"

"Sometimes there's a bidding war between a couple of men, in which case, if the girl wants to, they can go into a private room, and yes, she opens her legs."

Her grimace wasn't lost on me.

"Why do I keep getting the feeling this isn't for you?" I reached into my handbag and pulled out a checkbook. "I can't give you ten thousand pounds, but I can give you a month's rent until your dad gets a job."

Her eyes widened in dismay as she shook her head. "No. I can't. That's so sweet of you, though. My dad won't be able to work. He's got some kind of illness. I need this to help us get through so I can continue my studies while working part-time."

"Where's your mother?" I asked.

"She left." Her lips trembled, and I couldn't stand it anymore.

I scribbled a cheque for two thousand pounds. I was about to become a millionaire. My twenty-first was only a month away.

She stared down at the cheque. "You would give me this? You don't even know me." A tear dropped on her smooth, pale cheek.

"Don't tell anyone. Now go away."

She stood and kept staring at me wide-eyed. "This won't do. I mean, can I still come and watch and decide then?"

I puffed. "Okay. But to be honest, I don't think you're right for this. If you haven't had a boy touch you, then how will you feel with an older man?"

"Maybe you can tell me what to expect?" She forced a smile.

"Have you ever watched porn?" Was I really having this conversation?

"No." She looked embarrassed, as though she were illiterate or had missed out on something as vital as basic education.

"Sit there and let me find something for you."

I opened my laptop, which was more the venue's official laptop. Something told me that Rey wouldn't be too worried about me showing porn to a prospective client.

He did make a twenty percent kickback on each auction and was raking it in, as was I from the two percent I got. Last month alone, I had banked fifty thousand pounds.

I found a guy fucking a girl from behind, knowing that most men liked that position and that Sapphire would have to get on all fours at some point should she decide to go down this jaded path.

Peyton had me sucking his dick and doing all kinds of acts within one week of us hooking up. But he had a small dick, so it wasn't so painful.

I studied Sapphire's face as the blonde girl on the screen screamed out while a guy with a massive cock rammed into her. His hands squashed her big tits.

Sapphire's eyebrows knitted as she looked on in horror. Or was that fascination? Porn didn't turn me on. The only thing that turned me on was the thought of Drake ramming his dick into me.

But he was off in his world of older women in tight gym wear.

I gazed down at my watch. I had an elocution lesson at eight.

"What do you think? Could that be you?"

"She looks like she's in a lot of pain. And he's so big down there."

I nearly laughed. "Well, they tend to use guys with big dicks in porn. Women love big dicks. Haven't you heard?"

"It looks painful. Where would it fit?"

"Have you masturbated?"

She shook her head.

I picked up the cheque. "Here. Take it. Please. Don't tell anyone about this. Okay?"

She nodded meekly and hugged me tightly. "This is so kind of you, and I will try to pay you back."

"Forget it. Now off you go. I'm busy."

CHAPTER 2

Drake

CARSON STEPPED OFF HIS motorbike, removed his helmet, and nodded at me. "How's it going?"

"Okay, I guess. I love your new wheels."

"Oh, she's smooth, all right." He ran his hand over the seat like he might a woman's curves.

I unlocked the door to Reboot and stepped away for him to enter. "How was France?"

"Fantastic. We traveled around the Mediterranean on a yacht. You got my postcard?"

I nodded. "Sure did. You look tanned and healthy."

"I feel great." He wore a rare smile. Carson had never been that kind of happy-go-lucky guy, but married life seemed to suit him.

He followed me into the kitchen, and I turned on the kettle. "Tea?"

He nodded, and I made tea before my client arrived. I always liked to get in early for a cup of tea and sit by the wall of windows to stare at the forest. It was a nice way to start the day. After living in a council estate for half of my life, the only nice view I got from our tiny balcony was the sky on the days when it wasn't choking on fumes. Other than that, it was nothing but concrete and crowds of people moving about.

"We'll have to go over the rosters, I guess." Carson took the cup from my hand. "I need to employ a couple more instructors. I might need your help in the office since you've been running this place in my absence. Do you mind having more to do? You'll get more money, of course."

"That sounds fine to me. Won't say no to more money." I chuckled. "I'm paying off my apartment and plan to get my mother something nicer."

"How's she doing?"

"She's okay. She has good and bad days, I guess."

He returned a sympathetic smile, then switching back to business, he asked, "You mentioned in your text someone's coming in this morning for the training job?"

I searched for a file on the desk. "Sorry, it's a bit of a mess. I was planning on cleaning before you arrived, but I had back-to-back training sessions yesterday."

"No worries, mate. What time's the interview?"

"In about fifteen minutes."

"Right." He nodded, then looking a little distracted, he crossed his fingers. "Look... um... thanks for covering for me with the cops."

I shrugged it off as though I lied to cops all the time. "That's okay. I just told them you were at mine watching Arsenal and Liverpool."

He returned a strained smile and a nod. "I'm sorry to put you on the spot like that."

"Hey, it's cool, mate. I don't mind. I get it. The guy was a fucking pig—after what he did to Savvie. Had it been someone I loved, I would've done the same thing."

"Mm..."

He didn't contradict me, which only fuelled my curiosity because, though it had been a straight-out overdose—not that shocking for a junkie—I wondered if Carson had anything to do with Bram's death. I kept that tight to my chest.

"A detective's still sniffing around. He spoke to me a couple of days ago. I told him the same story. Don't worry," I said, noticing Carson's frown.

"I'm sure you're wondering, so this is really what happened. I don't want you to think I had anything to do with his death. Savvie knows, as does my mother-in-law since she sent me there. Not that I needed fucking convincing." He pulled a half smile. "I was heading there, anyway."

The front door rang, and with piqued curiosity left hanging, I had to control the urge to roll my eyes. "That must be my interview. She's early."

I peeked through the glass door, and instead of the new instructor, I spied Kylie almost bouncing on the spot, giving off an intense and troubled vibe.

My shoulders tensed. She'd become a problem.

If only that drink she'd invited me to hadn't turned plural. One shouldn't blame booze for their actions, I knew, but if I'd been sober, I might have put professionalism before allowing a client to suck me off in her car.

"Shit."

Carson looked up from the desk. "Who is it?"

"It's Kylie. One of my clients. She's kinda stalking me." I brushed the hair away from my forehead. I needed to cut it off, but Manon kept on about how she loved the way it fell on my face.

Why am I thinking of her?

That kiss, stupid.

I shut the door and whispered, "I fucked up." Kylie could wait.

"Oh. You guys fucked?"

"More a blow job. She kinda lured me into her car."

Carson seemed to suppress a laugh. "You're rather popular with the girls. We have noticed."

"That's why I'm hiring female trainers. We need balance."

He nodded. "Totally agree. You better get out there and see what she wants."

I puffed out a breath. "Can't you tell her I'm not here?"

He chuckled. "I could, but I think your interview's arrived." He slanted his head towards the window as a young woman appeared. "She's pretty too." His eyebrow raised.

"They're all fucking pretty."

None compared to Manon, though.

Carson rose. "I'm sure there are lots of guys who'd love that problem. You better get out there. Don't worry, she's not about to eat you. She's not a tiger."

"No. More like a cougar." I left him there grinning.

Kylie stood by the mirror. Body obsessed, she had a thing for staring at herself. Whenever we trained, she checked her arse or lifted her tits.

"Hey, Kylie. I didn't know we had a session booked." I tried to sound casual.

She ran her hands down her blonde hair, smoothing it, something she did regularly.

"You haven't returned my calls." Kylie didn't do no. Like the world owed her or something. Or was that a quirk of the rich?

"I'm sorry, I've been busy."

She adjusted her shoulders. Something she did when she was about to pounce.

I didn't want to be with her. If anything, in the morning's light, and stone-cold sober, I didn't find Kylie's manicured looks attractive.

Manon overdid the makeup, but at least her lips hadn't gone all duck-like and her tits were real—from what I could see in those tiny tops she favored that always made me forget my name.

A young blonde girl stood awkwardly at the door. I welcomed the interruption because I didn't know what else to say. Small talk had never been my forte.

"You must be here for the job."

Kylie looked the girl up and down. "You're hiring?"

"We need instructors. And I believe Terese runs Pilates classes too." Terese nodded.

"Oh. I already have a class I go to. I like the personal training myself."

Kylie gave me a flirty smile, and I cringed, hoping Terese hadn't noticed.

I turned to Terese. "Can you give me a minute? Perhaps have a look around, and I'll be there in five."

She nodded and smiled. "Of course. Thanks."

Once Kylie and I were outside, I scratched my neck, heating into a rash, something that happened whenever I felt uncomfortable. "About the other night..."

Kylie looked over my shoulder, and I turned to find Manon, who looked at me, then at Kylie, suspicion written all over her pretty face like she'd found us naked.

"Oh, is this a private moment?" Manon asked.

I opened my mouth to respond with a resounding "no" when Kylie answered, "Yes, it is." She eyeballed Manon, and the woman who had hijacked my sanity looked at me with a "how could you?" glower, then off she went.

I just froze like an idiot.

How could I allow this misunderstanding to escalate? I hadn't exactly done anything. Had I?

CHAPTER 3

Manon

THERE I WAS, ABOUT to invite Drake to the birthday party my grandmother had offered to throw for me, and I found him lost in a deep and meaningful with Fake Tits. I stomped off instead.

I tended to overreact. Always had. Some days, my blood boiled over the smallest things. But this wasn't trivial. This was Drake. The guy I'd been wanting to fuck forever. At least, from the moment I'd caught him shirtless, shoveling dirt.

Squeezing my mouth tight to block a scream, I shook my head.

What does he see in older women?

Was it because they were more experienced? Did those cocksucker-pumped lips give great blow jobs?

Or did Drake need the woman to do all the seducing?

I was the one who had pushed him against the tree for that kiss. Wasn't that me taking the lead?

He nearly ate my mouth. What a kiss. Passionate. I'd never had someone kiss me like that before.

I hadn't exactly had a lot of experience. After Peyton, I'd stayed away from men. My body was a commodity, as my dear mother reminded me. I wouldn't allow myself to go all silly over a boy or a man, not like some girls I grew up with. I would use it to get the richest man I could find.

A good-looking one like Peyton. Then I met Rey. And well, he was richer than Peyton but creeped me out big time. So, I got him girls instead.

The feeling of Drake's lips on mine had become my go-to daydream, and how he'd made my body burn for his hands. I'd even had to finger myself later that night to extinguish my relentless ache. Peyton had taught me all about my pleasure button—his cute term for my clit. But I hadn't been into playing with myself. Until that.

Damn Drake. Why did he have to be so hot?

Unable to resist, I took another look. Her hand moved up his arm, all the way to where that snake tattoo wrapped around his bulging muscle.

My heart sank.

Was it Drake who wanted her? Or vice versa?

She gave off an aggressive vibe. Drake looked like he was trying to get away. Or was that guilt over me finding them?

Wearing a blue T-shirt with the Reboot logo and jeans that showed off his long, muscular legs, Drake looked even hotter than the last time I'd seen him. I loved how his hair had grown longer and the way it fell over his face.

My unrelenting crush had to stop. Drake wasn't interested.

Then why kiss me like that?

He'd practically dry-humped me. Or was that how he treated all girls, including that overly made-up woman? I mean, who wears that much makeup in the morning? The trick to good makeup during the day was to make it look like one wasn't wearing any.

I'd made a career out of that skill.

My morning had started with a real buzz, and Drake was the first person I'd wanted to invite to my first-ever birthday party. Mummy didn't believe in them. She didn't believe in much. Only money, shopping, and rich-guy hunting.

Other than Sapphire, who'd become a friend of sorts, Drake was the only person I'd thought to invite. After all, we'd connected. I knew it was just a kiss, but he'd touched my bum... well, more squeezed it.

I couldn't stop thinking about how he'd pressed himself against me. I even felt sticky and swollen. That didn't happen from a kiss normally. I would have let him fuck me, but he'd pulled away, telling me it was unprofessional of him.

Unprofessional?

What a shit-poor excuse.

Maybe he just didn't like me. But then what was that big fat boner poking into my tummy as he pinned me against the tree?

So, if it was too unprofessional for us to get all hot and steamy, why was that client about to shove her tongue in his mouth and the rest? They weren't exactly doing chin-ups. Or did she perform her stretches in bed with him?

Enough already. He can go fuck himself and his faked-up cougars.

I had nothing to whine about. I was about to be rich. Living the high life with a credit card, which meant I no longer needed to steal.

As I headed back to Merivale, I ran into my grandmother and Cary, with Bertie trotting along at their feet.

In all the time I'd been there, I'd never seen my grandmother in anything but Louboutins, so I stared down in surprise at her ankle-strapped wedges. Her style was effortless, though, in pink fitted ankle-length slacks and a floral linen shirt.

Unlike my mother, who had to work hard to make herself look anything but gutter in designer. But I guessed it was true what they said: 'You can take the girl out of the gutter, but you can't take the gutter out of the girl.' That would never be me. Even if it involved a brain transplant, I would never become my mother.

"Pleasant morning for a walk," I said, trying to sound chipper.

With her arm linked to Cary's, my grandmother was in love, and that brought a smile to my face.

That was me in the future.

It went a little deeper than just her being my role model, however. I loved my grandmother. At first, it was gratitude for accepting me despite my crappy behavior, but then, warm feelings kept growing as if she were that mother I wished I'd had.

I still couldn't believe she'd forgiven me for hocking her ruby neck-lace—a necklace that Will had stolen as a gift to my mother and that I then stole from my mother. A guilt-free transaction until my under-standing grandmother had told me to keep the money. Something had changed in me that day because I'd expected a slap, not a kiss.

Will was at fault. I think my grandmother understood that. He was the bad one, along with my mother, who'd plotted to steal from Harry Lovechilde. I'd heard them scheming. It had been her idea, even though he was rotting in jail.

On top of everything, Grandmother then invited me into her home, to live there like family. I couldn't believe it. Even after Savvie complained about me stealing her clothes—which were hard to resist since my aunt had style dripping off her—Grandmother had turned a blind eye.

She looked at Cary. "Manon turns twenty-one in a few weeks, and I suggested a party at Merivale."

Cary's eyebrows rose. What was he expecting? Me to invite a bunch of party animals from London?

He had nothing to worry about there. When it came to friends, I hardly knew anyone. I'd always kept to myself.

Sapphire kept calling. I even offered to meet in London for a spot of shopping and ice cream. I couldn't exactly suggest the Fox and Hound, seeing as she was only sixteen. Besides, I wasn't much of a drinker. One glass of champagne, and I talked shit.

Sapphire kept thanking me and wanted me to know how her dad was doing and that she'd enrolled in a course. It felt good to help. A strange experience because I'd never actually given money away.

I bent down to pat Bertie, who licked my hand. He sometimes slept at the end of my bed when I put him there on those nights when the wind made all the doors creak.

"I'm free this afternoon if you want me to read your essay," Grand-mother said, talking about the online course I'd enrolled in to develop my vocabulary.

I shifted on the spot. I didn't want anyone else to know about my study just in case I failed to complete it or flunked the exams. At least,

I'd gotten my beautician degree, but that had been dead easy. I loved makeup. I'd since discovered I didn't mind reading, either, despite being challenged by big words.

She turned to Cary, who looked puzzled for some reason. "Manon's enrolled in grade-twelve English."

His face brightened like I'd single-handedly rescued a whale. "But that's marvelous news."

My grandmother wore that proud, motivating smile that drove me to do better than become that big-tits-and-tight-vagina girl my mother claimed to be my only useful purpose.

"Did you choose the book?" she asked.

I'd never been much of a reader, and suddenly, I was having to read books with long words. The Harry Potter books were the only ones I'd read. After discovering one lying around at school, I devoured it. Couldn't put it down, and even thought of myself as Hermione there for a while, a welcomed escape from all the sleaze at home.

"Um... I'm finding it hard to make a start, to be honest." I shifted from leg to leg. I hated admitting that I couldn't focus, mainly because of working late four nights a week for Rey and all the daily admin involved with interviewing the girls.

"What have you read?" Cary asked.

He was a writer, so I suppose his curiosity made sense.

"I read Tess of the d'Urbervilles."

"Oh, Hardy. Great story. Influential writer." He spoke like they were best friends or something.

"I liked it." I hoped he wouldn't ask me to go into great detail. My grandmother almost wrote my essay on it. "It was a bit difficult to understand in parts."

"She had a difficult time with the vernacular," my grandmother added in a gentle tone.

Cary gave an understanding nod. "Dialogue in those nineteenth-century stories can be rather challenging to navigate. Dickens, Hardy's younger contemporary, also had an endless cast of characters speaking in their local tongue."

"I think I prefer happy endings. I hated what happened to her."

Cary wore a sympathetic smile. "Quite. Back then, books were not intended to evoke comfort for the reader but to shed light on human struggles."

"She was raped," I said.

"Tragic. I know." His mouth twitched into a sad smile. "I can think of several books from the eighteenth and nineteenth centuries that portray the difficult plight of women—Clarissa, Madame Bovary, Anna Karenina. Just a few that come to mind."

"I've seen those on my reading list, but I'd like something that leaves me with a smile when I finish."

"Then you'll have to read Jane Eyre. That ends well. Or Pride and Prejudice. Not Wuthering Heights though."

"Oh, I don't know," my grandmother said. "Heathcliff ends up with Cathy in the end. Their spirits meet on the moors."

Instead of falling into a literature rabbit hole, I wanted to talk about my party, but it was nice to have them show an interest in me.

"Manon did well with an essay on a Shakespeare monologue."

"Oh." Cary's face lit up. That was his world, after all, in the same way as eyeshadow and clothes were mine.

"She scored a distinction for Juliet's famous soliloquy."

"Really? Which one?"

She looked at me, and I bit my lip.

"As I recall, it was act three," she said.

Cary was clearly enjoying himself. "Gallop apace, you fiery-footed steeds..."

He even recited it with a girlish voice, and I had to giggle. "That's the one. Wow. I'm impressed. Do you know it all?"

He nodded. "I played Mercutio back at college, during my fifteen seconds of fame treading the boards."

"Mercutio's part goes longer than that," my grandmother said before turning her attention back to me. "Did you start on Virginia Woolf?"

"I've started on Lady Chatterley's Lover."

"Oh, that ends well." Cary looked chuffed like it was him having to read the book.

Still, it motivated me to sit by the duck pond with the musty, yellowing-paged copy I'd found at Merivale's library.

"I like a plot."

He nodded, holding his chin. "Then try Somerset Maugham. He's a giant. Of Human Bondage. A splendid book."

"It's not BDSM, is it? I liked Fifty Shades but not the whipping parts." I'd only ever seen the movie, but I wasn't about to admit that.

He looked at my grandmother and smiled. "Nothing like it. And now that I think about it, that book's rather depressing. But a brilliant, life-changing read for me, at least."

On that bookish note, I left them, thinking that if I wanted to develop my brain, Merivale was the place to be.

A text arrived from Drake. "Hey, nothing was going on there. Did you want to see me about something?"

"Maybe." I kept it short and sweet. I wanted him to come after me for a change.

CHAPTER 4

Drake

TERESE SEEMED A PERFECT fit for Reboot, and at least she would be my excuse for leaving as soon as more instructors signed up. I preferred working outside and had my sights on the organic farm. Declan had already offered me work there, but with the personal training and after-hours security work, I didn't have the time.

Tired of being a personal trainer, I'd become drained by people's unrealistic expectations. The men wanted instant results, while some women had distorted views about their bodies. One needed to be a psychologist or therapist rather than a body coach.

Lost in my head, wondering what Manon might have wanted earlier, I almost jumped when Kylie cornered me.

"Oh, you're still here." That shouldn't have come as a surprise. Kylie didn't do "no."

She ran her tongue over her lips, and her eyes softened. Yes, she gave great head, but I should never have gone there. It was one huge fucking mistake.

Blame it on beer and an overactive male gland that had become even more active thanks to Manon. It didn't take much around her for my heart to race like I'd run a marathon.

Manon's tits pressed against me and her soft lips on mine kept replaying in my head after the best kiss I'd ever had.

"Where are you off to now?" Kylie asked.

"I'm about to go for a run." To make a point, I kept walking towards the forest, which was probably a bad idea with Kylie following along.

The thin fabric of her top clung to her nipples. Not that I was looking, but with those ballooning breasts, I found it difficult not to notice.

I had to say something. "Um... about the other night."

"You liked it, didn't you?" She smiled.

I gritted my teeth, and before I could respond, she pushed me against a tree and rubbed my dick while running her tongue over her lips.

"Oh, that feels nice. You're a very big boy. Wouldn't you like me creaming all over that fat cock of yours?"

She kept squeezing my dick, and it went hard. I tried thinking of something else, like the fact that I had to drive to London to visit my mum.

I pulled away. When she started playing with her tits, I knew I needed to get away fast before she lifted her top. I was too late, because the next minute, like swollen balloons, her tits sprung out, and she jiggled them. I almost started laughing. The whole situation was ridiculous but also dangerously public. People often walked that path.

I heard heavy panting at my feet and looked down. Bertie, Merivale's corgi, wagged his tail, looking happy to see me while licking my trainers. From a distance, Caroline and her boyfriend approached arm in arm.

"You better go. Please. I can't be caught like this."

I bent down to pat Bertie. "Thanks for the shoe clean." He always did that. Must have been that bone I gave him.

Kylie clucked her tongue and rolled her eyes. "Tonight. At mine?"

I shook my head. "That was just once. I'm not really..."

I looked over her shoulder, and she'd just covered up when Caroline and Cary spotted us.

I waved at them, and they looked at Kylie, who gave them one of her sexy smiles. I wanted to die on the spot.

"Nice day for a walk," I said.

"You saved me a call." Caroline gave Kylie a passing glance before returning her attention to me. "There's a party in three weeks for

Manon's twenty-first. Do you think you could do some security work for us?"

"Of course." I smiled.

"Good. I'll send the details." She called out to Bertie, who'd scampered off into the scrub.

I waved them off and turned to Kylie. "I've got to go."

"What about your run? I can think of something nicer to get your heart pumping."

"No." My voice had that edge.

My head filled with thoughts of the party, wondering if I would have received an invitation. I would have preferred to be a guest rather than work, but Caroline had asked, and the money would come in handy. I planned to pay off my apartment as soon as possible.

Kylie followed me back to Reboot, and I stopped walking. "Look, it was just once. Okay? Now, I've got to work."

Her mouth turned down. "But you were so into me the other night."

I took a deep breath. "I'm not looking for anything right now."

She inclined her head. "We can just do casuals."

"No." My shoulders tensed. It was getting ridiculous. "Now, please go."

"Oh... it's like that, is it? Then I'll make a complaint about how you touched me during my press-ups."

"That's bullshit, and you know it." I turned away.

"Oh, you're so hot when you're angry." She smiled.

I puffed. "I'm sorry if I gave you the wrong idea the other night. As I said, I'm not looking for anything. Okay?"

She seemed on the verge of tears, which made me regret my harsh tone.

"We'll catch up soon, okay?" I gave her a small smile. "For a training session, I mean."

"Mm... maybe. You took advantage of me, though." She turned away abruptly and walked off.

I stood there shaking my head, hoping it wouldn't come back to haunt me.

I needed to tell Carson about what had just happened with Kylie, if only to get some advice, should her threats become a reality. As I entered the gym, I found Carson and Savvie cuddling and kissing.

They saw me and stopped.

"Sorry." I lifted my palms.

Savvie looked like she'd been crying, despite her bright smile. That confused me. Carson also had tears in his eyes. I felt like a first-class prat for arriving at some kind of special moment.

"I should leave you to it."

"No. It's okay. My beautiful wife was about to go."

She slanted her face and smiled sweetly.

They made the perfect poster couple for a happy marriage, and I thought that if ever I married, I hoped that would be me.

Savvie turned to Carson. "You can tell him."

"We just found out that Savvie's pregnant."

I hugged Savvie, then Carson. "That's great news. I'm so happy for you both."

Carson kept shaking his head and staring at his wife like a miracle had happened.

Despite needing Carson's advice about Kylie, I didn't want to crash their moment of bliss and pretended I'd left something behind instead.

I exited Reboot, weighed down with anxiety.

Was Kylie about to stir trouble?

CHAPTER 5

Manon

THERE WERE NERVOUS GIGGLES everywhere and girls talking over each other. I'd turned into everyone's big sister by helping with makeup.

Summer looked all doe-eyed at me as I added a little more lipstick to her plump lips. She would do well. Four men had already made a bid on her.

Watching me in the mirror, she wore a grateful smile. "You're great at this."

"Thanks." I tousled her blonde hair a little more.

She went to smooth it down. "I like it straight."

"Trust me, you'll get more if you look like you've just gotten out of bed."

Her strained giggle revealed her anxiety. Something I'd become alarmingly accustomed to while working at Cherry, which affected me too. My mother's tough outlook had not quite set in, despite my best efforts because becoming detached from situations or people would have helped.

Putting aside the participants' nervous anticipation, which was present pretty much every night at My Cherry, it had been an easy night so far. No drama. No pep talks. And after making sure the girls looked the part in their sexy lingerie, we were ready to start.

Darkly lit with lamps at each table, the purple room had an arty touch with tasteful black-and-white images of nudes on the walls.

Rey sat at the bar, chatting with one of the clients, who I hadn't seen before. The waiting list was long. They came from everywhere.

Apart from filling Rey's already-overflowing pockets, My Cherry also fulfilled his appetite for the young and untouched. He always bought a girl. One a week. The man was insatiable.

I'd asked him why he didn't just get a girlfriend. He pulled a face like I'd suggested he get a mohawk or something just as ridiculous.

"I don't do attachment. It's all about sexual pleasure. Speaking of which..."

I rolled my eyes. "Photos are the best you'll get from me, Rey. And I'm not ready yet."

That was me bullshitting again. I just needed those five million pounds in my bank account, then I could walk away from all the sleaze. My birthday couldn't come quickly enough because, at last, I could be independent and make choices unrelated to capitalizing on my so-called physical assets.

Rey knew so little about me. He still thought I was pure. What a laugh. My mother kept telling me to keep him close so that he'd marry me, but Rey wouldn't marry.

If I gave myself to him, I would be a million pounds richer, but I would face being booted out of Merivale. My grandmother had made it clear that if I went with Rey, she would turn her back on me.

Even without the money, I still would have chosen my grandmother over Rey. I enjoyed being there, and as a bonus, I could now have the best of both worlds: an apartment in London and a room at Merivale.

"Is she here?" Rey asked after the girl I'd lined up for him.

"Natalia's keen on being auctioned. She's got her eye on the big prize. And something tells me that ten thousand won't cut it."

"If she's worth it, I'll bid. Can you arrange a private meeting?" His eyebrow flew up.

We knew what that meant. I'd watched. Couldn't help myself. I was too curious for my own good. The girl would be taken to a private room where she would strip naked and open her legs wide. I swore I could hear the men grunt, and the room had this thick, musky stench, which I suppose was the smell of lust.

"I'll have a word with her now if you like."

He nodded. "Before the doors open. I don't want anyone else having her."

"She thinks she's here for an auction. As I said, she wants the lot. A holiday. A big deposit. A credit card."

"Is that an assumption?"

"She told me when she applied. I sent you the details."

"Yes." His blue eyes had a hungry, must-have glint, as though he were about to gorge himself on something.

"I'll send her to the private room, then?"

He nodded.

I returned to the dressing room where Natalia was clipping on her stockings and running her hands up her long, toned legs.

After I explained Rey's offer, Natalia just crossed her arms. "I want more than one thousand pounds to show myself to anyone. I get more than that on OnlyFans."

I knew what she meant. I'd already done that. Took it down. Couldn't stand the idea of being wanked over by a bunch of desperados, even if the money was good. I'd never stooped to show images of me with opened legs, however. Way too personal.

Back when I was fifteen, my mother had accused me of being a prude for refusing to strip for a man she'd brought home hoping to sell me. Just as I was about to run away, she introduced me to Peyton, who hadn't expected me to open my legs for a gawk. Instead, he'd taken me to dinner at a fancy restaurant, filled me with wine, then fucked me raw.

"He will want to see all of me?" she asked.

"You'll have to strip naked."

"Will I get to go to Paris or somewhere nice?"

With those big tits and pretty face, she could name her price, I imagined. And didn't she know it. She was a tiger, and Rey liked the chase. For a twenty-year-old, she seemed mature, making me question whether she was even a virgin.

"You can discuss that with him."

"But I need to know how much."

"That's why he would like to see you and discuss it directly with you. Yes?"

"Do I at least get a deposit just in case?"

I smiled. "That's the one thousand pounds you get to come here."

"Mm... what's he like, then?" Natalia had a heavy accent.

"Are you legal?"

"I'm from Serbia, and I'm here on a visa."

"He's filthy rich."

"The marrying kind?" Her eyebrow rose.

I shook my head. "Few of them are. But hey, they'll set you up, and you can marry someone you're into."

Her mouth turned down. "Fuck that. My mother married for love, and my dad ended up being an arsehole."

I had to smile sadly at that. Heard that story one time too many. I thought of my real dad. He was an arsehole, too, but I still thought about him a bit too often for comfort. My mother wasn't exactly doting-wife material, so I imagined she'd made him that way. Maybe that was why he hit me.

The private viewing room came with a bed, a velvet sofa, and moody lighting. I gestured for Natalia to enter.

"You are coming too? I won't go there alone."

Imagining that Rey wouldn't be pleased by my presence, I followed her in.

Wearing a silk robe covering her nearly naked body, Natalia's only other coverings were a thong and a tiny bra. Her round, firm arse poked out, and her double-D tits were all hers. She must have been raking it in with OnlyFans, I could only guess. It begged the question of why she needed an old man's dick inside of her for cash.

She could have gotten someone younger, hotter, and rich just from hanging at the right bars. I wasn't about to give her that information. I didn't like her attitude. She struck me as arrogant. Perfect for Rey.

He stepped into the room and gestured for me to leave them.

"No. She stays," Natalia demanded.

"That's not how this normally works." A smile twitched on his thin lips.

"Then I auction like other girls." Her heavy, slightly husky accent made her sexier.

Rey looked at me, and I shrugged. He pointed for me to sit in the corner, away from the bed. Fine by me. I wasn't into the whole gynecological thing myself.

"Remove the robe," he said.

Natalia let it drop to the ground.

His eyes ran up and down her slender, curvy body. "You've never fucked?"

She shook her head.

"That comes as a surprise."

I had to agree there.

"I've been saving myself." Natalia put on a softer voice.

They all say that.

"What were you hoping for?"

"I want a residency and a rich husband."

I had to squeeze my lips together.

"The first I can probably arrange. The second, well, I don't doubt you can find one, but it won't be me."

She tilted her head. "Pity. I rather like you."

I wanted to vomit. Talk about peppering him up.

"I'm not the marrying kind, Natalia. But you're a stunner. And if I'm to give you your price, I need a sample."

I squirmed. I did not need to see that.

She ran her tongue over her lips. "I am happy to suck your dick. But for a price."

"Um, can I go now?" Watching a blow job wasn't my idea of fun.

"No. Stay." Her tone had that cold, hard edge to it.

"How much do you want for her to go?"

"Mm... fifty thousand." She held up her finger. "But you just get a look and maybe a little touching. No fucking. Yet."

Rey had his back to me, so I couldn't see his face, but I got the feeling that the girl had him in knots.

Fifty thousand was a night at the casino for him. I'd seen him sink that much at Salon Soir, which struck me as odd since he was the owner. But he told me afterward that he was a sucker for a good poker game.

"All right." He fluttered his hand for me to leave.

Happy to comply, I scurried off and made sure the other five girls were ready to be paraded before a bunch of horny men.

CHAPTER 6

Drake

My mother stroked my face. "Every time I see you, you're even more handsome. You must have the girls going crazy."

Crazy's right. Only the wrong girl.

I loaded groceries into the cupboard and fridge. It was my weekly visit to my mother's council flat in Lewisham. We'd moved there when I was ten, after my mother, unable to work, could no longer afford the mortgage payments for our Brixton home, where I was born and which had come with a backyard.

Now that I was earning a good wage, I paid for my mother's food and bills. She struggled on her disability pension, and an apartment for her in Bridesmere sat at the top of my wish list.

"You've put on more weight too." She looked pleased.

That was how weird life was: my mother wanted me chubby while the rest of the world preached how being buff and lean would win us a healthy, happy life. Though pumping iron and running made me feel less anxious and healthier, I didn't care how I looked. Especially after witnessing how body-obsessed people wasted so much time staring at themselves in the mirror, craving perfection.

I made us a cup of tea and sat down in front of the television. My mother could move around on good days, but on bad days, which she associated with the weather, was riddled with pain.

"Thanks, love." She picked up her cup and took a sip. "So, have you asked out that girl you like?"

I shook my head. "I don't know. She seems like trouble to me."

"She's young. They're all trouble at that age, darling. If you like her, though, you should at least get to know her."

Wise words. Perhaps I was being too presumptuous about Manon. If only she didn't work at that sleaze bar, and I wondered about her relationship with Crisp. I'd seen how she flirted with him at that Merivale party.

The thought that she might have slept with him sickened me, despite my having no claim on her, but Manon had gotten under my skin. And that kiss. Whoo. I hadn't gotten that out of my body and head yet. Maybe I never would. I'd never nearly come from snogging before. But then, I'd never squeezed an arse like Manon's before. I needed a cold shower just thinking about her rubbing her tits against me and how soft her lips felt, and I could swear I still smelled her floral perfume.

"Do you want me to order pizza?" I turned on my phone to make a call when a crapload of messages from Kylie rolled down my screen.

Shit.

"Are you sure you can't stay for dinner at least?" she asked.

Tugging at my heart and protective urges, her eyes shone with a hint of need, though she would have been the first to deny it. My mother hated being a burden to anyone. She was far from that to me. That was why I wanted to move her closer to where I worked, so I could drop in more frequently.

I even suggested her meeting someone, but my mother scrunched her nose at that idea, reminding me that my father was the love of her life and that she had his memory to keep her warm at night.

That warmed my heart because etched in my memory was an honest, kind, and loving father who liked to kick the ball around with me, took me to games, and hugged me a lot.

I still remembered with frightening detail how everything had spiraled out of control the moment that call had arrived. I was at my grandmother's house, where I'd often stayed whenever my parents went out on Saturday night.

Blood had drained from my body, and tears had blinded me for days like my eyes had sprung an unfixable leak. My legs could barely hold me up, and someone had reached into my chest and ripped my heart out, squeezing the life from it.

And somehow, in that twilight zone of excruciating pain, another being had taken possession of me. After that, I had gone from being that kid that always helped the older lady next door with errands to an angry, withdrawn kid who hated the world. Maybe I should have gone to church, like my mother had suggested, instead of street fights.

Like my mother, I carried my father's memory with me everywhere and even talked to him from time to time. He guided me, and I was a better person for having known him.

Also, thanks to Declan Lovechilde, I'd exorcised my inner angry person and had made peace with myself. A proper legend in my eyes, Declan did so much to help me and other troubled youth, just by trusting and giving us the support we'd always needed and by showing us what a strong, honest man looked like.

"We'll go shopping tomorrow for some new clothes. Yes?"

Stroking my cheek again, she smiled. "You don't have to, love."

"And Sunday we'll go visit Betsy if you like."

"Oh, and bore you with all her retelling of books she's just read?"

I laughed. My mother had met Betsy, who had no family, at a group she'd just joined and liked to visit her.

"I don't mind."

"You're a good boy. I'm so lucky to have you. You could have gone bad like all the other boys around here with their drugs and goodness knows what else."

That could have been me, easily. But I kept that to myself.

"Billy and I are heading to the city for a drink, then I'll probably crash at his place."

"I prefer that to you drinking and driving, love." Worry swam in her eyes.

My mother hated me driving full stop. After sustaining life-changing injuries from that crash that had killed my father, she suffered anxiety just from being in a car. That was why I did her shopping and made sure she got to walk a little at the tiny park up the road. I'd even made her do rehab stretches, despite her protests, and it was why I wanted to move her to Bridesmere—so I could monitor her health.

I loved my mother. It was just us. And even though she had my aunt and a couple of neighbors she caught up with occasionally, my mum kept to herself. A big reader. She went through library books like no one I'd ever met. She loved murder mysteries. Our shelves were filled with Agatha Christie and P. D. James's novels.

I ordered a delivery pizza, then kissed her cheek. "Okay, then. You're all set. Now promise me not to finish that entire bottle of wine."

She returned a "who me?" look.

I PULLED UP OUTSIDE Billy's two-story Peckham brick home, where he lived with his disabled mother. We shared that in common, only his mother was wheelchair-bound after slipping on an escalator.

Despite having help, he was his mother's carer. He never complained, and Sarah, his mum, could do most things for herself. She was tough and an inspiration.

Billy had his own space at the back of their house, which was where we hung out and where I crashed on our big nights out since the cab ride was cheaper to his place whenever we hit the city.

He answered the door and stepped out. "Hey, ready for a big one?"

I nodded. "There's a pint of Guinness with my name on it."

We rode the tube to Piccadilly, then walked to our favorite pub for a few drinks before going to see a band. We preferred live gigs to clubs. Techno overwhelmed me with all those pulsing lights and digital music. We didn't do drugs. Just booze. We shared lots in common like that and were the best of mates.

Bouncing along and joking, we were on Regent Street when I saw a girl with long, dark hair, tight white jeans, and the kind of body that sparked all kinds of dirty thoughts. As we neared, I saw it was Manon swanning along with another girl.

My heart picked up its pace, and again my brain went numb. All the blood must have drained from my head down to my dick.

"Oh, it's you." She forced a smile.

"Nice to see you, too, Manon." I cocked my head and smiled.

I introduced her to Billy and back.

"This is Sapphire," she said, introducing the pretty blonde girl, whose eyes remained on Billy's a little longer than usual.

Popular with the girls, Billy, with that red hair, had a Prince Harry look about him, but with more muscles.

"So, where are you off to?" Manon asked, taking the lead as always, which suited me, given how tongue-tied she made me.

I looked at Billy as though I did not know.

Come on, some smooth talk, you fool.

"Um, we're just off to a pub."

She kept staring at me. I even wondered if I had a stain on my face or something. Or was she wanting an invitation?

"Why don't you join us?" Billy suggested. He was always the one who pulled the chicks.

Good lad.

She turned to her blonde friend, who I imagined was not of drinking age, and Sapphire gave a nod to that suggestion.

"Okay, then, show the way," Manon said.

"So, are you here for the weekend?" I asked.

"I am. Just doing a spot of shopping for my party next week. You are coming, aren't you?" She stopped walking and faced me again.

"I'm working there."

Her brow creased. "Oh? I tried to invite you, but you were busy with your girlfriend."

Billy opened the door to the noisy bar, and we all stepped in.

"She's not my girlfriend." I rolled my eyes.

"I wanted you to come." She looked upset, which I found rather nice. "Can't you get out of it?"

I looked at Billy, who was also doing a spot of bouncing work while completing an online computer course.

He shrugged. "Sure. I can stay at yours?"

"You sure can mate. I just bought a sofa bed."

Manon's face brightened. "Then I'll talk to Grandmother and tell her, shall I?"

"I can do that." I smiled.

Billy rubbed his hands. "Okay. So, what are we having?"

We found a table, and Billy brought over a tray of drinks and passed Sapphire a coke.

"Are you sure you don't want me to get you a proper drink?" he asked.

She shook her head. "No. I'm good. I don't want to drink."

"Have you ever?" he asked, passing our drinks then sitting down next to her.

"Yeah." She made it sound like he'd asked a silly question.

"So, how did you two meet?" I asked Manon, switching my focus from her to her young friend.

Manon regarded Sapphire as though she needed permission to answer that simple question, which struck me as strange, as it did Billy, going by his puzzled look.

"She's a friend of the family," Manon said at last.

I couldn't understand why she'd found that response difficult.

We spent the next couple of hours talking about football and movies and all kinds of silly things. Lots of jokes, thanks to Billy, and time flew. It was the first time I'd actually sat down with Manon and chatted normally, and thanks to beer, I could even hold a conversation with her without sounding dumb. She liked to giggle, which was cute and sexy. Everything about Manon was sexy. I could have stared into those pretty, dark eyes all night.

The pub closed at midnight, and we spilled into the street along with everyone else.

A few of the lads were pushing each other around, looking for a fight, and one started to hit on Manon.

I looked at Billy and rolled my eyes.

"Hey, why don't you drop those losers and come with us instead?" a heavily tattooed guy said to Manon.

"Don't think so. You're not my type." She might as well have told him to fuck off.

He stumbled closer.

"Here we go," I said under my breath.

"You're not sticking around these poofs, are ya?"

Looking scared, Sapphire hid behind Billy while Manon confronted him with her hands on her hips, sneering at him.

I gently took her by the arm. "Hey, let's go. The guy's pissed. Don't play him."

"He's a dickhead if he thinks I'd go off with someone as ugly as that." She said it so loudly that he heard.

"Hey, now listen, bitch…"

That was it. It started with Billy, who was a hothead at the best of times, throwing the first punch. The idiot guy fell back on his arse while his mates, five in all, jumped in, and there we were, punching into each other.

We took them down, two against five before the cops arrived and bundled us off as Manon yelled abuse, which didn't help.

Sitting in the back of the police car, Billy looked at me and shook his head with "we fucked up again" written all over his face.

I sucked it back and stared out the window at the noisy, crowded streets, suddenly wishing that was us bouncing along.

"They started it," I explained to the cop after we got to the busy station.

We'd been there often enough.

"You've got a record, I see." He stared up at me from the counter.

"That was a long time ago. They picked on my friend and were hitting on her."

"Yeah, yeah. Heard it all before. You need to learn to control your fucking temper."

Manon burst through the door.

The cop peered up from his glasses. "This is your girl?"

"Yes. I'm his girl," Manon answered for me. "And they started it. One of them touched my tits. Drake was only defending me. And then all the others jumped in. Five against Drake and Billy. They had a right to defend themselves, you know."

That was bullshit about her being assaulted, but who was I to contradict her? Manon could have won an academy award because she nearly had me convinced, despite knowing otherwise.

The cop looked her up and down. Dressed in skin-tight white jeans and a pretty blouse that left little to the imagination, Manon was literally out there. I could read his mind. "Dress more modestly next time, and maybe the drunks might not notice you."

"Hello, stop blaming the victim," she sang.

"Can anyone corroborate, miss?" the officer asked Manon after she made her statement word for word so he could take it down.

She held up a finger, and a few moments later, Sapphire slipped in.

The older, pissed-off cop looked close to retirement. I imagined he'd seen his share of Saturday-night brawls and had listened to tons of stories just like ours.

Sapphire nodded to everything and gave her details.

The officer studied her closely. "You're a little young to be out and about."

"It's okay. She's a friend of the family, and she didn't drink," Manon interjected.

The cop puffed out a frustrated breath. "Okay. Get out of here. All of you. Unless you want to press charges?" He looked at Manon.

Her decisive shake of the head had the cop's eyes narrowing.

At least we were free to go.

"Where's Billy?" Sapphire asked as we were leaving the station.

"He left in a hurry after making his statement. Cops freak him out. He can't afford another conviction."

"Oh, really? He's been in trouble before?" she looked alarmed.

"Let's say we both had difficult pasts." I looked at Manon, who I imagined understood the meaning of that because I was sure she also had a troubled history.

CHAPTER 7

Manon

WE JUMPED IN A taxi and dropped Sapphire off at her house. "I'll call you tomorrow. We can go shopping again if you like."

She smiled and gave me one of her uncertain nods. I think she couldn't believe my sudden attachment.

I'd never really had a girlfriend before. I guess it helped that, despite her sweet nature, she was half broken like me, given how her mother had left them when she was young. Also, her angelic innocence played on my heartstrings and somehow sparked this desire to support her by buying her things. Before meeting up with Drake and Billy, we had done a spin around Oxford Street, where I'd bought her a pair of jeans. She hugged me, leaving a teary stain on my silk blouse. I didn't mind. It felt nice.

Perhaps subconsciously, I craved some of that hopeful, blind trust she put in people, which was the opposite of me. I put my walls up, assuming everyone had ulterior motives, which made me paranoid. I hadn't exactly had outstanding role models.

Over and above everything, however, helping Sapphire gave me deep satisfaction, even more so than when I bought myself something. It was the same warm, fuzzy feeling I'd only experienced once after my grandmother had accepted me and even suggested I change my surname to Lovechilde. After I got over the initial shock, I fell in love with that idea. Who wouldn't want to be known as a Lovechilde?

I'd even noticed my grandmother smiling more lately, which was probably due to love. The only time a smile came naturally to me was around Drake.

Was I in love? Maybe in lust. But then, he wasn't exactly throwing himself at me.

Maybe I was too young for him.

Strange how the world was—older men wanted younger women, and young guys gravitated toward older women.

I planned to change that. At least with Drake. I couldn't discourage girls from tossing themselves at older men to secure their futures, however. I wasn't superwoman.

As we drove to my place, I sat close to Drake. Our shoulders touched, making it the closest I'd ever been to him physically for a prolonged period. I could smell his soap and sweat. Or was that tension from the fight? Whichever way, sexy.

Going on his long face, Drake seemed shitty with me. I couldn't blame him. I hated myself for not walking away from those drunken dickheads. Me and my big mouth. It had just sprung out of nowhere before I'd even had time to think. Like there was a bad me lurking within, waiting to pounce and unleash a dark spirit.

Disruptor and provocateur, a therapist had once described me at the therapy session that was forced on me after being caught shoplifting.

I hadn't known what those words meant, but I'd looked them up, and my dark side had almost smiled. Better than being well-behaved and under the thumb, I thought. But currently, I wasn't so sure, because that react-first-deal-with-the-fallout-later programming had placed a wedge between me and Drake. Or maybe his coolness towards me was more to do with him not being interested.

Then why those long gazes at the pub? Like when I wasn't looking, which I still noticed, of course. I always noticed things about Drake. Even from across a large room, I sensed him gawking.

"That was some night." Drake sighed.

"Are you okay?" I asked, turning to get a good look at that beautiful face. Roughed up, he looked even better. "From where I was standing, you were blocking their punches. I didn't notice you take a hit." My voice sounded thin. I hadn't even apologized for inflaming the situation. "That was awesome, by the way. You and Billy on those five guys." I chuckled. "I bet they'll be sore tomorrow."

His brow puckered, and he gave me a piercing look. "You enjoyed that?"

His angry tone turned me to wood.

Tears prickled at the back of my eyes. That apology just couldn't make it to my mouth. Why was I so fucking emotionally constipated?

Given his rough tone, I was busting to give him the middle finger, but I dug my nails into my palms for a hit of pain instead. "Well, it's nice to have strong males fighting for my honor."

He laughed coldly. "You make it sound like something out of the fucking nineteenth century. The guy was a first-rate arsehole, but unless someone comes at you swinging, it pays to ignore them. Can't you see he was itching for a fight?"

Fire bit my belly. "Oh gee, thanks for the advice."

He just responded with a loud puff, and just as a trickle of sweat slid between my shoulders, we arrived at my mother's Knightsbridge house. She'd gone away to Paris with her rich boyfriend, which meant I had the house to myself.

"Do you want to come in?" I asked, trying to climb out of the black hole we'd fallen into.

"No."

I stared him in the eyes. "Are you staying at that cougar's place?"

"Fuck off, Manon."

"Ew. Aren't we shitty?" I sang, despite hating myself by the minute. Why couldn't I just be nice or apologetic or seductive?

I froze instead, waiting for something. Or was he really wanting to leave?

"Why don't you come in?" I bit into my cheek, then softened my voice. "I'm sorry. You're right, I shouldn't have done that."

He puffed out a breath and kept staring deep into my eyes. His big blue eyes filled with confusion. He looked so serious.

"Come on." I patted his large hand. "I won't bite. Unless you want me to."

He maintained a serious frown. He was either seriously sensitive or religious.

That kiss in the forest was not from the lips of someone who'd drank from the blood of Christ or swallowed the holy host or whatever consumables were foisted upon worshippers.

"You're too much for me, Manon."

"I'm too young. Is that it? You only go for older women with fake breasts?"

His unblinking stare burned into me. I'd offended him again.

The silence overwhelmed me. All I could hear was the ticking of the meter. The driver had turned off his engine. He probably got that all the time—the push and pull of couples. Either arguing or trying to convince the other to come in for a drink and a fuck. Only it was usually the man doing the coaxing.

After more of an awkward gap, and his spellbinding gaze making me forget to breathe, Drake grabbed me almost roughly, and his lips were on mine before I could open my mouth.

It was an angry kiss. But hell, it was fucking hot.

I could imagine him fucking me hard.

I wanted that. I wanted him to hurt me.

His dick ramming into me.

Pounding the ache out of me.

I finally pulled away only because I sensed the driver was having his own little show.

"Why don't you come in?"

He went to pay for the cab, but I stopped him.

"Please let me. I'm earning a lot more than you."

He continued to appear ruffled like I was messing with his head. It was pretty straightforward; I thought. I was earning loads more than him.

We stood on the path, and his eyes were at his feet like he didn't want to be there or something.

"I could've paid." He circled his foot, wrapped in Nike.

"I turn twenty-one next week, and I'll be a millionaire, Drake, so don't think about it for another minute. Okay?" I took his hand.

That kiss still warmed my lips, and I wanted more.

He looked up and down at the white, two-story Edwardian home. A moonbeam lit his gorgeous face, and a film of moisture remained on his lips from our kiss, which I was dying to continue.

The thought of his hot, hungry lips smothering mine sizzled through me. I was all sticky and swollen, and all I could think of was stripping naked and his hands all over my body.

"You live here?" he asked, following me up the path to the red door with the brass lion-head knocker.

"My mother does. I stay here sometimes."

After we stepped into the hallway, I tapped the sequence to disarm the alarm and turned on the lights.

He seemed to hover at the entrance. I couldn't believe how difficult it was for Drake. He was either seriously shy or just uncertain about me.

Probably both.

"Come on then, I promise not to make you do anything you don't want to do."

His mouth tugged slightly at one end. That was the most expressive he'd been since that kiss.

We entered a room filled to the brim with antiques. All were purchased by my mother, who didn't just copy Grandmother's style in hair and clothes but also furnishings and decorations. I even recognized certain pieces. My mother's time playing maid at Merivale had given her a lesson in taste.

"Can I make you a drink or something to eat?"

Drake settled onto the burgundy velvet sofa. In that fitted blue polo that accented and, therefore, made his eyes ever bluer and his regular Levi's that I'd already noted for the way they fitted his arse, he looked more like an intruder than a visitor.

But that was how I'd always felt in that house. Nothing seemed real. Everything in its place. My mother had become a stickler for perfection.

Once again, copied from her time at Merivale because before she'd moved into her rich woman phase, my mother had been a slob. Growing up, I had been the one who'd washed the dishes or put things away.

"No. It's okay."

I slanted my head. "Are you still pissed off with me?"

He crossed his large, bruised hands. His long pause confirmed that something was eating at him.

"You could have had that boy locked away for something he didn't do. Wouldn't that have bothered you?"

"No way. It would have taught him to stop acting like a tosser. He tried to hit on me, and he called me a bitch. Remember?" I walked off and grabbed some coke from the fridge and brought out a packet of crisps.

I poured him a glass of coke and passed it to him. "I can put some Scotch in that if you like."

He shook his head. "No. I'm good."

"You're so fucking serious, Drake. Lighten up."

I joined him on the couch and moved up close. "Are you gay?"

He sprung off the sofa like he'd sat on a spider. "Look, enough of the fucking games. I'm not fucking gay." He brushed away the lock of hair from his eyes. "I want you, Manon. Always have. From the moment I fucking laid eyes on you."

That made my cheeks warm. "You've got me. I'm here." I unbuttoned my blouse, and his eyes went straight to my tits, which spilled out of my tiny bra.

Normally, I manipulated the moment easily enough with a pout or bending over at the right moments, but Drake was deeper than that.

That was why I wanted him more than my next fucking breath.

I wanted his hands and mouth all over me. My panties were soaked, and there was this throbbing ache in my pussy. I didn't normally get so aroused from a kiss.

I undid my bra, and my heavy boobs fell naked.

His eyes went heavy with lust, and I noticed a bulge growing in his jeans.

I wiggled out of my pants and stood before him in my thong.

He parted his legs slightly, and he even touched his dick, adjusting his position, which I found very erotic.

Despite his eyes darkening with what I sensed was arousal, he remained seated. I was expecting him to pounce.

Peyton used to pounce before my tits grew too large and he couldn't even get a hard-on. That rejection had brought on a period of insecurity. An insecurity that had resurfaced with Drake.

Men did the undressing, the picking up. But then, those men hadn't made my pulse race like Drake did.

"What's the matter? You don't like what you see?" I inclined my head to the side.

I joined him on the sofa, and he jumped up like I smelt bad or something.

He raked through his hair with his fingers and stared into my eyes. Not at my half-naked tits, but into my eyes. Mesmerizing me with those big blue eyes, he fell into mine, like he could see behind all my bullshit.

"You're fucking gorgeous." He sounded in agony or that my being gorgeous was a serious problem for him.

I laughed. "Then what are you scared of?"

He brushed back the dark wave from his tan forehead. "It feels like you do this all the time."

I grabbed my shirt and covered myself. "You're fucking weird."

"Yeah, well, I am that." He turned on the spot, looking uncertain again. "I think I need to go."

"You're leaving? Why don't we just sleep together? No sex. Promise."

Why am I begging? Err...

He looked at me strangely, like I'd proposed he sleep with a snake or some man-eating beast. That comparison made me smile. I could be either of those things.

After what seemed like ages, he nodded.

Ten minutes later, we were in bed. Even that was weird, in that he had to look away when I stripped down, despite seeing me in nothing but my thong earlier. I lent him my toothbrush, and it seemed like we were teenagers having a sleepover. Not that I'd ever had any experience. My only reference to what a typical teenager's world looked like were those screechy teen movies, which I'd sometimes watched as a teenager. Only someone forgot to tell me that Hollywood didn't do normal.

I cuddled into him and breathed him in deeply. Drake was all firm muscle beneath his T-shirt. Just us there, with our warm bodies close, felt nice, despite the throb between my legs. I even contemplated using my fingers. I was seriously in need of a release.

Wearing my favorite silk nightie, I rubbed myself against him. I loved how he smelt. Dangerous. After that fight, his scent had changed.

I rocked into his body, and he turned to face me.

Moonlight pouring through the window of the upstairs room made his face appear older. Different. But still handsome. I knew he would get hotter with age, which only intensified my craving for him, and for us to make that journey together and not just end in a one-night stand. Even though that didn't seem possible, given how seriously Drake took things.

On the one hand, I appreciated he took sex seriously, while on the other, my body burned with frustration because I wanted him more than anything.

"Am I keeping you awake?" I asked.

"You could say that."

I felt his dick tenting his briefs against my stomach, which only fired me up.

He must have read my need because his mouth landed on mine, and that time, it was soft and explorative. Like he needed to understand my lips. Our tongues twirled together, and I fell into one of those flying dreams. All pinks and reds. And hoping never to wake up.

His hands traveled up and down my curves.

"You've got the most perfect body." He sounded in agony.

I allowed my strap to slip and slide down, and his mouth found my nipples as he fondled my tits.

His dick kept thickening against my thigh.

"I want to feel you inside of me."

He ran his hands over my body, exploring every inch of me. He sucked on my nipples, which were so sensitive I felt it in my clit.

My body gyrated against his, and as his fingers brushed my thighs, I opened my legs wide to encourage his finger to fuck me.

His finger entered, and an electric impulse struck me. Just that one action threatened to make me come. My pussy swallowed his finger with hunger.

"You feel hot." He groaned. "And seriously tight. Have you fucked before?" He pulled away to stare me in the face, looking almost frightened by that idea.

I almost laughed.

How ironic. Considering how everyone around me was obsessed with virgins.

"I have. But it's been a while."

"Why?" He looked surprised like we were talking about food and not sex.

"I haven't liked anyone enough to sleep with them."

"So... you're not fucking Crisp?"

"No. And never will either. Like... yuck," I sang.

A slow smile formed on his lips as he rolled his tongue over it, and the burn between my legs returned. If he didn't fuck me that minute, I was going to have to suck him off or do something radical.

He pushed himself onto me almost roughly. If ever I needed proof that he desired me, it was there with that big dick stretched to its limit against my belly and him unable to take his hands off my tits while he almost ate my mouth. Yep, he was as hungry for me as I was for him.

Pleasure didn't even describe how I felt at that moment.

"Your tits are perfect."

"I've noticed you looking." I danced against him, pressing myself to that enormous dick, teasing it to take me.

"That's because you wear tight, low-cut tops."

"You sound annoyed," I said.

"No. But it's distracting. It's difficult to think straight when you're around."

I rubbed his dick, which was so steel hard.

"Do you do this?" I pulled on his dick.

He removed my hand. "Don't."

"Am I hurting you?"

"Sort of. No... I mean... fuck, Manon. You're making me want to blow."

"Do you pull yourself off thinking of me?"

"All the fucking time." He sounded tormented.

"What am I doing in your head when you blow?"

"You're playing with your tits while I'm riding you hard."

The next minute, he traveled down my body and had his tongue on my clit.

"Oh..." My mouth parted. "You're great at this."

His warm, wet tongue licked me with just the right pressure to make me lose my mind.

The throbbing became so unbearable, I screamed for him to stop. He kept going, and I arched my back, then surrendered to an almighty orgasm.

I'd never had that happen before.

"Please fuck me." My voice was small and pleading.

"With pleasure." He broke away and reached for his jeans.

"No condom. I want you to come inside of me." I pulled down his briefs, and his dick was so big, I gasped. "You're huge."

He gave me a shy smile, reminding me that though he looked like a man, a very fuckable man, he was still that boy, too, which only deepened my attraction.

"Are you on the pill?"

I nodded.

He parted my legs, then entered me with a finger, followed by two fingers. "Is that okay? I mean, you're so fucking tight."

"I won't cry, promise." I giggled.

"I want you to come, not fucking cry."

Judging by how his tongue had made my eyes water, I had a feeling I might just do both. But I kept that to myself.

I spread my legs as wide as possible, and he entered me slowly, making me wince. It hurt.

I'd never had such a big dick enter me.

He stopped and looked at me. As he took his weight in his arms, Drake's biceps looked like the veins would pop. "Do you want me to stop?"

"No. But I'm not sure it's going to fit." I bit my lip.

He pulled out. "Maybe I can use my finger for a while."

"No. I want you inside of me. I'll be fine. Maybe go slow."

"Oh, I will. I don't want to hurt you."

I studied his face, and he looked like he was also in pain. "Is it hurting you too?"

He sniffed. "Um... no. Quite the fucking opposite."

"Oh?" I wanted to hear more about what he felt.

"I'm finding it difficult not to blow. Like even just then."

"Is it a turn-on?"

He rolled his eyes. "Like yeah. You're one big fucking turn-on, all right."

We locked eyes, and then his mouth ate mine again.

I took his throbbing, almost-purple dick and guided it in.

As I relaxed my muscles, the pain turned into something so indescribably pleasurable I became a dick junkie, there and then. Drake's dick, my heroin.

He rotated his dick slowly, and as he found that magic spot, I pressed on his firm arse to encourage him deeper.

I'd become addicted to the burn, which shouldn't have surprised me, given how pain was something I gravitated towards as an escape mechanism, but in this case, as he thrust into me, the pain was pure pleasure.

My heart pounded against him. Or was that his heart? Who could tell? His breath grew loud. He fondled my tits roughly while filling me to the brim. Each time he entered, he rubbed against nerve endings that set off sparks.

The build-up threatened to take me somewhere I'd never been before.

My moaning intensified the deeper and harder he took me.

"Am I hurting you?"

"No. I mean, yes. But I like pain."

Noticing his brow crease, I regretted that comment.

I pressed myself deeper so I could feel every inch. I squeezed his curvy biceps, which were slippery from sweat.

"Are you close?" he asked, as though in agony.

"Don't stop." Tingles sparked waves of heat. I knew that something magical was happening inside me, like nothing I'd ever felt before.

With his rough breath on my neck, he kept pumping deeply into me.

Fiery explosions came one after another. My body spasmed. The friction was so intense, I might burst. It was like his dick had grown even bigger.

As I released my contracting muscles, stars fluttered before me. My eyes watered at how full I felt with him thrusting deeply and at a piston rate.

My toes gripped as my fingernails dug into his hard muscles.

Euphoria rocketed through me, and I screamed.

I'd never screamed while fucking.

But this was something else.

Drake was something else.

He trembled while holding me. "Oh... Manon." My name flew out of his mouth as his pulsing dick poured an endless hot stream into me.

We lay in each other's arms, breathing roughly like we'd run up a steep hill. Only it was a million times better than any exercise I'd ever done.

He let out a breath. "Shit. That was insane."

I nodded slowly, then giggled. I didn't know why I giggled. Must have been the intensity of the situation.

"I didn't hurt you?" he asked.

"Yeah. You did. I loved it."

He pulled away and stared me out again. I could see he was trying to understand.

Good luck. I couldn't understand myself that well, so I couldn't imagine him getting anywhere.

CHAPTER 8

Drake

AFTER WHAT HAD BEEN an insane night, I almost stumbled back to my mother's. I wished I could just drive back without seeing her. She would know I'd been with a girl. My mother missed little with me.

I found her in the kitchen, preparing pancakes. After any big night out, she always made me a fry-up.

Bacon on pancakes with spinach. It was a crazy breakfast, but I loved it. And no one made them like her.

"There you are, my darling."

She smiled brightly, and I hugged her.

"Your hair's still wet. You should dry it," she said.

After I'd woken up half-disorientated and still buzzing from what had been the greatest fuck of my life, I had intended to rush off, but Manon had insisted I shower.

She'd then joined me, gotten down on her knees, and tried to suck me off. It hurt—her teeth. But it was sweet anyway, and I didn't have the heart to tell her. In many ways, her lack of experience made me glad, for some unclear reason.

As her firm, curvy arse danced against my cock, I almost crushed those tits that I couldn't stop fondling while I thrust deep into her. She was a wet dream come true.

I'd never come like that before. She was more than I'd ever imagined, a drug that I could see myself getting hooked on—only drugs were dangerous.

Was Manon bad for me?

Just as I was zipping up my jeans, her mother arrived with George, the rich boyfriend, and things got pretty weird.

"What's he doing here?" Bethany asked.

"I'm allowed to have who I like here." Manon looked at me and rolled her eyes.

And before the argument blew out, I scuttled off without even kissing her.

Manon followed me to the door. "Why don't you wait, and we can go for breakfast somewhere?"

"I have to be back at Bridesmere this morning. I've got a client."

"Kylie." She gave me a dark grin while slanting her beautiful face.

"No. A male client."

"Oh, that's a pleasant change."

I pecked her cheek, despite the urge to devour her lips again. Something we'd been doing all night. Between fucking, instead of sleeping, we'd kissed.

I'd never wanted to just hold someone all night long and kiss them. It felt nice. Too fucking nice.

Manon freaked me out. I couldn't tell if she had a dark heart or whether she'd adopted that rebellious nature as a protective front. I couldn't stop thinking about that scene at the police station. And though my body craved her, my need for a sane, honest life warned me to run a mile. So I had, to the nearest station, where I'd ridden the tube home with dripping wet hair.

I poured tea from the teapot into a cup for my mother, then one for me.

She passed me a plate filled to the brim with pancakes, and my stomach groaned with delight.

"Thanks, Mum."

Sitting down, she took her cup and poured milk into it. "So, how was your night? You look flushed."

"We had a good night." I munched on a piece of bacon.

"You didn't drink too much, I hope." Her eyes landed on my bruised knuckles. "Oh, Drake, you didn't fight again, did you?"

"Just had to defend a girl. Some losers were trying it on."

She nodded. "I hate it every time you go out. It's becoming more violent these days. All those Middle Eastern gangs."

"These were white guys, Mum. English. Like us."

"Oh, well. At least you don't go to the football. That's where all the trouble starts."

I had to smile. It was a mother's role to worry.

I kept seeing the look of horror on Bethany's face like I was some street sleeper who'd crashed her privileged life. George hadn't seemed too bothered with me being there, but the mother had other ideas, it seemed, for her daughter.

What ideas did I have for Manon?

All I could see was her gyrating on my dick while playing with her big, firm tits. My dick went hard just thinking about her.

I also felt a powerful urge to protect her, which had little to do with my security training. There was something broken in Manon. And what were those cuts between her thighs?

When I'd asked, she'd changed the subject, which only roused my suspicions.

"Did someone do that to you?" I'd persisted.

"No. I cut myself with a razor."

"Up there?"

She had a hairless pussy, so it made sense, but why did she seem nervous when I asked?

Eating breakfast like a man who'd fucked his brains out all night, I pushed away thoughts of Manon and focused, instead, on my future. Which didn't involve personal training and security work. I was young enough to explore options while saving like mad to secure a comfortable future for both me and my mother.

I LOVED MY NEW studio apartment. Though small, the space seemed larger, thanks to a superb view of the pier and the ocean. I enjoyed watching fishermen bringing in their catch and loved that the apartment was all mine, despite ten more years of mortgage payments.

Buttoning up my black cotton shirt, I prepared for my gig at Salon, where I'd be working five nights a week. And while I wasn't Reynard Crisp's biggest fan, the pay was too good to ignore.

Checking myself in the mirror, I tucked my shirt into my black pants and practiced my tough-guy stance. I'd gotten better at it, even though I had to watch myself when women smiled at me. My instincts were to smile back. Something frowned upon in that role.

My phone pinged just as I was about to leave for work. It was from Manon, and a smile grew on my face.

She had me eating out of her sweet little palm. One couldn't have a girl like that and not get a little attached, and I couldn't wait to see her again.

"Are you in Bridesmere? And can we catch up later?" she wrote.

"I'm at Salon until two in the morning. I'm heading there now."

"Then I'll drop in because I'm at Cherry."

"Huh?"

"It's my name for Ma Chérie, which sounds pretentious if you ask me."

It sounds more than that.

"Fitting, I suppose." I sighed. I wasn't about to tell her how much I hated that venue.

"See you then."

"Great. Bye," I signed off. My heart raced.

That night of hot sex came flooding back to me. All I could see was Manon rubbing herself against me, and if I weren't running late, I would have had to relieve myself. Again. The girl had me on fire.

Her involvement with Crisp's girly bar didn't sit well. There were rumors. Everything about my boss was shady. Like those Eastern European heavies who kept coming in, night after night, which had been going on for the past month.

Caroline Lovechilde had asked me to inform her if I noticed anything unusual at the casino. So apart from working as security, I'd somehow become her spy. She was Declan's mother, and I owed so much to him, so I didn't have to think twice about helping.

Overall, though, it had been smooth sailing at the casino. No fights. Only the odd drunk to deal with.

It wasn't my idea of a brilliant career, but I had a meeting with Declan in the morning to discuss an administration gig at the organic farm, which would suit me better. It would also free up my nights for dirtier pursuits, like exploring more ways to make Manon scream my name.

Crisp was talking to a young woman when I arrived. Giggling and getting all touchy-feely, she was young enough to be his girlfriend, knowing how he liked them young.

As long as he kept his sleazy hands off Manon, who was I to judge?

Acknowledging me, he nodded, while his girlfriend looked me up and down, wearing a flirty smile.

"Aren't you going to introduce us?" she asked with a heavy Eastern European accent.

"This is Drake. He's on the door." Crisp turned to me and gave me that keep-your-hands-off-her look.

I nodded, keeping a straight face, thinking of the thousand pounds he was paying me for five nights' work. Cash, and no questions asked. At first, it surprised me he'd even asked me, given our history with that minor episode at Merivale when I pushed him off Manon, but it wasn't spoken about.

I thought about Manon's twenty-first. "Um… can I have a quick word?"

Crisp gestured for his girlfriend to go inside. She gave me another lingering look, then swanned off, swaying her hips. Manon was playful compared to that girl, who I sensed was outright dangerous.

Crisp watched her walk away, then returned his attention to me.

"I need next Saturday off. There's a party I'm invited to," I said.

"Okay. Sure." He went to walk away when he turned. "That's Manon's twenty-first I take it?"

I nodded.

"You're together?" His eyes held mine for a tense gap.

It was no secret that he had the hots for Manon, but then he had his own young, sexy thing, so, what was the big deal?

"Well, she's a friend, you could say."

"In other words, you're fucking?" He smirked.

I went to respond when I heard gunfire. Instincts kicked in, and I pushed him away. The bullet that had just passed my ear by a whisker was obviously meant for him.

He scurried inside, and I pulled out the gun Crisp had given me. I hadn't been too happy taking it, but I could see why he'd insisted on me carrying one while on guard.

At least I knew how to use it, having practiced at a range when I was sixteen in prep for joining the army.

I gripped the pistol and stepped away from the light, but the black SUV took off.

The other security guard, Novak, a new guy who I hardly knew, arrived and positioned himself by the door, and Crisp gestured for me to follow him into his office at the back of the casino.

He pointed to the seat, then poured himself a whisky and offered me some, but I declined.

"Not a word to anyone," he said at last.

Somewhat stunned, I nodded slowly, as it was only just dawning on me I could have just died.

While Carson had put me through the ropes and trained me in security, part of which meant danger and even taking a bullet to protect the public, I hadn't prepared myself mentally. I had to cross my fingers to stop my hands from trembling.

Crisp gulped down half a glass of whisky—the only sign that the near-death experience had ruffled him—then scribbled in his checkbook and handed me a cheque for fifty thousand pounds.

"Here, for saving my life. There's more where that came from. From now on, I want you on my team."

He said it as though I should be grateful for the opportunity.

"Well, I'm working at Reboot as a trainer, and I have an interview in the morning…"

"Name your price."

I thought of that apartment for my mother and how I could pay mine off sooner.

What was my price? And would I still be alive to enjoy a debt-free future?

"Apart from working here, I have an estate not too far from Merivale. I'll need you there some nights. You'll be well paid."

He scribbled something on a piece of paper and passed it to me. I read five thousand pounds. I wondered what that meant.

He read my mind and said, "That's a week. For a twenty-two-year-old, that's not a bad sum."

"It's not." I took a deep breath. "What exactly would you expect?"

"You'd sign a privacy agreement. No talking to anyone about what you see or hear." His raised eyebrow had me thinking I was about to do a deal with a devil.

"Look, I don't know if I can turn a blind eye to girls being—"

"Nothing like that. Don't worry. Contrary to rumors, the club only deals with consenting, legal-aged girls."

I nodded tentatively. "Can I think about it?"

He leaned forward. "Not a word about what happened tonight to Caroline Lovechilde. Especially Manon." He rose and stretched his arms. "You'll have to stop seeing her. That's the only stipulation."

My back went rigid. I dropped the cheque on the desk and rose. "Then, forget it."

I went to walk off.

"You really would sacrifice all that money for someone like her?"

I turned to look at him and was about to speak when a knock came at the door, and a couple of bald, heavily tattooed men rocked in.

"It's here," one of them said.

Crisp looked at me and fluttered his hand. "We'll talk later. Think about it."

The fifty-thousand-pound cheque sat on his desk. He picked it up. "Here, you forgot this."

"But I'm not sure—"

"You earned it. Take it. For your silence."

His eyes crept over to the dark, heavy guys, which I read as a threat. Or it might have been sudden jitters because there was something seriously slippery going on in there, and I wanted to be alive to see my thirtieth birthday.

Seriously shaken, I grabbed my stuff and went out the back way into the dark night. I looked around me, but it was quiet. My phone beeped, and I read a message from Manon. "Are we still meeting at two?"

After what had been a harrowing experience, a sexy distraction was just what I needed. Even if I couldn't stop thinking about that troubling expression in Crisp's eyes when he told me to stay away from her.

"Can't wait. What color are your knickers?"

"I'm not wearing any."

That made my cock thicken and my heart race in a nice way. Manon had unknowingly saved me from working for an evil man because, for a minute there, that five thousand pounds a week had looked tempting.

What really bugged me, though, was why Manon continued to associate with him.

CHAPTER 9

Manon

DRAKE LOOKED A LITTLE pale as he let me into his apartment. "Hey, are you okay?" I placed my bag on the sofa.

Sipping beer, Drake seemed a million miles away. "Sorry, I didn't offer you a drink. Do you want one?" He held up his bottle.

"Just water, I think." I followed him into the tiny kitchen, which extended into the living space.

His apartment reminded me of a place I'd stayed in East London after my dad left us. One room for everything—sleeping, eating, arguing, and loser male visitors, which meant I had to leave for a few hours, traipsing the streets and shoplifting for an adrenaline hit. At least Drake's studio apartment was new and had a great view, so I didn't feel so claustrophobic.

He passed me a bottle of water and then returned to the sofa.

"Are you too tired? Or is it something else?"

Looking very serious, he stared at me with those large, hypnotic blue eyes. "Are you fucking Crisp?"

I squirmed. Not this again. "No way. I've told you that."

"Then why this affiliation with him? He's fucking dangerous and associates with some pretty bad types."

"Can we not talk about him? I just want us to..." I unbuttoned my shirt to reveal a new red lacey bra.

Intensity faded from his expression as his eyes grew heavy with lust. He swept his tongue over his pillowy lips, which hadn't so much as curled since I'd arrived.

"Do you like it?" I tipped my head with a teasing smile.

"Of course, I fucking like it."

He sounded gruff, like I was getting on his nerves, but it still ignited a spark in me. His alpha side made me want him even more.

"Then, what's wrong?" I hated how whiny my voice sounded.

"I just don't want to be with you if you're going to work at that Cherry place." His mouth curled slightly. "As you call it."

"I plan to resign. I just have to find the right way to tell him."

"What the fuck has he got on you?"

I winced at his rough tone. "He thinks he can own me, like some pretty ornament, I guess." Reluctant to give him the full story, I kept it short and sweet. I couldn't imagine Drake liking the fact that I'd been seducing Rey with my little virgin act all those months. Put it down to naivety, but if I could go back and do it again, I would never have done that.

But then, I hadn't known my grandmother was going to make me a millionaire.

Somehow, I didn't think Drake would accept that as an excuse. After all, I had a job and a career in beauty. I just liked the idea of living in luxury.

Who wouldn't after the crappy life I'd lived?

"I'm waiting for my birthday, which is like next week, and that fat cheque in my account, then I'll be independent. Don't worry. He has nothing on me. Honest."

That explanation worked because he drew me onto the sofa, and I landed on top of him. He removed my bra, almost ripping it off, and with his breath all hot and raspy, he ran his hands over my tits, groaning. And as he sucked on my nipples, almost devouring them as one would a sugar hit, my brain emptied. It was all about us in that sexy moment and nothing else.

His mouth landed on mine. He tasted different, still like something I couldn't stop wanting to taste, but I sensed danger. Or was that just raw lust? His tongue fucked my mouth as though it were his dick.

I unzipped his jeans, and the red head of his dick, dripping in pre-cum, peeped over his briefs.

I rose and stripped out of my jeans and felt the heat of his gaze traveling up and down my body.

He clutched onto my bum and pulled me close to his face. He put his tongue on my pussy, and I was so thick and sticky my legs went all quivery.

Drake was an expert and much better than Peyton—the only other person who'd ever used his tongue on me.

Bliss blasted through me as my muscles relaxed. His large hands clutched my arse, holding me up because my legs had turned to jelly.

When he entered with his finger, I came so hard I had to bite my lip to avoid crying out.

"Ooh…" he gasped. "Fuck you're so wet."

"I'll be wetter if you show me your dick."

He removed his jeans, then his briefs, and his dick sprung out all thick and veiny and almost purple-red.

"I'd love a photo of you," I said.

"What would you do with it?" His mouth curled at one end.

"I'd touch myself while looking at it."

"Show me," he said.

I sat in the opposite chair and spread my legs, getting off on how his hard dick twitched against his belly button.

"Go on, then. Touch yourself," he said with a hoarse voice.

"Only if you play with your dick."

There we were, me finger fucking, and him pulling at that big dick that I wanted so badly inside of me.

I went over and slowly lowered myself onto it. My eyes watered from the intense stretch. Pleasurable and painful. His slow groan sounded like he was in agony.

He sucked on my nipples while he held onto my bum, carefully guiding me up and down over his dick. Allowing my pussy to adjust and take him all in. I felt so full like I might burst any minute. Nice though.

The friction from his thrusts sparked warm bursts of pleasure.

The faster he moved, the hotter I became, as uncontrollable spasms shot through me.

Our moist bodies squelched together as his groans merged with my moans.

He smelt of sweat, bath soap, and my pussy. I could taste my cum on his pillowy lips as our mouths crushed like our bodies.

"Oh, fuck, Manon." He fondled my tits roughly as he pounded into me. I closed my eyes and saw an explosion of reds and oranges.

I came so hard I cried out his name.

I'd never orgasmed like that before, and it never seemed to stop.

He grunted loudly, and as his orgasm gushed deep inside of me, I surrendered to another moment of intense bliss.

After my breathing had evened, I untangled myself from his arms, smiling like a happy kitten. "Oh. My. God."

His face had gone a healthy shade of red, and he smiled for the first time. "You're not wrong. That was hot. You're hot."

I fell into his arms, and we cuddled, which was like that dollop of cream on an already-delicious pie.

I WAS WALKING THROUGH Harrods when I bumped into Savanah, alone and minus her screechy girlfriends.

"Hey," I said with a bright smile.

I'd spent the night with Drake, and nothing could bring me down. Not even my mother, who had been on my tail, ever since I'd stupidly told her I was about to inherit. I mean, she had a billionaire boyfriend. What did she need with my money?

"Oh." Savanah's greeting was normal for her. Like I was an interruption or something.

"What are you up to?" I asked.

She looked at me as though I might have lost the plot. I couldn't blame her, considering how I would normally say something bitchy. But that jaded, shitty-at-the-world version of me I'd sent packing.

"I'm just killing a bit of time. I've got a doctor's appointment at three." Her phone went off, and when she read the message, her face dropped.

"Nothing serious?" I asked.

"No." She sounded disappointed.

"So, congrats, by the way. That's awesome about you being pregnant."

"Oh, you heard?" Savanah's flat response made me wonder if I should have kept that to myself.

We stepped away from a crowd of elderly shoppers wheeling in for their special day out.

"Yeah. Well, um... Drake mentioned something." I frowned. "Aren't I meant to know?"

She shrugged. "I guess it's fine. Everyone knows anyway, and hopefully..." She sighed. "I'll be showing one day soon."

Savanah struck me as stressed. "Are you okay?"

"It's just that Carson was meant to meet me for the doctor's appointment, and he's stuck in a traffic jam."

"I'm free. Do you want me to come along? I don't mind. I'd like to."

I might as well have offered to deliver her baby. Suspicion shone from her shocked look.

"I...I... tried to call Jacinta... um... but she's away."

Her stuttering caught me by surprise. She'd always been so confident.

"We're family, aren't we?" I played with my fingers. "And well, you know, I'm over all the fights. And I know I stole some of your clothes, but I returned them. You noticed... didn't you?" I also stammered. Apologizing wasn't my thing. Or I should say, I didn't normally admit to doing the wrong thing, but weighed down by all my bad actions, I thought it was time to embrace my better half. At least, not steal from those close.

Perplexed, Savanah looked as though I'd fallen out of the sky. "I think so. I generally can't keep up with my clothes." A faint smile grew on her face. "I suppose it would be nice to have someone with me."

She gazed down at her stunning diamanté watch, which during my bad days, I might have tried to steal.

"We've still got thirty minutes. Care for a juice?" she asked.

I smiled. My heart felt light. I'd always had a soft spot for my aunt. "I'd love that."

She kept staring at me. "What have you done with Manon, that little smart-arse, light-fingered niece of mine?"

I giggled. "Oh, she's still here somewhere. But I thought it would be nice to make a few friends."

Her jaw opened, and her eyes sparked. "It's because of your party. You want people to come."

I shrugged. "That hadn't crossed my mind. But sure, it would be nicer if people sang happy birthday and not something like rot in hell."

She chuckled. "Mummy's cohort are all too well-mannered to do that."

"That's a relief. I wondered if they were going to whisper horrible things about me."

"Oh, they might still do that, but at least not to your face."

I sniffed. "I guess I have it coming."

She returned a sympathetic smile. "Who are you inviting? And please don't say your mother."

We stepped into the juice bar and made our orders before settling on stools by the window bench.

"Don't worry, she won't be there. I'm not in the mood for more family drama. It's a big night for me."

She nodded pensively. "You become a millionaire."

"Well, it's not just that. But sure, that's exciting."

"What about Ma Chérie and Crisp?"

"I've left."

Her eyebrows flung up. "Well, good for you. But that sleazehole remains."

"Mm... maybe it won't."

She inclined her face to the side. "What do you know?"

I splayed my palms. "Nothing."

I wasn't about to tell her that Crisp had hooked up with Natalia, who had taken over my role. I'd since learned that her arrival was no coincidence. Crisp didn't seem to blink at the fact that Alek and Goran, those heavily built guys I'd seen hovering around the casino, were her brothers.

"That's colorful." I pointed at the purplish drink she'd just had delivered.

"Beetroot, carrot, and ginger. It's about as exciting as it gets these days. I'm not even having coffee." Her mouth turned down.

I grimaced. "Difficult. Coffee can't be bad, though."

"I'm not taking any risks with this miracle pregnancy."

She explained how Bram had damaged her chances of getting pregnant.

"I've heard that doctors aren't always right." I smiled sympathetically. "How far are you?"

"Three months."

I noticed the glass trembling in her hand, and I touched her arm. "Don't worry. I'm sure you'll do good. You've kicked booze, I take it."

"Oh, God yeah. It's amazing how clearheaded I feel. I'm even designing Kelvin's new house."

"Is that the guy who wears the tinselly jackets?"

She laughed. "Yep, that's him. You should see the color scheme. Oh my God, it's right out there. But fun."

"You'll have to show me some photos."

She pulled out her phone and showed me a collection of rooms exploding in color.

"You weren't kidding. One would have to wear sunglasses inside."

"Kelvin said that life was too short for beige and white." She laughed again. "But it's cool. Don't you think?"

"It's very seventies."

"That's what they're going for. I even designed the wallpaper."

She showed me a print with eyes, fish, and all kinds of strange creatures floating around. "It's like someone on magic mushrooms might have designed that." I gave her an apologetic half-smile. "I meant that as a compliment. I've never taken any, myself."

"I've had them, and one does see odd things. Mainly you laugh, though. Or at least I did. Ethan and I ate some when we were teenagers. We spent the whole time giggling at ducks and watching trees move around."

I shook my head in awe and envy. "I wish I had a brother I could do that with."

"Not a good idea. We were young and stupid." She chuckled. "Instead of magic mushrooms, I drew inspiration from Dali when coming up with the design."

"Who's that?" I felt dumb, as always, around my worldly relatives.

"The Spanish artist, Salvador Dali." She scrolled through her phone and pointed to an image of a woman with drawers coming out of her body.

"I love that." Fascinated, I felt a sudden urge to go out and find his book.

"Very twisted and imaginative at the same time. I love him. I'll lend you a book."

It was the nicest we'd ever been with each other, and it felt great.

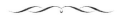

WHAT A DAY. I wanted to see Drake right then, but he was nowhere. I'd even worried something had happened to him. He wasn't answering my phone, and we were meant to catch up.

I couldn't stop thinking about Savanah and how she'd turned pale when the doctor had given her the sad news that her baby's heart had stopped beating.

Her sobs made me teary. A rare reaction. It took a lot to make me cry. She nearly squeezed the life out of my hand, but I didn't mind. Whatever the poor girl needed as she drowned in grief.

"Where's Carson?" she kept asking as we made our way out of the clinic after the doctor had given her a script and rattled off the need for a procedure while Savanah bawled her eyes out. I wouldn't want his job for anything.

With me clinging onto her, just in case she fainted, Savanah kept saying, "I need Carson."

I led her to a bench, and her phone buzzed.

With a trembling hand, she took the call, sobs spilling into her words. "Our baby is dead."

It was the afternoon, and people stared at us like we were weirdos. I even gave one woman the finger for staring that little too long.

"What's up your arse?" I couldn't help myself. People gave me the shits some days.

Savanah ended the call and sat there, frozen. I gave her space, unsure of what to say. I mean, I couldn't keep saying "it will be fine" over and over, which was what I'd said probably twenty times. I hated my lack of experience in tragic situations. As an only child with a mother whose emotional range comprised anger, spite, and suspicion, I didn't exactly have a role model when it came to soothing people. I did, however, feel very teary. My heart felt heavy like it was me who had lost the child.

"He's on his way." She quietened down after saying that.

We sat in silence, staring at life rushing by. A double-decker bus raced past. People coming and going filled the street—a reminder of how overpopulated London was. I wasn't about to let her in on that thought.

She exhaled loudly, then got up. "Come on, let's get drunk."

My eyebrows flung up. "Oh? Okay." I wasn't much of a drinker. I had to watch it. Two champagnes and I turned into a maniac. Either uncontrollable giggling at all the wrong times or talking shit.

We passed a pub that looked a little rough, mainly men who came from anywhere but the nice part of town.

"That will do," she said.

"Shouldn't we cab it back to Piccadilly?" I asked.

She looked like she was in a daze. "Nope. This is better. I don't want to be around cheery people having a great life. I might scream at them."

I nearly laughed. That was me. My aunty and I shared that in common. On my bad days, I felt like screaming at people.

"And Carson?" I asked as we stepped into the pub.

"He's coming. I'll send him the details."

"Why don't you sit somewhere, and I'll get the drinks?"

She nodded, and as I was about to head for the bar, she grabbed my hand. "Thanks."

A knot in my throat tightened. The sight of her puffy, sad eyes stirred pent-up feelings, but I managed a strained smile instead.

I was certainly out of my comfort zone because, were I to unleash what I really felt, especially with Savanah reaching out to me like that, I would cry for days. But that was not me. My mother had bludgeoned toughness into me. She believed tears and emotion weakened us. But since being with Drake, I'd become so raw and exposed, it felt like I might burst.

"What would you like?"

She opened her purse and removed a credit card. "Get me a double vodka tonic."

I didn't take the card. "It's okay, I can afford it."

She shrugged. "Make sure you get something, too. I don't want to drink alone."

I smiled. "Okay."

I stood at the bar and was careful not to lean too close or place my elbows on the sticky counter while waiting for the barman to lumber over and take my order.

The patrons perched against the bar turned and stared at me like I was an alien. I guess I was. They all looked like they were growing out of their chairs like they'd been in that same place all their adult lives.

I turned to the chubby, bulbous-nosed man closest to me. "You got a problem?" I hated people staring.

He turned away and continued drinking—all alone, like the rest of the sad creatures drowning in their pints of beer. I could only guess they hadn't had a chance in life. Or maybe they were too weak to go looking for it.

My mother always said that losers made their own beds. Had they tried harder, they would get jobs and do well.

I wasn't sure about that, because there had been days when I couldn't face myself, let alone people.

Thanks to Drake and my grandmother, that was no longer me.

I returned with our drinks, and like everyone there, we drank in silence while staring out the streaky window. If one could smell poverty and loneliness, that stale beer mixed with unwashed bodies would be it.

A couple of men, maybe in their late twenties, wearing Liverpool T-shirts, burst through the door and, zeroing in on us, strutted over.

"Here we go," I muttered.

Savanah was lost in her own world as she drained her glass.

"Hey, girls. Need some company?" one of them asked.

"Nope." I kept it short and sweet.

"You both look so sad." He pulled a tragic clown face. "Have you been dumped? Or is it the wrong time of the month?"

I rolled my eyes and remained silent, despite my inner bitch stirring.

"They must be lezzies." He turned to his mate.

"Nuh. They're too pretty to go for carpet munching." The other guy laughed.

I smashed the small prosecco bottle I'd just poured into my glass and held it to his face. "If you don't fuck off, I'll cut that smile from your ugly face."

Bewildered and wide-eyed, Savanah turned sharply to look at me.

I just eyeballed the dickheads, and they walked off.

Once the adrenaline had drained away, I got up and went to the bar. "Give me a dustpan and a cloth."

The barman handed it to me without batting an eyelid.

I cleaned up my mess, then ordered another drink for Savanah.

When I sat down again, Savanah shook her head slowly. "Holy fuck. That was insane."

"Sorry." I sipped my prosecco, and while my heart still thumped after what had been an out-of-body experience, I stared out the window to calm my nerves.

"That was ballsy." She shook her head in disbelief. "Where did that come from?"

I could see she would not let that violent outburst slide.

"Let's just say I grew up on the tough streets. We had to fend for ourselves."

She nodded slowly, giving me one of those I-think-I-finally-get-it looks. "I know nothing much about you. I'm sorry for hating you." She started on her second drink.

"That's all right. I hated all of you for a while there."

We looked at each and smiled.

Carson entered and went straight to Savanah and hugged her. He kept holding and rocking her, and I wasn't sure whether or not to stay.

I rose.

Savanah broke away. "Stay. We'll give you a lift back if you like."

"No. It's cool. I've got my car. Remember?"

She nodded. "You should have seen Manon," she said to Carson. "She smashed a bottle and threatened a couple of guys trying to hit on us."

"She did what?" Carson's eyes nearly popped out of his head.

I forced a smile. "Sorry."

He looked at me as though trying to solve a hard puzzle. "This is a rough joint." Carson turned to Savanah. "And what the hell are you doing here?"

She shrugged. "I don't know. Rough is good sometimes."

They had another one of their lingering moments, and I collected my bag for a quick exit.

"I'll be back at Merivale soon. Like in an hour or so. If you need anything..."

Savanah rose and hugged me. And that lump in my throat thickened. What an emotional day it had been, not just for Savvie but for me too.

"Thanks, niece."

We shared a smile, and I left them there, with Carson holding Savanah's hand. They were so into each other that nothing else seemed to matter.

I wanted that.

CHAPTER 10

Drake

WHILE WAITING IN AN office overlooking the farm, I watched workers lifting boxes of cabbages and spinach and wondered if my life would ever be the same after what had happened at the casino. Though I thought I'd shaken it off, I kept hearing the bullet ringing in my ear. I could have died saving Crisp. Why?

Put it down to instinct, I supposed, because I hadn't even had time to think.

While my head filled with gunfire and fiery sex with Manon, who I also couldn't stop thinking about, Declan entered the office and shook my hand.

He showed me around the office. "We just need someone to oversee the running of the farm and help with administration."

I nodded. "I'd love to give this a go. Thanks for giving me a chance. I need a break from the gym."

"Carson mentioned that you've grown a little too popular with the older female clients."

My face heated. It irked me knowing that I'd developed a toy boy reputation. "It was unintentional."

He smiled. "It's all good. Carson's just contracted a couple of new trainers. Are you still doing security for Crisp?"

I took a deep breath as the blood drained from my face. "I left last night. He wasn't happy."

He nodded slowly. "Can I ask why?"

"Why he wasn't happy?"

"No. Why you left?"

My stomach did somersaults. I hated lying to Declan, who felt like that older brother I'd never had. "I don't like the late hours, which reminds me, I hope your mother doesn't mind me not working at Manon's birthday party. I've been invited as a guest."

"You're seeing her, I believe."

"Well, kind of." I frowned—from one awkward subject to another. "How do you know?"

"My darling wife knows everything. I think she ran into Manon one morning leaving your place. You know small villages: everyone knows everything." His grin faded, and he turned serious. "Are you trying to keep it a secret?"

I shrugged. "No. But it's complicated."

He gave me a knowing look and nodded.

"It's just this thing she's got going with Crisp bugs me."

"Yeah... well, that's understandable. We're doing our utmost to see the back of that"—holding his fingers in quotation marks—"men's club."

I returned a smile at his reference to that sleaze bar.

I followed him into what was to be my new office, and he passed me a sheet that explained my tasks. Administration wasn't something I'd imagined ever doing, but I was good with computers.

Staring out the window, I noticed the construction of a new building. "What's that going to be?"

"That's our new indoor market, enabling us to sell to the public five days a week. We plan to not only stock organic veggies but other organics, like meat and vegan alternatives. Mirabel and Thea are keen on organic beauty products and cleaning materials that don't affect the planet. All locally sourced, of course."

"That sounds fantastic."

"We're launching in time for the summer solstice. We'll be hosting a fair."

"It's quite a community you're building here."

He smiled, looking proud. "That was always my intention. Keep the land producing and stave off development."

"I guess you've got that on the other side of Merivale with Elysium, the spa, and the casino."

He rolled his eyes. "Apart from the spa, which had little impact on the farmers, I was never a fan of Elysium, and I hate the casino being there."

If only he knew what went on in that casino. "This is so good of you to give me a go."

"As I recall, you were the one who got your hands dirty when we first started this project. You seemed to enjoy working in the dirt." He chuckled.

That was a guilty reminder of me and Billy messing around and having mud fights on those wet days at boot camp when instead of doing a ton of push-ups, we dug up a patch for veggies. Though I might have been cynical at the time about being forced to train hard, my life had changed for the better.

I hated to imagine where I would be without it, consumed by anger and doing crappy, underpaid work in London. Reboot had trained the hot-headed brawler out of me by giving me focus and an opportunity to grow into a better man. Something I would never forget.

I remembered, before arriving at Bridesmere, how I'd grumbled when the corrections officer had offered me an olive branch known as Reboot.

That was two years ago. I'd found well-paid work and was paying off my own apartment. I lived by the sea and dated one of the most beautiful girls I'd ever laid eyes on. She just needed to reserve her inner wild child for the bedroom and not the public. I loved her wild and untamed but only when alone with me.

She shoplifted, too, I'd only just discovered, having spotted her slip something into her bag at the supermarket.

"What?" she'd responded as though it were no big deal. Like she'd only taken a flower from someone's garden.

"I could have paid for that. Why didn't you ask?"

"Where's the fun in that?"

She'd shrugged, shoving the chocolate bar in her mouth like it was a cock, and I'd flipped from being shocked to horny.

As we stepped into Declan's office, he asked, "Can you start next week? Murray, who's a whizz kid with IT, will show you the ins and outs. I can pay you what you're getting at Reboot."

"That sounds good to me. I'll also do some night shifts for Carson's agency. I hope that's okay."

"That won't clash. There'll be no need to work late."

"I want to buy my mother a studio apartment around here."

"My mother's hiring kitchen staff, which comes with a residency at Merivale."

"In normal circumstances, I'm sure she'd jump at that opportunity, but she's got health issues."

"Oh, I'm sorry to hear that."

We shook hands, and off I went, feeling more relaxed than how I'd arrived.

As I entered Reboot, I caught sight of a man in a suit talking to Carson, so I went into the gym and did some weights while waiting.

Carson entered and rolled his eyes. "That was about Bram again."

"Oh?" I frowned. "They haven't questioned me."

Carson rubbed his head. "I've had a shit week, and now a fucking cop's hassling me." He sighed.

"Is it that bad?" Since I was his fake alibi, I had a hit of nerves.

"I'm not worried about the cops. It's just that Savvie lost the child."

His eyes went watery as he took a steadying breath, and wiping them with a tissue, he forced a smile. "Sorry. It's been tough. I'm becoming a bit too emotional, I'm afraid. Savvie even wanted to have a funeral." He shook his head. "I talked her out of it. Do you think that was right?"

He looked lost at sea.

"Um... I don't know, man. I mean, I lost my father, and some days I still feel like crying. Emotions will make us feel and do all kinds of strange things. If she wants some kind of private ceremony, then maybe there's no harm, I guess."

He held my stare and nodded slowly. "Yeah. Perhaps you're right. A ritual of sorts." He released a heavy breath.

"I'm sorry." I touched his arm.

"Don't worry. We're getting through it. As long as she's well, that's all that counts to me. I'm just sad for her. She's gutted." He sighed. "I couldn't be with her. I got caught up in fucking traffic. At least Manon was there."

I frowned. Manon hadn't mentioned that. "Really?"

He nodded, looking just as surprised as me. "Holy crap, she's something else."

Tell me about it.

"Manon's got balls. I'll tell you that much. And a fucking dangerous temper to boot."

"How? What happened?" I asked.

He recounted how Manon had threatened to glass some dickhead, and my jaw dropped. I was speechless. Her screaming at that pissed idiot outside the pub came to mind. Manon was a hothead all right.

Dangerous, but kind of admirable too. I was a sucker for someone who stood up for their mates.

"Anyway, I'm sorry to put you in the middle of this Bram bullshit case."

"They're still investigating it?"

"His father's appealing the verdict. He can't believe that his son intentionally shot himself up with heroin." He gave an ironic sniff. "He obviously turned a blind eye to his son's fucking track marks."

"He sounds deluded." I exhaled. "Anyway, don't worry about me. It felt like the right thing to do."

I recalled the day the cops turned up at Reboot, and when I'd heard them questioning Carson on his whereabouts that night, I'd jumped straight in. I knew Bram was a woman-bashing junkie causing hell for Savanah. Therefore, it had been easy for me to say that Carson had watched a game with me that night.

"Feel like a walk?" he asked.

"Sure. I was about to go for a run to the cliffs. But a walk through the woods is always nice."

We'd been walking for a while when he said, "Look, about Bram. Only Savvie knows this, but I feel like I owe you some explanation. I don't want you to think I had something to do with his death."

"Even if you did, I wouldn't blame you. The guy was a cunt."

"Can't argue there." He stopped walking. "Look, I went to see him. But when I arrived, he'd already ODed. He was at some run-down warehouse. No CCTV or anything. I just left."

"Then you're innocent," I said.

Lost in his thoughts, he nodded distractedly. "As a soldier, I was never faced with that gut-wrenching do-or-die situation where I had to kill a stranger or two or many. Lots of soldiers have been, many of whom are so haunted by the experience that they come back changed men. But Bram, and the danger he posed to my wife, sparked my dark side. Had he not injected himself with a bad batch of junk, I would have done it for sure."

Looking as haunted as the soldiers he'd just described, Carson turned his eyes to me, seeking some kind of response. I sensed that the issue had been eating away at him.

"I get it. If anyone tried to hurt my mother, I'd fucken kill."

He gave me a sad smile. "Thanks, mate. I feel better for having told you. I know you won't talk."

"You can rely on me. And anyhow, I'd end up in jail for perjury, or is it obstruction of justice? I don't mind the occasional episode of Law and Order." I chuckled.

His brow smoothed, and he smiled. "Hey, race you to the cliffs?"

"You're on."

We charged off. I didn't go full bore. As a sprinter at school, I had that competitive streak, but I had nothing to prove. Only friendship.

CHAPTER 11

Manon

DETERMINED TO END MY twentieth year on a high, I headed to My Cherry earlier than my usual starting time to meet with Crisp. He'd asked to see me, which was interesting. I expected him to say that Natalia, his latest plaything, had taken over. She already had from the looks of things, which suited me fine. She struck me as ambitious, and I sensed she'd planned it, through her brothers, to attach herself to Crisp.

One didn't need to be a genius to add the dots with Crisp. He could dab all that Dior Sauvage he wanted, but the stench followed him around. Speaking of which, he was soaked in it when I walked into his office—the smell hitting me immediately. His ruddy complexion suggested he'd been doing something lascivious—my new word for the day. I'd decided to use a new big word every day until my brain absorbed them.

Despite that noble ambition, reading had become a little difficult with all that was happening, and I preferred exploring Drake's penis rather than navigating D. H. Lawrence's complicated vocabulary. I could have tried another book, but I wanted to impress my grandmother and her smart boyfriend, who liked to talk about books—often leaving me bewildered. He was like a walking library. There wasn't a book he hadn't read, and he sure loved discussing them. I didn't mind, really. Anything that brought me closer to my grandmother.

Crisp sat back on his leather chair, balancing a scotch and a cigar in his large hand as carcinogenic vapors exited his mouth. Since I'd given up that dirty habit, I resented being a passive smoker.

"So, you wanted to see me?" I sat down in front of him.

"Yes. I've got a proposition for you."

My brow pinched. "What is that exactly? I was about to hand in my resignation."

An arrogant smile traveled from his chilly blue eyes to his thin lips. "Oh, that's right, tomorrow you come into your inheritance. Five million, I believe."

Of course, he would know. I hated that he knew everything. Grandmother had to stop his association. And I planned to tell her everything I knew about the horrid man, hoping to turn her.

"So? That's my business."

He leaned back and puffed smoke in my direction as though on purpose. Like a threat. "Oh, but that's where you're wrong, pretty girl. Because you are my business."

My brow squeezed. "You want me to continue working here?"

He shook his head, and my spine relaxed.

"I want you to marry me."

My jaw dropped, and a squeaky laugh flew out. "This must be a joke. Yeah?"

His deadpan silence answered that question.

"But I haven't even let you fuck me."

"That has been a bone of contention—you leading me on like that. I'm not an idiot." He slanted his head, wearing a cocky smirk. "It didn't take me long to discover you weren't pure, despite those lurid photos you so assiduously doctored."

What?

"I'm pure of heart." Puke. Did I really just say that? "Not like you, you dirty old man."

He laughed. Crisp loved being mocked. Perhaps he was into one of those weirdo fetishes of being whipped by a rubber-outfitted girl.

"You flatter yourself, dear girl. Your heart's far from pure. You stole from Harrods. I had to pay them off to avoid you being charged. I could open that case up if you like. At my request, they've kept the CCTV footage."

My fingers were so tightly crossed, I nearly snapped them off. My shoplifting habit had come back to haunt me. It wouldn't be the first time being caught. No one knew. Only Drake and my mother, who'd encouraged me to steal when I was little. She figured they wouldn't pick on a kid. I got good at it too. Stealing food at the supermarket, then clothes and makeup and all kinds of things.

I got off on the adrenaline, especially when pushed into a corner. Like at the Pond, after I screwed the owner and all the gossip and backstabbing that followed—stealing helped me deal with the stress.

"So, if I don't agree to marry you, you'll get me convicted for shoplifting?"

My grandmother had forgiven me for pawning her ruby necklace and even let me keep the money. If she could overlook that, then shoplifting paled in comparison.

"Do your worst. And by the way... I quit."

I was about to walk off when he pointed to the chair.

"Sit." His scraping tone felt like a whip lassoing me back onto the chair.

"You always said you weren't the marrying kind," I protested as my spine shivered at the thought of sleeping with him every night.

"I need to legitimize my empire by having a wife who can make me look good."

Another snort issued from my mouth. "And you think that's me? I'm not exactly upper class, am I?"

"More a work in progress. You're dressing more modestly. You look good and possess your grandmother's stature. Good paparazzi fodder. It doesn't hurt that you're photogenic."

Hearing I had a bit of my grandmother in me helped thaw some of the ice in my veins.

"And your noteworthy attempt at dropping that East London accent also helps."

"I'm not doing it so I can become your trophy wife. Far from it. No fucking way." I purposely reverted to cockney, hoping he would drop his ludicrous marriage proposal. "But really, why me?" I had to ask again if only to understand his true motives.

He poured himself another shot of whisky and offered me one, but I declined.

"Because you know me." His eyebrow lift spoke volumes.

"By that, you mean my knowing of your hunger for young flesh?"

Yep, he sounds like a fucking cannibal. More like a devourer of souls.

"That's part of it, of course." He relit his cigar. "I'll reciprocate, of course. You can screw whoever you like. Only it must remain clandestine."

"And if I say no?"

"Then the world will learn how you've been pulling tricks for money. Which includes me. You led me on. All that silliness about me having to pay you millions."

"That's a fucking lie!" I leaped off my chair and planted my fists on my hips.

"Keep your voice down," he growled.

"You're not my fucking father," I snapped.

"No, I'm not. I've met him. He's nothing like me."

I fell into the seat, and my jaw dropped. "How have you met him? Where is he? I've been looking for him."

He took a sip and wiped his mouth. "Easy to find. He's a kept man who sends out his high-powered lawyer wife to work while he sits back and does little."

"You've met him?" I couldn't believe it. "Where is he?"

"Notting Hill. I can give you the address if you like. I'm sure he won't want to see you, though. When I brought you up, he flinched and asked that his past remain buried."

"That's because he fucking beat me, the arsehole."

"Then why do you want to see him?"

Good fucking question. "I don't know. He's my father, I guess." I sighed.

"I got the feeling he wasn't too keen on seeing your mother."

"Yeah, well... that doesn't surprise me. They weren't exactly compatible."

That image of my father's hands around my mother's throat after discovering her fucking for money came to mind. That was the final straw. He left us after that.

"He didn't expect to marry a whore, I suppose." He grinned, clearly enjoying himself.

I shook my head and sprang up. "You have no right to discuss my family. And I'd prefer to beg on the streets in tattered clothes than marry you."

"But you will marry me."

His snaky smile made my skin crawl. I sensed he had more in his arsenal with which to destroy me.

"Why are you even here?" I had to ask. "I don't get it. Isn't London a bigger oyster for you? My Cherry stands out here. People hate it."

"You're turning it into a mockery and something sordid by calling it that."

"Well, excuse me, but a bunch of horny old men chasing virgin pussy is just that. I thought it was rather apt. And where's your sense of humor in all of this?"

"Hmm..." he grunted. "I'm here because of the prestige that comes from associating with old money, and the Lovechildes are of the finest pedigree. Though I question the marriages all three children have made. Lovechilde offspring marrying commoners was never in Caroline's narrative." He smirked. "She even came crying to me after Declan fell for that maid, then Ethan followed suit by marrying a hippie. She didn't seem to mind Carson, though. I suppose having someone looking after her damaged daughter played into that."

"Inbreeding makes unhealthy kids. And English aristocracy is famous for inbreeding. Something you wouldn't know about, since I imagine, like me, you sprang from some dark seed."

Instead of taking offense, he nodded, looking impressed. "Dark seed... my, you're demonstrating a poetic streak."

"Let me get this straight. By marrying me, you remain close to the Lovechildes. Is that it?" I needed to understand what was cooking in that evil head of his.

"I'm already in thick with Caroline. Always will be. But I need that extra leverage."

"What are you planning?" I had to ask.

He looked pleased like I'd asked the kind of question that enabled someone to sing their own praises. "I'm planning a lot. The Lovechildes own half this region, which doesn't just include farm acreage but also numerous crumbling estates occupied by financially stressed heirs." Wearing an arrogant smirk, he stared into my eyes. "And with you as my doting wife, we can build an empire. You'd like that, wouldn't you?"

"But Declan and Ethan won't sit back and allow that."

"Everything, bar that hippie enclave Declan's developing by Chatting Wood is in Caroline's name. Ethan's got the hotels, which he's expanding worldwide, and Savanah's sitting on a couple billion pounds."

I shook my head. "You know so much about this family, don't you?"

"Oh, I've made it my life's work to know everything." His satisfied smile made me want to pick up the ashtray and smash it over his head. With that long face, he looked like he'd already had his head squashed between two bricks.

"What about if I move to London and leave all this behind?" I asked.

"That's perfect. You can be my wife for all those important events, and behind the scenes, you can have your cavalier servente."

"I do not know what that is."

"Look it up. You're studying English lit, I believe."

"Why don't you groom Natalia? She strikes me as keen."

"She's not a Lovechilde, and I don't like what comes out of her mouth."

Then stuff your tiny dick in it.

"So if I refuse, you'll tell everyone I was whoring myself and shoplifting?"

"You won't refuse. Oh... and by the way, you need to stop seeing Drake."

"What?" I exploded. "Fuck you. You can't tell me what to do."

"Remember what that video did for Savvie?" he asked.

"You have nothing on me."

"Oh, we can do anything. You know that. After all, you doctored those porn images for me."

"I hate you. I'm not fucking marrying you."

"I thought you'd say that. So, right now, I have someone waiting for my call and your darling Drake will take a nice long holiday somewhere far, like Australia. You'll never see him again."

"You can't. I'll tell everyone."

"I don't think they'll believe the words of a thief and the plaything to rich men. Let's not forget Peyton."

I wanted to crawl into a cave and hide. Hide from my ugly past and the man in front of me who made Peyton look like that nice guy who would donate his kidney to a stranger.

"So, you knew all along I wasn't a virgin, and you still pursued me?"

"Once I discovered your blood association with Caroline, I stuck around. I knew, one day, you'd come in handy for something."

"But everyone knows you're not the marrying kind."

"A person can change." He strained a smile. "And I didn't expect to fall hard for someone."

His blood-freezing chuckle made me want to stick my hands down my throat.

He fluttered his hand as a king might to his servant. "Now, off you go and get that wedding party set up. Let's go all out, shall we?" He grinned. "Maybe a spread in Vogue?"

Drunk on anxiety, I felt my head spin out of control. "And if I say yes, Drake will be safe?"

"Safe to enjoy his farming life with Declan and keep fucking rich older women."

"But I want to be with him."

His mouth turned down with patronizing sympathy. "Oh, dear girl, he's too nice for you."

"Then you fucking young girls at My Cherry won't go down well if you're married, will it?"

"That's about to move somewhere away from prying, puritanical eyes."

That news would at least please everyone, I thought, leaving with a heavy heart.

What the fuck am I going to do?

CHAPTER 12

Drake

WHILE ON MY DAILY run up to the cliffs, I bumped into Theadora with her son and their Jack Russell.

"Hey there." She waved.

Julian, who looked more like Declan each time I saw him, tossed a ball to the dog.

Wiping my brow, I pointed at the frothy waves pounding against the towering, chalky cliffs. "Nice view, isn't it?"

"Stunning. I never tire of coming here. Any excuse. And the steep ascent is a good heart work out." She giggled. "Look at you, running all the way up. I'd need constant breaks."

"I've trained myself. In the beginning, I had to pause for the odd breather."

Her face sparked up. "Hey, it's Declan's birthday, and we're having drinks at the Mariner tonight. I wanted to throw a proper party, but he didn't like that idea." She rolled her eyes. "In the end, he agreed to drinks at our local instead. Mirabel's performing a set."

"That sounds great. I have noticed that the Lovechildes throw lots of parties."

"It's fun, though. I enjoy being social. I never used to, but since joining the family and becoming one of them,"—she raised an eyebrow as though that had taken work—"I rather enjoy them. As next week is Manon's twenty-first party, I don't think Declan felt like combining the events."

I remained tight-lipped despite Theadora pausing for a response. Maybe she noticed me flinching at the mention of Manon. I couldn't exactly hear that name without a bodily response.

Her constant text messages with the occasional sexy image of her in a skimpy bra kept this thing between us bubbling away, or more like steaming.

Crisp demanding that I stop seeing her still made me anxious, and I'd knocked back a load of cash too. But a deal with the devil wasn't on my bucket list.

"Are you going to Manon's twenty-first?" she asked.

I nodded.

She tilted her head. "You're still seeing each other?"

"It's kind of complicated." Switching the subject, I asked, "So, what time are the drinks tonight?"

"Around eight. I hope you can make it. Should be fun. I might even play a tune or two." She smiled shyly.

"You guys are legends. I love Mirabel's mermaid song. It's amazing."

"Yeah. She's so talented and creative."

"So are you. You're such a skilled musician. Are you still teaching children?"

She nodded. "I love it. We've got a concert coming up. Mirabel and Ethan's boy, Cian, is playing a tune. He's talented for a five-year-old."

My eyebrows rose. "Wow. That's young."

"That's how prodigies are made."

"His parents want him to become a concert pianist?" I asked.

"I don't think they mind what he becomes. But he seems to enjoy it, and he practices."

"And is Julian also musical?" I cast an eye at Declan's little double.

He threw the ball to the unstoppable canine, Freddie, whose whole meaning in life seemed to revolve around chasing that ball.

"He's a little too distracted to practice." She shrugged. "I don't mind. There are a ton of musicians in the world. He seems more obsessed with planes and trains."

I laughed. That sounded like me as a kid.

Julian tugged at my leg. "I'm taking swimming lessons today." He looked all excited.

Theadora laughed. "He loves the water. Cary's teaching him."

"Really?" That took me by surprise. "Whenever I run into him at Merivale, he's either writing on a notepad or reading."

"I guess that makes sense. He's a writer. Apparently, he was a champion swimmer in his young Eton days and even trained swimmers for a while."

"Gee, that's unexpected. I know little about him. I guess I know little about everyone here. Except for Declan and Carson, of course."

"There are a ton of secrets." She giggled. "I suppose you can't have a family history going back hundreds of years and not expect all kinds of hidden information locked away." She held my stare. "Speaking of secrets, have you seen those heavies hanging around Salon Soir?"

That shot ringing past my ear was still causing me nightmares and night sweats.

"I've seen a few guys coming and going. But I'm no longer there."

"Oh? I thought you were doing security. Every time I've been there, you've been working as a bouncer."

A bead of sweat that had nothing to do with my running dripped down my neck. "I've moved on. I'll work for Carson's team when he offers the odd gig, but I'm happy at the farm."

"Declan's happy to have you." She smiled. "Rumour has it that drug dealers are laundering their money at the casino."

Theadora seemed determined to keep the discussion open.

"I saw all manner of people coming and going. I'm just happy to be out of there."

She nodded. "Julian, come along."

Her son raced off down their path, chasing Freddie.

"We'll see you tonight, then," she added.

She kissed me on the cheek, and I ran off.

I'd forgotten to ask if they had invited Manon. My heart hoped so, as did my body. My head, however, was in another universe. Crisp wasn't someone to fuck with. But I hated being told what to do. My mother was the only person who had that privilege.

Maybe Manon too, when she got all bossy and demanded I show her my dick, which turned me to putty. Obviously not my dick, which went rock hard just from seeing her pink tongue brushing those beautiful rosebud lips.

MY AFTERNOON SPED ALONG. Time flew at the farm, which I preferred to watching the clock, as I often did when working as security.

In fact, I preferred the farm over every other job I'd done so far, including training. Sometimes I even helped with sowing or weeding and spreading compost. I enjoyed getting my hands dirty. Though employed in the office, I soon discovered each day offered something different.

After what had been a big day dealing with builders for the new market, I rode my bike back to the village to my apartment. Then Kylie appeared out of nowhere. Taking a quick diversion, I turned into a side street, and when I heard my name, my shoulders slumped.

I had to stop riding and acknowledge her, despite wishing I could summon my inner arsehole and tell her to fuck off. Being rude wasn't my thing—unless someone pushed a few buttons one time too many. And Kylie was close to doing that.

"You're not returning my messages," she said.

"Kylie, look." I took a breath. This was not me. I wasn't the breaking-off type of guy.

Since when did a blow job constitute a relationship?

Manon was as serious as I'd ever gotten with a girl. And for me, at least, it felt serious, considering I'd just knocked back a ton of cash to keep seeing her. Before her, I just saw girls as fun, even though I hated the idea of hurting anyone. I'd even thought of staying away from sex for a while to avoid all the mess that followed.

With Manon, it was different, and it was more than just the hot sex. I enjoyed being around her. Despite her stirring trouble now and then, she fascinated me. The last time we'd been together, she'd spoken about the books she'd been reading. I could see she was trying to improve herself. I appreciated that in any person because I wanted that for me too.

Kylie stroked my arm. "Mm… you're a little sweaty." She ran her tongue over her plump lips.

"The hills are steep." I brushed my hair away from my brow. "Look, Kylie. I don't want this to continue. I've already told you that."

"Mm… you have. But I'm sure you wouldn't mind this." She grabbed my cock, and I had to look around to make sure no one saw us.

I stepped away. "This is turning into fucking harassment. Leave me alone."

"I don't want to." She made a sad face. "Do you want me to tell everyone that you touched me inappropriately while being my trainer?"

"That's bullshit. Do your fucking worst." I turned my back.

"Oh… you don't know how fucking hot you make me when you're angry."

"Fuck off, Kylie."

I jumped on my bike and pedaled off with force.

THE MARINER HAD BECOME my favorite place. Being the only pub in town, I had little choice. As I entered, I found the Lovechilde clan milling around at the bar. Ethan was telling some joke about an Irish cocksucker to which Mirabel accused him of being racist.

"Okay, he's an English cocksucker then." He laughed.

"Punch line, please," Savanah prompted.

"He got a mouth full of feathers."

Ethan killed himself laughing while everyone else went "Ha ha ha."

"Hey, there you are." Carson slapped me on the back. "Good to see you made it. We've been missing you at Reboot. Especially the girls."

I rolled my eyes. "I thought this would give me a good excuse to get hammered." I chuckled.

Carson already knew I wasn't a heavy drinker, despite my being tanked up on the odd occasion, mainly around Billy, who was a bad influence and could drink anyone under the table. He had the liver of an Irishman, as my mother often claimed.

I joined Declan. "Happy birthday. I only just heard today. I was on a run up to the cliffs when I met your wife, and she invited me."

He looked pleased. "Happy to see you here. And by the way, thanks for helping with the builders today. I was called away."

Theadora, who was standing close, added, "To his shiny new toy."

Declan chuckled at her dry comment. "I've just upgraded my plane."

He said it like he'd just traded in a car. I'd never met anyone who owned his own plane before—a reminder of my boss's considerable wealth and how he used it to give people like me a chance.

"Wow. That's cool," I said.

"We're off for a quick trip to Spain." He smiled at Theadora, but she didn't look that excited.

"You're not a happy flyer?" I asked her.

"I am slowly getting used to it. I just fear for Declan's safety when he goes off on his rescue missions."

Ethan jumped in. "That's Dec. The do-gooder of the family."

"I'd prefer if he'd volunteer at a dog rescue shelter or something," Theadora muttered.

Declan placed his arm around her and drew her in tight. Her face softened. If ever I needed a picture of love, I had it there with Declan and Theadora.

Just like Ethan, who also had his arm around Mirabel.

"I didn't know that about you," I said. "Have you rescued anyone lately?"

"Last week, we had to winch up a man who went off course in his boat in rough waters."

Both surprised and impressed, I nodded. "That must have been on the television."

He shrugged. "I prefer to fly under the radar." He smiled.

I was about to respond when Manon entered.

As she swanned in, Manon made heads turn, especially the male patrons. She smiled over at us, then her eyes landed on mine and held me captive. I'd never met a woman who could do that, but then, Manon was a unique experience.

"Someone invited Manon?" Ethan frowned.

I knew they hadn't exactly warmed to her. Manon had admitted that she wanted to be accepted and regretted rubbing her new family the wrong way.

She leaned in and kissed Declan and handed him a gift, then Savvie stepped in and hugged Manon, which drew a sunny response from Manon.

After all the greetings had happened, Manon turned to me. "Back in a minute."

Off she went, swaying those hips and looking even more beautiful than the last time I'd seen her.

"So, who invited her?" Theadora asked.

"I did," Savanah said. "We've gotten close."

"Even after she stole your clothes and made all those bitchy comments?" Mirabel asked.

"Let's just say we've bonded, and she's not that stirrer anymore."

"Working at that fucking Cherry bar isn't exactly helping her cause," Ethan responded.

"I hear she plans to leave, and anyhow, she was there for me at the hospital." Savanah pulled a sad smile, and Carson put his arm around her. "She's young and had a tough upbringing. We all fuck up. Don't we?"

"I guess you're right. And imagine having Bethany as a fucking mother. Beelzebub in Prada." Ethan grimaced.

Mirabel left to perform just as we all got our drinks.

The pub filled steadily as more people arrived to join our group. The Lovechildes knew everyone in that village it seemed, and Declan, I soon discovered, had placed his card down at the bar to shout the whole pub and had catered with finger food.

Three craggy old fishermen sitting up at the bar lifted their pints in gratitude.

"They remind me of the trio in that 'Old Greg' skit from Mighty Boosh," Ethan said.

Declan laughed loudly.

"I've seen that on YouTube. It's fucking hilarious. Those three men stuffed together in the overgrown jumper playing Irish jigs," I said.

Everyone joined me in a laugh.

Manon returned and pulled a face. "What's everyone laughing about?" Her pretty eyes did a sweep of the group before landing on my face and making me forget what we were talking about.

"Just this skit in a crazy Brit show," Theadora said.

"Oh. I don't watch television. Haven't got the time." She sounded a little uncertain as she spoke.

I wondered if something was wrong.

She stood next to me, and then, much to my horror, Kylie arrived. Given she lived in the village and that was the only pub, I shouldn't have jumped to conclusions about why she was there.

Just as I was inventing some excuse for leaving, jasmine hit my nasal passage—a scent that conjured up all kinds of sweet, dirty memories—radiating from Manon's long, dark hair.

I wasn't going anywhere.

CHAPTER 13

Manon

"You invited her?" I asked.

"Nope." Drake gave off an edgy vibe. He kept sweeping his hand over the curl that fell across his forehead, and all I wanted to do was suggest we leave so I could seduce him.

Fuck you, Rey. I'll keep seeing him if I like.

"Oh. Here she comes, looking like she's ready to pounce. Maybe I should say hi to Max." I cocked my head towards a laborer from Declan's organic farm who, though kind of hot, wasn't Drake.

No one was.

I cringed at how childish I sounded, trying to make him jealous.

However, the thought of Kylie or any other woman fucking Drake made me green with jealousy.

Drake belonged to me.

If only Kylie wasn't so gorgeous, with her thick blonde hair, big boobs, and long legs.

"You can do whatever you want." I was just about to give him the middle finger when he added, "I'm not into Kylie. You know that. I've told you often enough."

His tone was rough and almost angry, which only made me want him more. I wanted him to be rough with me. Physical pain was preferable to the crazy shit in my head.

Savanah joined me at the bar. "How are you? You look a little off-color."

"I'm okay." I sighed. "Just man problems."

She smiled sympathetically. "I thought you and Drake were together?"

Kylie had cornered him for what looked like a heart-to-heart. I couldn't see his face, but she was almost on top of him.

"It looks like he's got a girlfriend."

I kept stealing glances and comparing myself to her in that hot-pink, skimpy sheath that just covered her bum and showed off her long, toned legs. She could have her fair share of men.

Unlike Kylie, I was no longer dressing like some perv magnet. I'd only found that wearing skimpy gear attracted wankers and old sleazy men. In any case, designer made me feel sexy.

"He looks a little rattled, and it seems like he's giving her a tongue lashing," Savanah said as she snuck a peek at Drake and Kylie.

"Mm... as long as it's directed at her face and not her fanny."

Savvie nearly spat out her drink with a giggle. "That's amusing. I'm sure he's more into you. He keeps looking over here."

Mirabel strummed her guitar, and everyone's attention went to the small lit-up stage.

"Hey, thanks for inviting me," I said.

Savvie smiled. "You're part of the family."

That was what I wanted to hear. Being a part of something that didn't involve scams and lies mattered to me. Even when they were hating me, for which I couldn't blame them, given my bitchy behavior—I quietly admired my uncles and aunt.

As always, Mirabel stunned for all the right reasons. People just couldn't take their eyes off her. She commanded such a presence on stage. Wearing a slinky green dress, she captured everyone's attention not just because of her witchy songs but by her unique style. Fashion didn't mean a thing to her, yet she always looked amazing. And Uncle Ethan was so in love with her. It was written all over his smile.

"Does Mirabel wear anything other than green?" I asked.

Savvie chuckled. "I asked her the same thing, and she said that green's the color of Venus."

I nodded. "Nice. It suits her with that lustrous red hair."

"It does. I love this song too."

"Me too." Instead of watching the man I loved being seduced, I turned my attention to the stage.

The music swept me away to a magic forest filled with fairies and witches and sexy men in capes who looked like Drake. Her poetic words, sung in that husky voice of hers, gave me a break from the storm brewing within me.

After singing three songs, Mirabel welcomed Theadora onto the stage. My uncle's wife sat at the piano and performed a solo as her fingers glided over the keys in an impressive, effortless fashion.

As I glimpsed Uncle Declan looking like a proud and smitten husband, I wondered if I would ever make my future husband proud—a question I never even would have considered once. I used to think that having me naked in bed was their special gift from me.

I couldn't help but envy Mirabel and Theadora for their art. And Savvie, too, who was great at design.

What am I good at?

I regretted leaving school at fifteen, which was my mother's doing. She'd paired me off with Peyton, and I'd ended up living a lazy life in his double-story Chelsea home, where I'd learned how to fuck. He'd made me prance around the house in lingerie, and in return, I had a credit card I could spend to my heart's content. Only I rarely smiled. Funny. As I thought back on that time, I couldn't recall ever smiling.

Kylie had attached herself to Drake, and I wanted to tear her eyes out.

I joined them. After all, he was my boyfriend.

Wasn't he?

We hadn't been together for a few nights, which stung. He'd pushed me away and wasn't returning my texts. I couldn't figure out why and even wondered if I'd upset him. Perhaps it was because he'd run off with Kylie.

Drake headed off to the men's room, and unable to control my inner bad girl, I approached Kylie.

"You seem pretty close to Drake," I said.

She stared me down like I was some worthless being. "He's my boyfriend. Who are you?"

"Your boyfriend? He's been with me for the last month or so." I exaggerated because it had been less than that.

"Not anymore if I can help it."

Pouting with that unnaturally plump mouth made her look comical, I thought.

"He forced himself on me," she added. "I've forgiven him. He's too nice to ignore. And though it was like rape, I don't mind."

What?

When Drake returned, I turned him into a devil. Horns and all. A fucking gorgeous one.

But then the devil would be, wouldn't he?

"What's wrong?" he asked, looking from me to Kylie.

"You're evil." My eyes burned from the threat of tears. Refusing to give Kylie the satisfaction of seeing how she'd affected me, I turned my back to her sharply and marched to the loo, head held high.

The emotional pain intensified with each breath I took. I couldn't believe I'd allowed myself to fall so deeply in love.

My mother was right about love weakening us.

Once I was in the toilet, I rummaged through my bag and driven by frustration, I emptied the contents on the ground and picked up the flick knife I'd been carrying around since thirteen.

London was a dangerous place. I'd already defended myself once when some junkie had tried to rob me. I hadn't stabbed him, but I'd flicked the knife close to his heart.

Recalling how freaked out Drake had been at seeing those cuts on my inner thigh, I opted for my outer thigh instead. Whenever something dragged me into a dark place, cutting was my only coping mechanism. Alcohol didn't remove pain, and I hated the way drugs made me feel.

A deep sting took my breath away, and as I bled, pain transferred from my heart to my wound.

I sopped up the blood with toilet paper, and knowing it would probably show on my jeans, I decided I would make a quick dash for the exit.

I couldn't hang around, watching Drake getting all hot and close with another woman.

But rape? That wasn't Drake. Was it?

Drake was always so gentle. Except for that angry kiss. And he did push me against the wall to fuck me from behind, but that was seriously hot.

Though he came across as sweet, I'd seen the fire in his eyes, especially when we fucked, and those gorgeous blue eyes burned into mine. When I'd asked why he kept staring, he'd said he loved looking at me.

Was he just playing with me? If so, he was an excellent actor, or I was just a gullible stooge.

I sat there, buried my head, and cried.

The door flung open, and Savvie covered her mouth. "Oops. Sorry."

I stared up at her like a stunned rabbit. I should have locked the door.

Her eyes landed on my cuts and widened in shock. "What the fuck? Mannie?"

She called me Mannie. That was all I could think of at that moment. Drake had called me that once, and it had made me feel like a different person. Like we'd known each other forever.

"Your leg. It's bleeding." She pointed down at me.

I must have looked a sight. Sitting on the loo, my pants down at my feet. It took me a moment to realize what was happening. I'd been caught doing the unthinkable. People like me were freaks. Weirdos, who needed serious help. No one knew. Not even my mother. Not that she would give a shit.

"Did you injure yourself or something?"

Yeah. I cut myself because that's what I do when life sucks.

"There's a lot of blood." She opened her bag and brought out a plaster bandage. "Here, I carry them around for blisters when I'm breaking in new shoes."

"Oh, okay." I took it from her.

She looked down at the ground and saw the knife that I should have kicked away, but I was too shocked. It all happened so fast.

After staring at the blood-stained knife, as though trying to make sense of what happened, Savvie shifted her gaze to me. "Mannie, what the fuck have you been doing?"

I bit my lip, which trembled like mad. Normally, I would middle-finger anyone wanting to get into my fucked-up head, but Savvie had let me into hers, and I felt like I owed her something.

I picked up the knife, wiped it with toilet paper, flicked it back into its case, then popped it back into my bag.

Staring at me with expectation written all over her face, Savvie pointed at my leg. "Why hurt yourself like that?"

She unraveled the toilet paper and handed it to me. "Here, clean yourself up, then we can put a plaster on it."

I sat there on the toilet, looking pathetic, I imagined, unable to move. The shock of being caught overwhelmed me, and tears poured out like the blood spurting from my cut. I'd cut deeper than usual.

My heart felt like it was going to tear apart. I couldn't face her, let alone all my shit buried in a cupboard, bursting with torn memories that needed mending or to be tossed out.

Burying my face in my hands, I wanted to curl up somewhere and hide.

She joined me on the ground and held my hand.

"Listen. I thought of killing myself a few times. I know how you feel. Like you're being swallowed up by a dark cloud and can't find a way out."

That, I wasn't expecting. Savvie seemed to glide through life, even when walking like she was about to burst into a dance.

"Oh?" was all I could say. I wasn't good at that kind of deep reveal. No one had ever been interested enough to confide in me before. "But you have everything." I went to the basin, where I cleaned and bandaged my cut.

"There were some pretty dark moments in my life with Bram. I'm sure you know what I mean."

"Oh, that sex tape." I grimaced. "Sorry for making fun of you that time. I wasn't really in a good place. I'm still not." I gave a dark chuckle at that understatement.

"Anyway, Mannie." She smiled tightly. "You don't mind me calling you that?"

"No. I love it." I smiled, and a streak of sunshine melted some of the ice in my heart. Interesting what a chat with someone who'd also done some freaky shit could do.

We stood at the mirror, and I fixed my face. I dabbed my eyes to clean away the makeup. "So much for waterproof."

She nodded. "Tell me about it. I've had my tear fests and ended up looking like some psycho clown."

I laughed at that silly image before going dead serious again. "Please don't tell anyone. Not even Carson."

She crossed her heart. "No. I get it. But hey, you need help, sweetie. It's not good to do that. How often have done this to yourself?"

I stared down at my feet. "Lost count."

Her brows gathered. "Really? How old were you the first time?"

"Maybe seven." I swallowed tightly.

Shaking her head in disbelief, Savvie asked, "Why? I mean, doesn't it hurt?"

"That's the idea." I took a deep breath. Tears burned again. My throat choked back a sob. I'd never shared that about myself before.

"Oh. I'm sorry. Why don't we go somewhere for a coffee? I don't mind. Carson and Declan will understand."

"You'd do that? You'd leave what looks like a great night to listen to my crappy story?"

She smiled. "There are a million of these parties. You know that."

Yes, they liked to party. And I loved that about the family. Who didn't like a party?

"It's all good. I think I feel better now. Maybe we can meet in London to shop and have a drink. I'd love that."

"Sure. Always. I'll introduce you to my wicked girlfriends. Jacinta's having a party next week. She moved to Notting Hill. Why don't you come along? Carson hates parties, so it would be great to have someone to gossip with."

I laughed.

She hugged me, and another tear slid down my cheek.

"Thanks, Savvie, for allowing me in. It means everything."

She smiled. "Why don't we go out there and you flirt with your dishy Drake?"

"Kylie told me that Drake forced himself on her."

Savvie's head jerked back. "No. That's impossible to believe. He's a sweetie."

"That's what I thought, but they seem lost in a deep and meaningful."

She led me out. "Don't worry. She's just trying to force herself on him more like it. Don't believe everything you hear."

We'd walked another step when she turned and took my hand and stared seriously into my face. "Now, you promise me that if you're feeling that low again, you call me. Okay? Before doing that to yourself."

I bit my lip and nodded with a shaky smile.

Drake stood at the bar, and his eyes followed me. Kylie wasn't there, and the sting in my leg stopped more negative thoughts.

CHAPTER 14

Drake

"I HEARD YOU'RE NO longer at Salon Soir," Carson said as we leaned against the bar, enjoying our free pints of stout.

"Something's going on there. That Reynard Crisp's pretty fucken rotten."

"Huh." He sniffed. "You're not telling me anything new."

Overhearing us, Declan asked, "Have you seen something?"

"He's employed these Eastern European brothers. I'm not sure what they do, but they strike me as nasty." I shouldn't have said anything, but describing myself as bothered by what had happened during my last shift at Salon Soir was an understatement.

I could have died that night, and though I'd deposited that fifty-thousand-pound cheque towards my mother's new home, I needed to unburden myself because there was danger happening close to the Lovechildes. I owed more to Declan and keeping his family safe than I did Crisp. That cheque was payment for saving his life. Nothing more.

I turned to Carson. "Can we talk somewhere?"

He followed me out, and we passed Kylie coming out of the bathroom. She winked at me, and I gritted my teeth. I just wished she would find someone else to rub up against.

Carson laughed. "She's still got the hots for you, I see."

"It's driving me nuts. I might have to report her."

He frowned. "Why aren't you going public with Manon?"

"That's a long, shitty story. It all goes back to Crisp." I sighed.

Just as we were about to walk outside, I turned to scan the dance floor where a DJ had set up. I caught Manon and Savanah going crazy there, their arms waving and hips swinging, giggling like they were having a ball.

"Your wife and Manon have become chummy, I see."

"So, it would seem. I think it's a positive development for them both." Once we were outside, he turned to face me. "Tell me, what's up?"

I told him about the attack on Crisp.

"A pity the hitman was such a bad shot." He smirked.

"That was my doing. I pushed Crisp out of the way, and the bullet just passed me. I can still hear ringing in my ears."

He frowned. "You need to get your hearing tested, mate. The same thing happened to me. It's now passed, but it took some time." He shook his head as though what I'd just said had only just sunk in. "Shit. You saved the bastard."

"It's what we're meant to do as security. Isn't it?"

He nodded. "That's how we train our team. As you know. You attended the workshops." He paused. "And he bought your silence with a fifty-thousand-pound cheque."

"I shouldn't have taken it. I could have gone to the cops."

"No. He's too big for that. He's probably got cops working for him. I'd stay away if I were you. But I'll bring it up with Declan. Do you mind?"

"No. I trust Declan not to go around telling everyone."

"Caroline already knows there's large-scale drug importation happening there."

My eyebrows rose. "You're kidding, and she's, like, allowing that?"

"It's his venue. His world. She's disturbed by it for sure. But Crisp has her wrapped around his crooked finger. Not a word to anyone about what I just told you. Especially Manon." He cocked his head. "There she is now."

I turned and saw Manon sucking on a vape.

"Better go back in. Anything, and you come to me. Okay? You don't have to keep this stuff to yourself. I know how suffocating that can be."

He hugged me and headed back inside.

I wanted to leave. If only to escape Kylie. All my issues were turning me into a nervous wreck. I just wanted to hide in my room with my PlayStation or drink cups of tea with my mother. I needed her. She would calm me, and help me sleep better. Manon had helped that one night we stayed together after the shooting. I didn't even have a nightmare. With her soft, beautiful body in my arms and her sweet breath on my skin, life felt special, like I could do anything. Be anything.

I was about to turn away when she tapped me on the arm.

"Talk to me." Smoke poured out of that perfect mouth that fitted mine like it belonged on my lips.

"When did you take up vaping?"

"A few days ago." She looked sad.

"Full of harmful chemicals, Manon."

"So what? Better than harmful people."

We locked eyes, and all I could think of was us naked in bed.

"Your girlfriend's coming on pretty strong." She kept blowing smoke in my face like it was a form of punishment.

"She's not my fucking girlfriend. She's making my life hell. I don't want her." Anger built, and if I didn't walk away, I might explode and say something I would regret, like telling Kylie to fuck off. "I'm going. I'm over this."

Manon grabbed my arm. "Wait." Her eyes were wide and glassy. "Why are you being horrible to me? Why aren't you answering my texts? You're no longer into me?"

I raked my fingers through my hair. "Quite the opposite, Manon. I think I've made it pretty fucking obvious that I'm into you. It's not something I can fake. You, however…"

Her brow creased. "I'm not faking. I'm always calling you. It feels like I'm doing all the chasing."

We locked eyes once more, embarking on a wordless conversation. Something we did often.

Her eyes shone with want, uncertainty, and even a hint of fear, which struck me as odd. Manon had always seemed fearless.

Why did Crisp want me to stay away from her?

And why should I allow him to place a wedge between us?

Manon had me on a string and was in control of my actions.

She'd become a bit of an addiction I was trying to control, despite my hormones going into overdrive whenever I caught a whiff of her hair or those large, limpid, teasing eyes trapped mine.

"I think about you first thing in the morning and last thing at night." I kicked a stone around on the ground.

"Oh, you do?" Her forehead smoothed, and a wide smile grew on her pretty face. She put away her vape. "What do you think about?"

I shrugged. "Sexy things. Like you rubbing your tits over my dick."

She lifted her tits, and my cock thickened.

"Mm... now you're making me all hot," I said.

I took her hand and brought her up against me, then my mouth crushed hers, and I felt her curves pressed against my suddenly horny body. My dick engorged fast as blood pumped through me.

I broke away, despite the urge to fuck her there against a tree or behind a bush.

What I didn't add was that, apart from the smutty stuff, I also often relived that soulful gaze she would wear when our eyes locked, making my heart swell with a need to hold her—protect her.

Holding my hand, she followed me to my bike.

"You're not riding home after drinking, are you?" She sounded like my mother, which made me smile.

Her long, dark hair was tousled after I'd run my hands through it while kissing her. She was so gorgeous out there under the starry night, I could barely find words.

The staring continued as I held onto my bike. She reminded me of a girl trying to find herself. A little like I was doing. That was why I understood that I-can-do-better expression she sometimes wore.

I hated where she'd been, though, and wondered if I could trust her with more than just my body.

I knew that she'd gotten with some older man when she was only fifteen. That was sick. But I didn't blame her. Teenagers were easily manipulated. The arsehole pedophile, however, if I ever found him, that would be another story. Manon refused to tell me his name. I think I'd frightened her after I blew up hearing how her mother had sold her to a billionaire creep.

"I'll be there in five minutes."

"Is that an invite?" She slanted her face. "What about Kylie?"

"What about her? She's a fucking nuisance."

"Did you rape her?"

I rolled my eyes. "What do you think?"

She looked down at her feet and shook her head slightly. "I don't believe it."

"I would never do that."

"I believe you. Even when I threw myself at you, you wouldn't fuck me." She smiled shyly.

"I wanted you then like I do now." I stared into her eyes, which sparked with curiosity, like she couldn't get enough of my compliments. "Even though, in the beginning, you kind of freaked me out."

"Do I still?" Her gaze seemed to strip layers like I couldn't hide anything from her.

Manon had a key to my soul. I'd never given it to anyone before, but she somehow possessed it.

"Not as much. But I don't like the company you keep."

"You sound like my dad." She grimaced. "I mean like a dad."

Mm... back to fragile. I knew she missed her father, who, from what I'd gathered, had abandoned her.

Reluctant to discuss toxic people, I avoided the whole Crisp shit show subject. "Are you coming back, then?"

"Do you want me to?" She tilted her pretty head and was back to playing games.

"Um... like, yeah. It's obvious, isn't it?"

She shrugged. "I think so."

"See you in five, then?"

Giving me an I'm-going-to-suck-your-dick-till-your-balls-are-blue look, she wore a sexy grin, which made sitting on my bike painful.

AFTER I ENTERED MY tiny apartment, I tossed out empty boxes of take-away, drink cans, and bottles. I hadn't had time to clean, and my bed was buried under clothes.

As I was making the bed, a knock came at the door.

Manon walked in and dropped her bag. She then unbuttoned her shirt, beating me to it.

No more talk, just us naked and her creamy little pussy in conversation with my throbbing dick.

I sat back on the sofa, undid my fly, and let my dick grow as I adjusted it to remove the ache that had started the moment those big dark eyes had entered mine under the stars.

CHAPTER 15

Manon

STRIPPED DOWN TO HIS black briefs, Drake's fat bulge made me burn for him. Legs spread slightly, he sat on the couch, enjoying my little performance.

He pointed. "What happened to your leg?"

Despite the slight throb of pain, I'd forgotten that I'd only just cut myself.

There I was, naked and getting all steamy when reality knocked me back to earth. "I scratched it. Something must have bitten me when I was outside."

A line formed between his eyebrows. He wasn't buying it.

I let out a frustrated sigh. "I cut myself."

I think opening up to Savvie, which had left me feeling lighter, had encouraged me to confess to something as fucked up as self-harm.

His face went from flushed and aroused to horror, as though I'd turned into Madame Medusa and my hair had morphed into hissing snakes.

"You mean by accident?"

I shook my head slowly.

"Like on purpose?" Shocked, he didn't blink as he eyeballed me.

"Kylie told me you were together, and that you raped her and couldn't stop touching her..." My mouth trembled so much I had to pause.

He shook his head slowly like he couldn't believe what he was hearing. "But you just told me you didn't believe her."

"Now I don't. But you were ignoring me." I fell into the chair and held my head.

He came and knelt at my feet. "It's not the first time, is it? There were those scars between your thighs."

Tears drenched my palms as I hid my face from him. I wanted him to see me as happy and pretty, not ugly and teary.

"Look at me," he said.

"I can't. I look awful when I cry."

"No, you don't. Nothing makes you look ugly. If anything, you're even more beautiful when you open up and show me the real Manon."

"The real Manon?" I shook my head with a sarcastic chuckle. "Who the fuck is she? Everything about my life is an act."

He opened his palms. "What, even this? Us?"

"This is the only thing that feels real. Even my living at Merivale is like I'm tripping or something."

I couldn't say if it was the pity in his eyes or what, but the wire I'd used to bind myself in snapped, and tears streamed out of me like some angsty waterfall.

As tears melded with snot, I hated anyone seeing me like that, especially the love of my life.

Drake passed me a box of tissues, and I cleaned my face up a little despite the endless stream pouring out.

First Savvie, then Drake watching on as every rotten part of me spewed out like a stewing emotional volcano had finally erupted.

"I've seen and experienced a lot, I guess." I knitted my fingers. "And I quickly discovered that physical pain was better than heartache."

His frown deepened. "Who broke your heart? A boy? A man?"

"A man." I sighed.

"That pedo?"

I shook my head and bit a nail. Something I didn't normally do. I reached into my bag for my vape. "Do you mind?"

"No. If it makes you feel better. So, who is this man?"

"My dad. He left when I was young, and I felt so fucking alone. My mother had no interest in me. Only what money she could make from me."

"Bitch." He grimaced. "Sorry. I know she's your mum."

"No need to apologize. I hate her. She cheated on my dad."

"I still don't quite get why you cut yourself," he persisted.

"Because it was the only thing that helped. Daddy used to hit me, and though it frightened me and made me cry, I still preferred that to him being absent. After he left, I guess I discovered physical pain was better than emotional pain. Or something like that. Shit. I'm not good at self-analysis. I've read a few books on it recently, and I prefer novels about fucked-up women and their relationships. It helps me better understand myself to know I'm not alone."

"Oh, you're not alone, Mannie. There are a lot of messed-up people out there." He released a breath.

His eyes entered mine and held me there, like some gorgeous drug that made me warm and safe.

I sucked on the vape then turned it off.

"We've all done regrettable shit, Manon."

"Call me Mannie." My mouth trembled into a smile. "It feels like I belong to something, that I have a close friend."

He placed his arm around my shoulders and drew me tight to his warm body.

We remained quiet and close, and never wanting that moment to end, I registered it in my soul.

"Will you promise to call me instead of doing that to yourself?" he asked.

I nodded and gulped back another sob. "I love you, Drake."

His big blue eyes went watery, then a tear slid down his cheek. "I love you too, Mannie." He held my hand. "I know we've hardly been together. But I've never had this with anyone. I think about you all the time. I find it hard to breathe sometimes when you're in the same room. Your beauty robs me of everything."

My heart melted, and like a rising sun, a smile bloomed not just on my face but in my chest too.

As we held each other, I absorbed every bit of him, like I wanted his vital organs to entwine with mine—his heart, his cock, his brain, his soul.

I wanted all of him. Inside of me.

Flooding warmth dried my tears.

Drake loved me.

That was all that mattered.

No one had ever told me they loved me.

Not even my dad.

No more words. Our lips crushed in what was the longest kiss I'd ever experienced.

Drake loved to kiss, and I loved his lips.

His mouth explored mine like it was our first kiss.

I guessed it was our first time because now he knew the real me.

Only he didn't know about Crisp's marriage proposal and the filthy secrets that threatened to destroy us, should I refuse to marry that creep.

He carried me to the bedroom and stroked me. Though I wanted him inside of me more than anything, I also needed the softness of his touch and those blue eyes burning into mine, showing me how much he wanted me.

It was love. I'd never felt that kind of overwhelming sense of peace, warmth, arousal, and everything in between.

I would die for him.

As he poured his orgasm into me, I wished I wasn't on the pill. I wanted to have Drake's baby.

I could love no one like I loved Drake.

It wasn't just the hot sex or how gorgeous he looked with all those changing faces of his that I was only just discovering. It was because he still wanted me after learning about my train wreck past.

It was like he'd forgiven me for being me.

For someone who'd hated herself forever, that was huge.

I was even liking myself for a change.

Now that I could never have imagined.

We made slow, heart-melting love all night, and as we showered to-gether the following morning, he entered me in one hard thrust from behind. My palms lay flat against the steamy glass barrier, holding me up. Already raw from having him inside me all night, I groaned as he filled me to the bursting point.

"Fuck, I love your body." He bit into my neck and sucked on it.

"I love your dick inside of me."

"I love you creaming all over it."

Our sweet, dirty little banter went something like that.

Just us opening up to each other.

No rules. Just passionate sex and sweet love.

As we were drying ourselves, a dark cloud floated over me. "I don't want this to end." I turned down my mouth.

What was I going to do about Crisp? I couldn't bring myself to tell Drake. But there was that threat of Drake being taken from me.

How could I live with him?

"It's been quite a night." He smiled.

With just a towel around his waist, Drake brought a smile to my face, and all I could see was us and that moment, while pushing back those ugly thoughts crashing into my bliss.

Drake was my bliss.

He was my everything.

Did that make me weak?

I'd promised myself never to depend on anyone, but I'd never count-ed on falling madly in love either.

"Do nothing." I held up my finger. "Stay the way you are." I grabbed my phone and photographed him.

He laughed. "Hey. I'm not wearing anything."

"You're in a towel, silly." I giggled. "Though I'd love a picture of your dick. Can't you, like, make it hard again?"

He rolled his eyes. "I'm not sure I can do that. It's tired, to start with."

I ripped off his towel, got on my knees, then sucked his dick until his veins throbbed against my tongue.

"There you are." I rose and studied his dick like I might a work of art I'd created since my mouth had contributed to the final result.

He looked worried suddenly. "Hey, what if your phone gets hacked?"

I took a couple of photos and laughed. "Then they'll see a gorgeous, big fat dick, won't they?"

"No face, though."

"Do you want a picture of mine?" I lifted an eyebrow. "Or will it be too ugly?"

"You've got a fucking hot-looking pussy." His face flushed again. Drake was one very horny male.

Good. As long as it's all for me.

"Let me come first, so I'm dripping wet." I smiled. "The way you like it."

He groaned. "Now you're turning me on again."

I sat on the couch, opened my legs, and played with my clit while he held his dick. It was easy to come watching him, and like Drake, I seemed constantly aroused. But only with him because, before Drake, I used to question whether I even liked sex.

Studying the photo I'd just taken of myself, I pulled a face.

"I can't understand how that would appeal to you."

He shook his head. "Oh, it's hot. Trust me."

"Will you wank to it?" I slanted my head, wearing a little smile.

"I would've preferred the photo showing your pretty face." He stroked my cheek and ran his finger over my lips. "I love seeing you when you come. These lips open and your eyes go all dreamy. You're seriously beautiful, Manon."

We locked eyes again, and I wished I could pause time so that moment remained forever.

He touched his thigh. "Here, come and sit on me."

I lowered myself slowly over his dick and groaned as the delicious stretch made my eyes roll to the back of my head.

CHAPTER 16

Drake

CAROLINE LOVECHILDE REMINDED ME of Nigella Lawson. Only she didn't look like she was about to orgasm over a chocolate chip pancake. If anything, the head of the Lovechildes rarely smiled, only when she was with her boyfriend. Her lack of warmth didn't worry me, however. What worried me more was why I'd been summoned.

My attention turned to paintings of horses, the sea, and landscapes that filled the yellow walls, then onto the many shelves of antique books. I might have been in a library or on the set of one of those murder mysteries my mother loved to watch, often set in mansions like Merivale.

Wearing a red fitted dress, she stood by the window that looked out at the sea, and on seeing me, she turned and nodded a greeting. I could see the similarity to Manon, giving me a glimpse of how Manon would look in thirty years.

Would I be around that long?

With Manon, it was anyone's guess.

When she'd uttered those words of love, a mixture of fear and happiness had seeped through me. She'd given off a vibe of something else too. I couldn't put my finger on it, but she'd seemed jumpy, and after I'd kissed her goodbye, she'd given me a strange look, like she had been trying to tell me something.

That could have been just Manon. She'd lived a complicated life. One that I was only just getting my head around. Her cutting herself had left me speechless. I'd heard about self-harming, but I'd never seen it firsthand. If anything, it had brought us closer, because I wanted to help her—to make it all go away by being there for her.

As I looked around that room filled with so much that one could never see everything, I tried imagining myself in that world. Manon had told me that, one day, she hoped to run Merivale and step into those very high shoes of her grandmother.

I loved how Manon's cheeks fired up whenever she got excited about something, and I admired that she was striving for a better life, even if she was—in my unspoken, humble opinion—reaching for the stars.

My only aspiration in life was to stay out of trouble, make sure my mother was happy and, one day, have a family of my own. Simple stuff. As far as careers, I was still a work in progress.

Declan entered and kissed his mother before patting me on the arm.

"How was Spain?" I asked.

"Great. Too short. But I had to return for the party this coming weekend." He looked at his mother.

"It's important for Manon that family attend," Caroline said.

A knock came at the door, and when Caroline saw it was Cary, her face brightened.

"I'm sorry to interrupt, but there's a parcel that requires your signature."

She held up her finger for us to wait, then she joined her boyfriend, and he placed his arm around her. Even in their day-to-day life, the two looked seriously loved up.

After I embarked on some small talk with Declan, who spoke about the joys of flying and his new plane, Caroline returned.

She sat at her large desk and played with a gold pen. "I called you here to discuss the casino shooting."

I looked at Declan, who returned an apologetic smile.

"It won't get back to Crisp. Don't worry," he said.

"I know he paid for your silence. You did the right thing telling Declan. This will not go past this room," she said.

The breath trapped in my lungs finally released.

"Tell me, have you seen this man?"

Caroline showed me a couple of photos of a bald, middle-aged, paunchy guy who I recognized because he always smoked outside. I remembered the smokers because they often chatted with us.

I nodded. "He's a regular."

She looked at Declan, then showed me two more images. "And these men?"

"That's Goran and Alec. They turned up at Crisp's office when I was there, telling him that something had arrived."

Again, she looked over at Declan. "You're no longer working there, I believe."

I shook my head. "His new terms were not something I could accept."

Her perfectly shaped eyebrows moved slightly. "Do you mind elaborating?"

I shifted in my seat. Did I really want to tell them about Manon? It wasn't a secret about us being together. "Well, he wants me to stop seeing Manon." I paused for her response, but she remained quiet. "I had to reject his offer of employing me for round-the-clock security at his manor."

"He requested your services at Pengilly?" she asked.

"I'm not sure of its title, but he described the estate as being close to Merivale."

She rose and stood by the enormous marble fireplace. "I imagine it was a fair sum you rejected in order to continue seeing my granddaughter."

Nodding, I took a deep breath. I couldn't exactly tell her that, after a month of passionate sex, I'd fallen madly in love with Manon.

She returned to her desk and sat again. "Would you be prepared to return to your role at the casino?" I went to respond when she added, "It would be just for a month. In return, you'll no longer have a mortgage to worry about."

I looked from her to Declan and back.

Could I do without Manon for a month?

As though reading my mind, Caroline added, "I'm sure my grand-daughter will understand."

Owning my apartment outright would enable me to use those fifty thousand pounds towards my mother's new apartment.

"That sounds good to me. Only what do I say to Crisp?" I asked. "We didn't exactly part on good terms."

She reclined in her chair and intertwined her fingers, which ended in long, pointy red nails. "Tell him you've had second thoughts and would like to accept his generous offer, but only for working at the casino."

"And if he refuses?"

"He won't. Good security is difficult to find."

"Why doesn't he just bring in some of his heavies that I've seen hanging around there? I'm sure they'd be up to the task."

She shrugged. "That's a riddle. Any insights about these characters would be useful."

"I can tell you that Alec and Goran are Natalia's brothers."

"Natalia's the illegal who has taken over for Manon?" she asked.

I nodded. "I've heard that the venue is about to close, by the way."

"Yes. Rey informed me. That's some good news."

"I noticed a van or two while I was working."

"And did you see what was coming out of the van?" she asked.

"Girls. Really young. Natalia was directing them."

Her wince wasn't lost on me. That was the most emotion she'd shown during that entire session.

"Both vans?" Declan asked.

"The other was parked at the back of Salon, but I saw nothing."

"Okay. I want you to be the eyes of comings and goings."

"I'll do my best." I rose. "Um... what if he doesn't want me?"

"You risked your life to save him. Heroic acts of the like aren't easily forgotten." Caroline gave me a faint smile. "Did you see who fired that shot?"

"Only a black SUV that quickly drove off."

Declan stood. "Okay then, I think that's enough for now." He turned to me. "I'm heading to the farm. We can walk together if you like."

I left Caroline's office thinking of Manon and how she would take me not seeing her for a month. My body was already complaining, given how insatiable we'd become.

"Let's go through the back way. I just want to check on Julian. He's here having swimming lessons," Declan said.

As I followed him through that fairy-tale mansion with its colored rooms, I couldn't believe the woman I'd lost my heart to lived there.

We stepped out into the courtyard and Bertie bounded over and jumped up to greet me, slobbering on my hand as I patted him.

"Hi there, little fellow."

Julian wore floaters on his arms, and standing thigh-deep in the pool, Cary held the boy's hands while Declan's son kicked his legs.

"Look, Daddy." Cary let go, and Julian swam, splashing water everywhere, while the corgi raced madly around the pool, barking in response.

I laughed and welcomed the distraction after that intense meeting.

"That's marvelous," Declan said.

Cary chuckled. "He's getting there."

"You're doing a great job. Soon we can hit the beach. I just don't want him going in until he knows what he's doing."

"That's wise," Cary said. "I went down for a swim this morning, and the currents pushed me out. It took me some time and patience to get back to shore."

Declan grimaced. "Don't tell Mother. She'll freak. There've been a few drownings this year alone."

"Caroline heard. She gave me a scolding." Cary laughed.

WE WALKED FOR A while in comfortable silence, something I found easy to do through that magical forest, where normally, instead of focusing on problems I faced, I would lose myself to nature.

Not so much currently, however, as nagging thoughts followed me.

Namely, Manon. How would she take us not sleeping together for a month? She was insatiable. Would she hook up with someone else?

I hated the idea of anyone going near her, let alone touching her.

That wasn't normally me. But then, I'd never faced that kind of burning passion for a girl before.

It wasn't just Manon, though, because the thought of returning to the casino spooked the crap out of me. That close shave had affected me more than I could have imagined.

"We'll equip you with a bulletproof vest," Declan said, synchronizing with my thoughts.

"That might be a good idea." I sniffed. "Who's the bald guy in the picture?"

"A cop who heads drug investigations."

I picked up a stick and dragged it along the ground as we walked. "You think he's on the take?"

"Probably."

Was this happening? Had I said those words? Suddenly, I was living in a real-life drama because that was heavy shit, and having watched my fair share of police dramas, I knew how those kinds of situations played out.

"I'm a bit nervous, to be perfectly honest."

He stopped walking and gave me a sympathetic smile. "That's understandable. But you're the best choice because we can trust you. Crisp thinks he can buy anyone, and by walking out on him, you proved otherwise."

I kicked a rock on the ground, choosing to remain silent because, had Crisp not insisted I leave Manon, he would have bought me.

One month without her, I could just do.

Not forever.

Life was way too short for forever.

We entered the farm, where the foundation for the market building was complete.

"That's coming along nicely," I said.

He nodded, looking pleased. "I'll leave you to it. I've got to meet my beautiful wife."

He saluted me and headed off.

CHAPTER 17

Manon

"WHO HAS A PARTY on a Thursday night?" I asked Savvie as we drove to Notting Hill.

"Jacinta and Sienna and anyone in our scene, for that matter." She giggled. "We're not exactly having to spring out of bed for anything."

No. She was right there. After leaving the Pond, I'd become rather fond of sleeping in. Drake rose early, however, often waking me. I didn't mind. I would have woken up at four in the morning for him. Especially when it involved hot, hard sex.

Our mornings were raw and wild. Drake was like an animal. Sexy though. I loved hearing his rough breath in my ear while he thrust into me.

The nights were more of a tease. I would parade in new lingerie and wait for him to pounce—passionate sex followed by soft touches, kisses, and more sex.

My heart bloomed just thinking about him, and I refused to allow Crisp to bring me down. There was hope on that front since he hadn't tried contacting me, despite insisting I marry him.

I imagined Natalia was keeping him busy.

Maybe she could convince him to marry her. I'd seen that sly, ambitious look in her eyes—my mother often looked like that whenever she was around wealthy men because, for her, everything had a price, and sex came with the biggest price tag.

Before heading for the party, I met up with Savvie to inspect apartments. Now that I had those five million pounds, I was ready to buy my own place.

There were stipulations, however. I was only allowed ten thousand pounds a month, but my credit card, in addition, came with a five-thousand-pounds-a-month limit. My grandmother probably wanted to make sure I didn't blow it.

As I sat in the lawyer's office, skimming over hard-to-understand legal language, my eyes landed on the following sentence: A predetermined limit has been established to mitigate overspending on frivolities.

I questioned him about that, and he suggested I talk to my grandmother.

She told me frivolities were things a person didn't need.

"Like shoes and clothes?" I asked.

"I'm sure you can make good with ten thousand pounds a month." She slanted her head, and we left it at that.

They allowed the purchase of an apartment, however. So in many ways, I wasn't free with that five mil, but it was way better than anything else I'd ever had. I'd also suddenly started to think about my future, something I'd never done before. I'd always assumed I would be dead by twenty-one.

Negative and dark, I knew, but after the shit I'd witnessed, there were days when I hadn't thought I could keep going.

Determined never to be poor again, I would learn how to control the urge to keep spending, even if my lingerie bill was huge—a small price for keeping Drake's dick nice and hard.

Was that what one did to keep a boyfriend? Or was that what Peyton had taught me?

Another toxic thought to bury. I had a ton of those.

As we drove along, I asked Savvie, "Do you think I should buy the Soho studio apartment?"

"A little squashed, but it's stylish. I like the high-beamed ceilings, and there's a balcony, which is always a bonus."

"And access to the roof garden," I added, getting excited. "It would make an excellent investment. Don't you think?"

She shrugged. "No idea. Anything relating to investing is Ethan's scene. You should talk to him about the money market."

"I will. Thanks for that."

She took my hand and squeezed it, and warmth flushed through me. I'd never smiled so much in my life.

If it weren't for Crisp, I would have been the happiest girl in London.

The cab pulled up at a two-story white Edwardian house with a willow sparkling with fairy lights.

We climbed out and heard booming music.

"The party's in full swing. Cool." Savvie adjusted her skirt, which resembled a modern art piece like someone had splashed paint over it. Stylish as always.

The door was already half-open, and as we entered, there were people everywhere talking loudly over techno music, which blasted from a large, cleared room with a DJ and people dancing.

Another new experience. Before Merivale, I'd never been to a party. As sad as that seemed, my upbringing didn't exactly lend itself to sleep-overs and girlfriends.

Weed smoke floated through the air, and a man in a multicolored striped suit and a funny hat kissed Savvie. "Darling, there you are." He brought out a tin and offered her a blue pill.

She shook her head, and his eyebrows flung up as though she'd turned down something that promised immortality.

"No. I'm clean. Married and trying to get pregnant. A few champagnes. That will do me."

"Oh, Savs,"—he pulled a sad face—"I hope you're not going all suburban on us."

She giggled. "Never. We're too rich for that." She turned to me. "You can have one if you like."

Though I'd had a few party pills here and there, I followed Savvie's example and declined.

We entered another room filled with antique furniture and splashy modern art. Looking like she'd just stepped out of one of the paintings, a blonde girl dressed in a kaleidoscope of swirly colors screamed, "There you are, you Minx!" and hugged Savvie.

After being introduced to Jacinta, I loved listening to them chatting about who was fucking who or who'd just been caught doing drugs and all kinds of gossip. Mainly about clothes. One thing I'd learned about the young and wealthy, they loved their designer and became almost hysterical if someone turned up in the same outfit.

Dancing, drinking champagne, chatting about makeup trends, and the latest scandals about some nobody reality star getting caught with a ton of dick pics on her hacked phone—I had a ball, and the night flew.

For once in my life, it felt like I was part of something. I was about to buy my own apartment in London. I'd made a few friends who I could meet for brunch at Harrods, and my plan to become a rich woman of style was on its way to being realized.

Where would Drake fit in?

I was too young to marry anyone, though he made my heart race, and I'd told him I loved him. Spur of the moment or not, I couldn't see my life without him. He would fit in nicely, like everything else, I told myself with a big smile.

After what had been a great night of dancing wildly, non-stop, we fell into the cab, giggling. I'd drank a bit too much champagne.

Savvie directed the driver to Mayfair, where I'd been invited to stay.

"Jacinta's wild," I said.

"She always has been. She's marrying soon."

"That's Alain?"

"Uh-huh. What do you think of him?" she asked as the taxi drove through London and over the bridge, crawling along, bumper to bumper.

"He seems nice. A little geekish."

Savvie laughed. "You got that right. Boring fuck, I believe. But he's loaded."

"She's marrying him for his money, then?" That surprised me. I thought Jacinta had her own money, going on her designer outfits, posh accent, and general vibe.

"Yep. Knowing Cin, she'll probably have a few playthings on the side."

I turned to read how she felt about that.

"You think that's okay?" I asked, recalling Crisp offering that cavalier servente option, which I'd soon discovered was something the Italians had done hundreds of years ago. Old, wealthy husbands allowing their young wives a young lover, which I thought was rather reasonable. Beat cheating and being caught and guilted out. That wouldn't be me. Through my mother's endless parade of lovers, I'd seen enough cheating to last me a lifetime.

"I don't know. Each to their own. I wouldn't do it myself. Too complicated."

"But you wouldn't need to marry for money, would you?"

"No. But I'd marry Carson even if I were fucking destitute."

"But that's easy to say, given you've never been destitute."

She turned and studied me. I'd hit a button of sorts. "Have you?"

I nodded. "It wasn't pretty."

"But wasn't Bethany hooking up with rich guys?" She frowned.

"That didn't mean she looked after me."

Her face crumpled in shock. "You're fucking kidding me."

"Hey, it's cool. I'm good now. I don't like to think about those times."

"Is that why you cut yourself?"

Having pushed that drama at the Mariner away from my memory, I squirmed. "Maybe. I don't know."

We'd arrived at the house just in time because I didn't want to talk about my past.

An elderly butler let us in, and we headed into the living room, where I expected Mary Poppins to ride down the staircase and land before me with her bird umbrella making eyes at me. The house, especially the living room, with its antique vases, statues, and lamps, reminded me of that movie.

Savvie made us a drink and ripped open a bag of crisps, and we made ourselves comfortable in the bright-blue living room.

"Sorry to bring that up earlier."

"It's fine. I'm in a bit of bother, though." I bit my cheek.

"What's up?"

I told her about Crisp and his threats to expose my shoplifting and the smutty, doctored images I'd sent him back in my desperate days.

"Ooh." She scrunched her nose. "He's a pig. Have you told Mother?"

"Not exactly." I knitted my fingers. "I'm ashamed of her knowing, to be honest."

She smiled sadly. "I get that. But hey, you've had a tough road, and shoplifting is nothing. Really. Lots do it. For the same reasons."

I turned hopefully towards her. "Have you?"

"I did not need to. Instead, I hooked up with slimy fuckwits like Bram."

I nodded slowly. "Oh well, he's not here anymore to hassle you."

"No. But cops keep sniffing around. Lord Pike's convinced Carson had something to do with it."

"Did he?"

"Don't know. Don't care. Had it been reversed, I would have done the same fucking thing."

Hearing that Bram might have been murdered left me rather speechless.

"So, are you going to leave Drake for Crisp?"

Gripping my glass, I sipped before answering. "I love Drake."

"You're still really young, sweets."

"I know. But what the fuck am I going to do about Crisp?"

She shrugged. "Talk to Mummy. She'll know. She always knows what to do in these sticky situations."

"But she's helpless around Rey. She couldn't even close the Cherry bar, could she?"

"No." She shook her head. "That is a bit of a mystery."

"You know that Crisp wants to build an empire around the land close to Merivale. Take over the farms and develop under his name."

Her eyes stretched wide. "Shit. That wouldn't surprise me. Only it's Lovechilde land. He owns some of it. We'd all love to know how that came about."

"He's obviously got something big over her."

"That's pretty established. But what? Do you think you could try to wheedle it out of him?"

I exhaled loudly. "Don't know. I hate him. I can't stand the smell of him. Don't even want to be in the same room as him. I just wish he'd leave me alone." A tear trickled down my cheek.

She touched my hand. "Hey, it's going to be okay. I'm sure Mother will sort this out. They'll get him in the end."

"I hope so because he's rotten."

"We figured that out years ago. I would just love to know why Mummy puts up with him. Can I tell Mother what you told me?"

I nodded. Even if Crisp would have my head on a platter for sharing details of our private conversation, I didn't care anymore.

The only things that mattered were Drake and my independence. Crisp's threats to send Drake somewhere far away kept hounding me, however.

I shared that fear with Savvie, and she scrunched her face. "This isn't the Georgian era, you know. We no longer send convicts of trivial crimes, like stealing bread, to Australia."

I giggled. She was right. Rey didn't have the power to have Drake extradited. It was all just a bluff.

Pushing nagging thoughts aside, I thought about my party and nice things, like Drake and me walking up the cliffs, holding hands, and staring at the ocean.

I WAS SO GLAD that Billy and Sapphire, who were now dating, made it to my party. At least they were genuine friends. Unlike the other guests, who turned up at all the Merivale parties.

Still, it would have been a sad outcome had I relied on my non-existent network.

My mother hadn't been invited, of course, but she called me. Any normal parent would have wished me a happy birthday, but she only called for an invitation and to ask about the money I'd inherited.

"You're an adult today," she said.

"Yep, Beth, that's right." I'd started using her name. Referring to her as mother felt fake.

She never even flinched at my calling her by her name. She hated being a mother—a fact that came up whenever she was blowing up over something like me refusing to shoplift a new shade of lipstick for her or hook up with some rich, ugly fuckwit.

"They're throwing a big party, I hear," she said.

"Yep. Nice of Grandmother, isn't it?"

I felt like rubbing it in. I knew my mother well enough. She would have loved to dress up and flirt with the rich and mighty.

"How did you hear?" I asked.

"Reynard told me."

"He's in contact with you?" I squirmed at the reminder of that terrifying marriage proposal.

"He felt the need to get my blessing for your upcoming nuptials."

"I don't want to talk about that."

"But there's the nice, big wedding to arrange."

"Not now. Bye." I hung up before I choked on my words.

Like with all the Merivale parties, people talked loudly, got drunk on excellent champagne, and munched on finger food that continuously came out on silver trays.

Drake looked sharp and yummy in a tux with silk lapels, especially in a white shirt that showed off his tan. I couldn't take my eyes off him, but then, neither could all the females and the odd male, it seemed.

I wore a hot-pink knee-length Dolce and Gabbana with a low-cut back. My grandmother had paid off my maxed-out credit card as another birthday gift, and I went on a shopping spree with Sapphire, where I ended up buying her a pretty Stella McCartney silk dress that she nearly stained with tears. She'd brought out the softy in me. I'd never felt so compelled to help anyone before, and the joy that radiated from her smile was priceless and beat any antidepressant I'd ever tried.

I went over to Drake, who'd been chatting with Carson.

When he put his arm around me, my heart sighed. Us was all that mattered. The guests just faded away.

"A bit of public display?" I giggled.

"I can't have all those randy, older rich guys eying you up."

"You're claiming me?" I cocked my head with a smirk.

Sapphire and Billy came over and joined us.

"This room is like an art gallery. I feel like I'm in an episode of Antique Roadshow." She giggled.

"You're not kidding," I said. "One has to be careful not to swing a bag or arm just in case you knock over some priceless vase or statue. There are so many stunning objects. I'm always watching my step."

Billy looked around as though he were worried about something.

"Are you okay?" I asked him.

He gulped back his beer and nodded.

"Billy's freaking out that Mrs. Lovechilde will whip him." Drake chuckled.

Billy gave him a dirty look. "That's between us, mate."

"Hey, Grandmother's cool," I said.

"She wasn't so cool when accusing me of stealing some necklace and setting the cops on me."

My breath hitched, and I hoped no one noticed, though Drake gave me a weird look. It was hard to hide anything from him; I was discovering. He was so locked in with me, which, in one sense, was touching—when I wasn't trying to hide guilty secrets from him.

The uncomfortable reminder of the necklace I'd stolen from my mother and pawned came back to bite me. At least I hadn't stolen it from the Lovechildes. Will had after my mother had asked him to take something of value from my grandmother.

I held my tongue just as Grandmother came towards me in a green sheath, looking much younger than her age. She could have been my mother's sister, or even my older sister, given that we shared a resemblance.

The guests stopped talking and gave her the attention reserved for a queen. That wasn't an exaggeration, either, because my grandmother boasted a commanding presence. She held her head high, especially with her long neck emphasized by a smoothly wrapped bun at her nape.

I'd always admired the way she walked and how she presented herself in a crowded room. She might have been an actress stepping onto a stage. Maybe that was how it had been for her in the beginning. She'd inspired me to keep my head up when walking into a room of people. I'd always stared downwards or into space. Never eye contact. Maybe I was frightened of what they might see.

"Say, your grandmother is so stunning. She should be in Hollywood."

I smiled at Sapphire. She sounded so young.

Grandmother came to me and touched my dress, giving me a look of approval. She liked that I'd stopped wearing tiny skirts and low-cut blouses.

Another habit I'd learned to shake off. My mother had drummed into me the importance of showing off one's assets to attract a better life. All my wearing little had done was attract dickheads.

My dress had an exposed back, however, which had been enjoying visits from Drake's soft touches, giving me goosebumps and making my nipples tighten.

All it took was a side glance for him to remove his hand, out of respect for my grandmother.

She knew we were dating. I'd told her. That was before the whole Crisp fake marriage bullshit story. At least that slime bag hadn't made a show to the party. Yet.

"You invited your friends, I see," she said.

Her eyes settled on Billy, and I noticed how he shrank on the spot. She could be very intimidating.

"I trust you got that letter of apology and cheque?" she said, looking straight at him.

He nodded slowly. "Thanks."

"Good. I hope you all have a lovely night."

She turned to me. "Can I have a word?"

I followed her out to the yellow room, known as the family room, at the back.

"Drake and you are official?" She sat down on a floral sofa.

I dropped into an armchair. "I love him, Grandmother." Two champagnes, and I'd gone all soppy.

"Rey tells me you're to marry. That you accepted his offer." She studied me for a moment. "To be honest, I was rather unimpressed. You've got a comfortable future without having to marry a man old enough to be your grandfather."

My chest deflated as I sighed loudly. "I don't want to. But he's threatening me."

Her brow creased, or at least tried to. Grandmother was rather partial to Botox, as I'd discovered during my time at the Pond.

Tears sprang out of my eyes.

"How is he threatening you? You don't have to marry him."

"But she does."

We both turned, and there was the man of my nightmares smirking back at us with those piercing eyes that seemed to x-ray through to my shaky skeleton.

Dressed in his signature blue velvet jacket, Reynard had that man-who-owned-the-world look about him. I thought about my mother and how she had gone on about the benefits of marrying someone rich and powerful.

She'd prattled, "Think about the clothes, private jets, the Riviera in summer, a large yacht. And you can have your boys on the side."

Were it not for Drake, I could have been coaxed into a life of luxury, but that version of me vanished the moment Drake kissed me. Maybe that was all the bad me had always needed—human warmth, passionate lovemaking, and tender touches.

"Rey, this was between me and my granddaughter."

"She's accepted my offer. And I think we can leave it at that." His stare lingered. Like they were having a wordless discussion. "Ma Chérie is closed. And now I think we can all get on like a family. Can't we?"

I rolled my eyes. I wanted to puke. My grandmother was fucking buying it, going on how her face relaxed.

She stood and, before leaving the room, placed her arm around me. "Happy birthday. This is between both of you."

And that was that. The only person who could help had left me to fend for myself.

Why the change of heart?

Crisp *did* have her wrapped around his crooked finger.

CHAPTER 18

Drake

THE PARTY WAS IN full swing. Everyone danced to a DJ under pulsating, colored lights bouncing from the carved ceiling of the large room that had been transformed into a dance club.

Coming towards me, Manon's eyes locked onto mine, causing everything around me to blur. Despite the swing to her walk, I read something dark in her stare.

"Can we go somewhere away from all of this?" she asked.

I checked my watch. "But it's only eleven thirty."

"Just come with me. Please." She looked like she'd been crying.

I touched her hand. "Is everything okay?"

She shrugged in response, as she often did when something troubled her.

"Okay. Show the way." I followed her, ogling her curvy backside, and leaned in close. "Have I told you how stunning you look?"

She stopped and smiled sadly. "A few times. But I don't mind hearing it again. You look pretty dishy yourself. I'm sure all the cougars are purring."

I rolled my eyes. "There's only one young pussy I'm interested in, and she's more of a kitten. A naughty little kitten." I rubbed her arm.

Instead of giggling, as she often did when I bantered, she remained stiff-lipped.

"Have I done something?"

She shook her head slowly, took my hand, and led me away.

When we stepped outside, we saw Crisp with a fat cigar chatting with a guest.

She backed up. "Let's go this way." Manon pointed to a path that led to the forest.

"You're trying to avoid him, I take it?" I had to ask.

I thought about my agreement to work for Crisp. Seeing her looking so beautiful under the moon made that decision difficult. But I could use the money, and if it meant that we would get enough dirt on Crisp to see the end of him, then it was worth one month without Manon, difficult as that was to contemplate.

She brought out her vape.

"You're still doing that?"

"It's either this or hurt myself in other ways."

I'd almost forgotten about Manon cutting herself. I'd probably buried that deep in the part of my brain where all the hard-to-process shit went.

"You haven't again, have you?"

Her eyes were so wide and lost I had to hold her.

I buried my nose in her soft, perfumed skin and could have stayed like that all night. Especially there in that magical setting under the stars with the earth under our feet.

"Are you going to tell me what's up?" I stepped away to get a good look at her face.

"It's nothing, really. I'm just bothered by how women are always eying you up and throwing themselves at you." She sucked on her vape like a baby would a bottle. "Let's go into there." She pointed at the forest.

"It's dark. A wild creature might attack," I joked.

She pushed me against a tree. "Now, I like the sound of that. I'm that wild creature. Now, fuck me." She unzipped my fly and reached in. "Mm... you're already hard."

"Just looking at you makes me fucking hard. And I love your hair up." I ran my finger along the curve of her long neck.

She smiled. "It's full of hair spray and stiff."

"Like my dick."

Her giggle relaxed the sudden tension. Something was eating away at her. But I wasn't about to interrupt the sudden heat between us.

She turned her back to me and rubbed her toned, round arse against my dick. "Take me hard. Hurt me."

"Huh?" I went to lift her dress but stopped.

"Go on. I need you inside of me."

Releasing a tight breath, I lifted her dress and ran my hands over her smooth, curvy butt. I then hooked my finger under her thong and rolled my fingertip over her clit, which swelled under my touch as I kissed her neck.

She trembled. "Oh... fuck me, please."

I rubbed my cock against her gyrating arse.

Her tits fell out of her dress as I fondled them. "No bra."

"No. Do you like them naked?"

"I love them naked. I've been perving on you all night, watching them bounce when you walk. You're getting bigger too."

I entered her with a finger, and her wet, tight pussy sucked on my finger.

"You're so hot and wet and ready."

"That's because I can't stop thinking about your dick inside of me."

I entered her in one thrust, and she gasped.

"Okay?"

"Yes. Please fuck me."

There we were in Chatting Wood. My hands against the rough trunk, I rammed into her, biting into her neck.

"Oh God, that feels so good," she said.

We fucked like wild animals; me pounding into her. Manon sounded like she was in agony, and I stopped.

"No. I'm close. Please."

We built and built, then I came like a rocket bursting out of me. It was intense. It always was with her. Like no one else ever. That was why she could get me to do anything. I'd become her slave. Only she needn't know that. I hated how weak that made me look.

It took me a moment to return to reality.

I puffed. "I've never fucked anyone like I fuck you," I said. "I've never felt a pussy like yours. You're fucking addictive. My dick loves being inside of you."

She turned and touched my hand, then leaned in and kissed me on the lips. "And I love your cock inside me. I also love sucking you off. I always thought I'd hate it."

"You've never blown anyone?" I had to ask. I didn't enjoy discussing her sexual history. It made me jealous, as unreasonable as that was.

"Well, Peyton…" She grimaced, knowing how much I wanted to kill that child molester. "Only he had a tiny little dick." She wiggled her finger.

"A micro dick that needs to be chopped off."

She took my hand. "There's only ever been us. There will only ever be us."

She held my eyes, and again, she'd gone deadly serious, like she was trying to say more.

That sounds like forever.

The way I felt, I could easily do forever with her. But was that just my dick dictating?

She stopped walking and adjusted her tits so they sat inside her dress.

"Hey, I was enjoying that," I protested.

Manon giggled. "I can't exactly go back to the party with my tits hanging out."

"No, you fucking can't."

Her brow pinched as she held my gaze. "Would it make you jealous if men were looking at my tits?"

"What do you think?"

"Well, I'd like to hear you say it."

"It would."

"What about if a guy touched me?"

"I'd knock his fucking teeth out."

An excited smile grew on her pretty face. "Ooh… you're hot when you're all alpha."

It was a cute game we played. But I kind of liked it, for some crazy reason. I drew her to me. "You belong to me."

"And you belong to me. I love you, Drake. No matter what happens, remember that."

It was my turn to frown. "What do you mean by that?"

"Nothing. Come on, let's go back in and get drunk and dance like idiots."

I reached into my pocket and took out her thong. "What about this? You can't go in there without knickers."

"Oh, but I can. Won't it make you hot to know my pussy's all naked?"

"Shit, Manon, you're making me hard again."

She rubbed her hand over my dick. "Oh, you are. Do you want me to suck you off?"

"Later."

Things went strange again. Instead of that cute, little wicked smile she got whenever we talked smut, she looked distant.

"Will you keep fucking me no matter what?" she asked.

"Why am I sensing something here?"

She puffed out a breath. "Why don't we go away? Just you and me. I've got enough money to keep us going for a while."

"I can't. I've got my mother."

"I can pay for her if you like."

She held both my hands and looked seriously into my eyes. She meant it.

I thought about the pact I'd made with Caroline Lovechilde. "Look, I've got something to tell you."

"Oh, please don't tell me you're going away. I couldn't stand that." She sounded so alarmed it surprised me.

Manon had attached herself to me, but instead of running, which would be my normal response to a girl wanting all of me, I stepped in close and let her have me. All of me.

"I've agreed to return to the casino. Just for one month. Rey doesn't know yet. The reason why I left last time was because he gave me an ultimatum to stop seeing you."

Her brow creased. "And you left?"

"Well, yeah. I wasn't exactly sacrificing my kidney."

"No. I guess not." She looked down at her feet. "Would you?"

Were we playing this game again?

"Well, if you needed my kidney. Yeah. Sure. To save your life."

"But what about for my love? If someone said, 'Give me your kidney, then you can have Manon,' would you?"

"That's fucking crazy. You know how I feel."

"Would you though?" Her searching stare gripped me. She looked almost haunted.

I'd met no one who needed so much reassurance. "Yes. I would."

"Why? Because you enjoy fucking me?"

"Oh God, Manon. What's this bullshit?"

She kept staring at me expectantly.

"Well, obviously, I love fucking you. But I want to be with you."

"Is that all?" she asked.

"I'm shit with words, Manon."

"You're doing pretty good so far."

She hugged me, and I relaxed.

"Your grandmother needs me to spy. So we might have to hang low. Just for a month."

She didn't respond, which I thought was strange.

As we stepped onto the lit-up grounds, Crisp, sucking on a huge cigar, stared straight at us, and I heard Manon say "shit" under her breath.

"Oh, Manon, there you are. I've been looking for you."

He looked at me as though I were trash, and I felt like smashing him in the face, but I controlled that urge. I was no longer that hothead, hit-first, question-later lad. In my bad days, just the hint of a snigger would have had me in a spin. And that was what Crisp's smarmy grin was, more of a sneer. I returned it with my own, despite my promise to Caroline to butter him up for a gig.

"This is Pierce, a close business affiliate," he told Manon, before turning to his mate. "This is my wife-to-be, Manon."

He ignored me, which was fine because, at that moment, I felt like I was about to spew all over his velvet jacket.

I turned to Manon and shook my head with my hands open, and alarm filled her eyes, as though confronted by a wolf, which she had. Crisp, in the meantime, wearing a predator's grin, looked like he was having some fun before the big kill.

I couldn't stand his smugness any longer, so I walked off.

She chased me. "Hey."

I stopped. "So, when exactly were you going to tell me?"

"I don't want to. I have to." Her voice cracked.

"Why?" I spread my hands again.

"I can't tell you. He's blackmailing me. It's bad. It will fuck my future."

"We can work it out. Just refuse him."

I couldn't believe I said that. Was I proposing to her? I wasn't exactly ready for that. But I wasn't ready to be without her either.

Tears poured down her face. "But you'll hate me."

Crisp came to claim her, and I turned my back on both of them. The ball was in Manon's court.

The fact that she couldn't trust me with more of her secrets kicked hard. Surely nothing could be as bad as her fucking that rich pedophile at fifteen.

CHAPTER 19

Manon

The pictures arrived just as I was about to call Drake again. It was the morning after my party, and I felt like shit. The forest sex had been so raw and magical we'd almost skipped back, or I had. I'd forgotten about everything and had even hatched a plan to run away.

We were happy and sharing our feelings. The storm in my brain had almost cleared until Crisp gate-crashed my bliss. He seemed to take delight in rubbing shit all over Drake. That ugly smirk on his pasty face even stretched into a rare smile.

Slimebag.

It wasn't the shoplifting that worried me but Crisp exposing me for sending pictures of my vagina, fakes of course, to lure him into marrying him.

I hated Drake hearing about that awful me—the girl who had stuck up her middle finger at the world while an inner war had twisted me into knots. And it had gone nuclear. Especially as I scrolled through the pictures that were not even my originals.

He'd had someone reconfigure a new batch, and they looked convincing. Bile rose in my throat as I scrolled through the fake images of someone's legs apart, exposing every little gynecological detail. I would never do that. Maybe for Drake, but no one else.

Drake would hate me, and I couldn't blame him. I looked like a complete money-grubbing skank.

MY GRANDMOTHER SAT BY the pool with Cary. They were having their breakfast, and while she read a magazine, he was with a book. What a picture they made, looking content and peaceful.

Could that be me in thirty years? Nothing would have pleased me more than to see me there with Drake, sharing tea and in comfortable silence while soaking up a sunny life.

She must have sensed me close because she looked up and gave me one of her welcoming smiles, which instantly put me at ease.

Around my mother, I always felt like an intruder. Particularly in the mornings, when some lover walked around in his briefs or with a towel wrapped around him after a night of noisy fucking. There was never a smile.

"Sorry to interrupt. Um... can I talk to you?" I asked, biting my cheek.

My leg stung with a fresh cut, and a trickle of blood embarrassingly ran down my inner thigh. I squeezed my legs together, which only added to the pain.

At least it took my mind off the ache in my heart.

"Give me ten minutes," she said. "We can talk in my office. Okay?"

Another smile, and I returned a quivery one, hoping she didn't notice the blood.

Drake refused to answer my calls, and with each call he ignored, I razored into my skin and was running out of hiding spots on my leg.

After cleaning myself up and dressing in a long skirt to hide my wounds, I went off to meet my grandmother.

She pointed at the seat, and I fell into it like someone doomed to an ugly future. I couldn't even straighten my back.

"I suppose this is about your upcoming marriage to Rey?"

I nodded. "I don't want this, Grandmother." My voice cracked.

"Quite. I'm surprised he's even taking this path. He's never been the marrying kind. I spoke to him afterward, and he's determined, Manon.

He explained how you'd been the one to initiate a commitment by enticing him."

I stared down at my nails and flicked at them. "Yeah... well... that was my mother's doing. She was on my back to marry someone rich. And to be honest, it was my only way out of a shitty—sorry, I mean, terrible—life. It wasn't fun growing up with Beth."

"No. I can't imagine what you went through." She had a distant look in her eyes, as though she'd had a tough time growing up too.

I didn't know who my grandfather was, and my mother never spoke about him. My grandmother's past remained a mystery, as Savvie had alluded to after I asked her whether she knew of my grandfather. My mother just told me he'd died and had nothing to add. Like it was a stain that needed to be removed.

"What can I do?" I asked.

"You can start by telling me what he's got over you."

I told her everything, blushing as I tried to skim over the finer details of those smutty images. I even admitted to shoplifting.

She shook her head. "Bethany had you doing that as a seven-year-old?"

"We were hungry." I stared down at my feet.

I'd distressed her.

She wore a look of alarm. Or was that guilt? Her hand even trembled. "I'm sorry," she said in almost a whisper, as though it hurt to talk.

"You gave my mother life. Something I'd often remind her."

"Her response?" Her unblinking stare made me shift in my seat.

"Um... she'd just complain how you had it all, leaving her with nothing and that a life in poverty wasn't a life worth living. Or something like that."

She walked to the window and turned her back to me. I sensed she didn't want me to see her reaction. Despite her coming across as tough most of the time, I'd sometimes noticed an occasional fragile flicker in her eyes that she would quickly shift out of. I read her well enough because that was me too. I hated people seeing me vulnerable.

With Drake, that tough layer dropped. I could be real with him, warts—or I should say scars—and all.

"I'm not fishing for pity. If anything, I would have gone through all of that again if it meant being here with you."

My grandmother wasn't easy to read, but I felt her relief at hearing me admit that.

"I just don't want to marry Rey."

Lost in thought, she nodded slowly. "Leave it with me."

IT WAS A PERFECT sunny day for a fair, and I was glad I let Savvie talk me into going after she caught me moping around by the pool, feeling sorry for myself.

Stalls selling food and homemade crafts were spread throughout the farm, and there was even a stage for local musicians.

Savvie hugged me. "Yay. You came."

"This is buzzing." I glanced at the brightly painted vans selling juices and vegan treats.

Carson joined Savvie. "It's a great turnout." He looked at his wife. "I'm going to that sausage sizzle. Can I get you one or two?"

She giggled. "No. I'm off meat. Remember?"

He looked at me and rolled his eyes, then kissed her and left us.

"What's that about?" I had to ask.

"Oh, we're having a food issue at home. He's, like, a huge meat eater, and having gone vegan, I've grown to dislike the smell of meat."

"That's tricky," I said. "Why no meat?"

"I read somewhere that it might help to detox, and I thought, why not? I never really liked meat anyway, and I feel healthier." She smiled.

She linked her arm to mine. "Come on, let's go for a spin and spend some money. Good to support the local community, and there are some nice crafty scarfs and beanies."

"It's summer," I said.

"It can get a little nippy when the winds blow."

We went from stall to stall. I bought some hand cream and lip balm, and there was even a stall with organic cotton underwear.

"These look comfortable," Savvie said, picking up a pair of long knickers.

I scrunched my face, and she laughed.

"Yep. Better wait until I'm forty and bored with sex for those," she added.

"You look too in love to get bored with sex."

Her eyes had that satisfied look of someone who had everything. "It just gets better. Even so, these do look comfy. I might buy a few pairs. And the singlets too."

I held back on the grandmother's underwear.

We ran into Declan and Julian at a wooden toy store.

"This is fabuloso." Savvie hugged Declan.

His son had fallen in love with a handmade wooden truck and was pushing it along the table, making engine noises. He was so cute. But up to his naughty tricks, he was about to knock over the entire range of toys.

"I'm pleased with the turnout," he said. "And the stalls specialize in local produce and crafts."

He took out his wallet and paid for the truck before his gorgeous-looking son destroyed the entire display.

"Where's Thea?" Savvie asked.

"She's with Mirabel somewhere. There's a local designer that's got them salivating. I think they're about to buy her entire range."

At the mention of designer, Savvie turned to me. "We better check it out, I think."

I smiled at my uncle. "It's such a brilliant scene. I love it here."

"Thanks. It's exactly what we wanted. And it will be a weekend affair. I've got Drake managing it. He's here somewhere."

I turned to look around, and sure enough, there he was—the man who'd stolen my heart, joking with a pretty girl. Tattooed with a pierced nose and long, dark hair, she wore that layered look favored by creatives. She couldn't have been more different from me. I wasn't keen on getting tattoos, even if I loved them on Drake.

I sighed, thinking of those muscly arms covered in ink wrapped around my body. The thought made my eyes water. Or was that seeing him chatting and smiling with young Cher's boho double?

Savvie helped snap me out of that pining-for-Drake moment and dragged me off to a colorful clothing stall where we spotted Mirabel and Theadora.

Mirabel held a dress against Theadora. "It's so nice. They've used sixties recycled clothes to refashion them. I love the patchwork skirt."

I noticed that the girl flirting with Drake was wearing one. And I suddenly wanted to change my clothes. I looked too synthetic like I should shop at Harrods and not an earthy market.

Maybe Crisp would hate me and move on if I embraced my inner earth mother and hippied out a bit. A rare smile touched me, thinking that.

"Perhaps I should go boho for a change." I inspected a floral full-circle skirt. "This would look great with boots."

Savvie nodded. "It's gorgeous. Would suit you. Anything would, Mannie. You've got a great body for clothes."

"You think so?" I smiled tightly. "Not just skin-tight stuff?"

"Oh God, yeah. Life's too short for activewear twenty-four-seven, and you don't have to wear Lycra to attract, you know. I hate it myself."

I nodded. She was right. There I'd been showing off all my skin, hoping it would bring me everything when all it had done was turn me into someone's fuck object.

After buying the skirt, we trundled about from stall to stall, with me sneaking glances at Drake, who was sucking on juice with that girl by his side. She seemed very expressive, waving her hands about and appearing to make him laugh.

Fucking great. A comedian too.

My heart shriveled, and I wanted to run away somewhere and cry my eyes out.

He'd moved on. He'd already met someone else. She was so pretty and earthy and natural. His sort of girl. I hated to be seen without makeup. Even in the mornings.

Savvie slanted her head and frowned. "What's wrong?"

"I need a drink."

"Good thinking. There's a locally crafted gin store I noticed over there." She took me by the arm. "Come on, let's get one."

I stopped. "Thanks, Savvie. You can't know how much this means, your being here for me."

She smiled sadly. "Come on. We'll get a drink. Sit over there at that nice bench under Wilbur."

"Wilbur?"

"That was our name for the old willow. We played here as kids."

I felt a stab of envy, having missed out on all those innocent, childish games.

As she headed off to get drinks, the girl who'd been chatting to Drake jumped up on stage with a guitar.

She's a singer? I hope she sings out of tune.

Bad me had made a show. I wanted to scratch someone's eyes out as I watched Drake help her with setting up the microphone.

Savvie passed me a drink. "Drake's become a roadie, I see."

"He's got a new girlfriend too." I didn't hide the edge in my voice.

"You don't know that. She might just be a friend. Weren't you two together? What's happened?"

I told her everything.

"Shit. And he's not giving you a chance to explain?"

I sighed. "He refused to talk to me unless I told him why I had to marry Crisp."

"Then fess up. I mean, is it that bad?"

I scrolled through my phone and showed her the images that I couldn't bring myself to show my grandmother.

Her mouth distorted like she'd seen something truly ugly. "Oh, that's right out there, for sure. And it's not you?"

I shook my head. "I had it coming, I suppose, after sending Crisp some fake images of my pussy to keep him on a string. That was before you guys accepted me and, well, you know, things changed."

"Then explain everything to Drake. I went through the same thing with that tape. You remember how bad that was?"

I nodded. "It's too late. He's got himself a new girlfriend. He won't even acknowledge me. I feel like shit." A tear slid down my cheek.

Savvie placed her arm around my shoulders. "Please don't cut yourself. Promise me."

Too fucking late.

I puffed out a breath. "I love him, Savvie. And he told me he loved me. And look how quickly he's moved on."

"You don't know for sure."

Just as she said that the girl wrapped her tattooed arms around him for a hug.

Shit.

"Do you think it's the tattoos?" I asked.

"I'm not a big fan. I like them on men though. Is that sexist?"

"I don't know anymore. I'm always offending someone for saying the wrong thing."

She laughed. "Me too. We share that."

"Hi, everyone," the girl announced on stage. "I'm Brooke, and I'm so happy to be at Gaia's opening. It's such a fantastic place. I'm just going to sing a few of my songs. Hope you enjoy it. I'm also selling some CDs for those who might be interested." She pointed at a box by the stage.

She ran her fingers smoothly over her guitar, and much to my despair, she was fucking talented.

"I'm sunk."

Savvie turned to me and pulled her sad face. "Don't jump to conclusions. But yeah, she's good."

Her voice, while not as great as Mirabel's, was sweet and tuneful, and I wanted to scream at myself for not being arty or talented. I had nothing to offer but my body.

That was all.

I hadn't even kept up with my course. I'd been too busy spending time with Drake and falling head over heels.

CHAPTER 20

Drake

I did my best to ignore Manon at Gaia's opening, despite the odd sneaky peek, and as I helped Brooke set up, I felt Manon's eyes all over me. I couldn't even bring myself to smile at her.

I missed her like mad, and I stayed busy to quash any memories of us together. The night was worse. I missed spooning her soft, warm body.

It wasn't just the sex, either, despite how hot we were together. I just liked her close.

Since I was back to working two jobs, I had plenty to distract me.

It was my fifth night at Salon Soir since returning. Crisp had taken me back with open arms. Maybe that bullet I'd nearly worn for him had something to do with how easy it had been to return.

Manon didn't even come up. No ultimatum. Just "Good to have you back. Remember what happens here, stays here."

I'd already seen that paunchy bald guy from the photo Caroline had shown me, and even spotted him having a heart-to-heart with Crisp.

That photo I'd snapped of them on my phone had proved tricky. I wanted to be useful. Standing at doorways always felt like a dead-end career that one day, after I paid all my debts, I would walk away from.

But at that moment, I just wanted to find dirt on Crisp. Whether it was so Manon didn't marry him, I couldn't say. I was still shitty with her for refusing to explain why she would destroy what we had for that old dick.

I WAS ONE WEEK into my casino gig when something significant happened. It was 2:00 a.m., and just as I was about to leave, a van arrived. The casino normally shut its doors at one, despite patrons connected to Crisp continuing on. The man was a vampire. I imagined he slept during the day.

The van pulled up behind the venue in a dark spot.

I quickly grabbed my backpack, and just as I headed over to Crisp, someone whispered in his ear.

I waved to show him I was leaving, and he nodded in acknowledgment.

Curious about that van, I went the back way, which meant crossing the forest. There were no lights, and wearing black meant I could sneak around unnoticed.

I reached for my phone and positioned myself behind a tree, where I had a good view of the two guys standing by the van. Another car arrived, parked next to the van, from which two men stepped out.

The four men started to push and shove each other in what looked like a heated exchange. One man from the car then brandished a gun, which was on a silencer. He shot dead the man from the van, then his partner took a bullet in the back while bolting off.

The remaining two men then opened the back of the van, removed sports bags, and tossed them into the boot of the car before driving off in the unmarked black SUV.

The next minute, Alec and Goran arrived and walked around the van, yelling something before bending down to check the victims' necks.

It all happened in a matter of minutes, even seconds, and I filmed it. My hands trembled holding the phone. I'd never witnessed anyone being shot before. I just stood there and froze. Severely shocked, I was almost drunk from the horror of seeing men fall to their deaths with such efficient speed. At least the Serbian brothers dealt with the bodies, because I was about to run over and see if they were still breathing.

At least I hadn't made my presence known, having just scored some compelling evidence of crooked activity.

As I traipsed through the dark forest, I kept looking over my shoulder while stumbling along with branches tearing into me. With the night moonless, it took some time for my eyes to adjust. I wanted to avoid using my phone torch. Rustling came from scurrying creatures, which had me on alert. Only nature wasn't about to kill me. Unless a hungry wolf had roamed into unfamiliar territory, but those furry monsters didn't freak me out as much as evil human ones did.

After watching my back through that noisy, dark forest, I was relieved to be home one hour later. I'd left my bike at the casino, and if Crisp commented, I would just tell him that the tire was flat or some other bullshit story.

It was quite a walk to the village, but I didn't mind, because it gave me a chance to clear my head. I tried to think of nice things, like the way Manon's eyes filled with lust when I entered her. Or the way her soft lips felt on mine. Also unwelcome thoughts in the end, given that I was trying to shake her off.

It was like Manon lived permanently in my head and body.

When I got home, I got myself a beer, stretched out on the sofa, removed my shoes, and pressed play on my phone.

The footage was grainy and dark, but the shooting was clear enough. As were the falling bodies and the bags then being removed from the van.

After a sleepless night reliving the same deadly ambush that I'd watched a million times on TV—but had never fucked with my head in the same way as seeing it in real life—I took a day off.

Merivale could wait until Monday.

Instead, I went for a run up the cliffs, in an attempt at working off dark thoughts. I'd never seen anyone die before, and suddenly, I had a disturbing scene on my phone, like some sick snuff movie.

The run helped because when I returned, I slept all afternoon.

IT WAS SEVEN O'CLOCK, and I headed off to the Mariner for a steak sand-wich, a pint, and to watch Brooke perform. She'd texted to tell me she was playing a set. I knew her brother from London, and she'd only recently moved to Bridesmere.

Brooke chatted with Olivia, her girlfriend, when I arrived. Just as she hugged me, Manon walked through the door. Manon saw me and pulled a face like I was evil before brushing past me, where she joined Colin, a local solicitor, who was always at the Mariner chatting up women.

For someone who didn't do jealousy, I felt a tug in my chest.

As Brooke and Olivia chatted with me, I watched Manon, who wore tight jeans and a low-cut blouse. Her sexy tits spilled out as she stood close to Colin, whispering in his ear.

Isn't she meant to be marrying Crisp?

"I better get up there and play." Brooke touched my arm.

I ordered another pint and enjoyed listening to Brooke's song about finding love. Her eyes had settled in our corner, focusing on Olivia. Only Manon kept looking at me with "What the fuck?" written all over her face.

I guessed she thought I was with Brooke.

The set was a blur. All I could do was watch as Colin's hand remained on Manon's arm.

Tired of the games, I told Olivia that I was leaving and to pass onto Brooke that she was awesome.

As I stepped outside into the dark, a "Hey" came from behind. I turned and discovered Manon running towards me with a question in her eyes like I had something to tell her.

"What?" I stretched out my hands.

CHAPTER 21

Manon

DRAKE LOOKED ANNOYED. NOT even the slightest smile. He gave me nothing like I was a pest. An interruption.

I'd gone to the Mariner because I'd heard that Drake's new girlfriend was performing. Masochistic of me, maybe, but curiosity had gotten the better of me.

Mirabel was the only person who knew Brooke, I'd been told. So on the pretext of asking Uncle Ethan for advice about investing, I'd visited them, only to discover his wife was away in London. At least Ethan had seemed keen to advise me, which was nice. When he'd hugged me, my eyes had even misted over. I couldn't believe how supportive everyone was towards me. Had the situation been reversed, I wouldn't have been so forgiving.

As soon as I noticed Drake with his new girlfriend at the Mariner, I pounced on Mariner's number one player, Colin, a hot solicitor, who invited me over for a drink. I couldn't even find a spark of interest, though. My heart and body had turned to ice.

I missed Drake badly. He was my soulmate. I'd known that from the moment we kissed. I would never feel like that for anyone. Love at first sight. Naïve, maybe. But the heart knew what the heart wanted. And Drake lived in my heart.

Even my throbbing wounds hadn't masked the ache from not being with him.

I couldn't just sit back and accept that we were over. That he'd found a girl and I was doomed to marry someone I loathed.

I had to speak to him.

Drake's gaze was full of hate. Then he turned his back on me and walked away.

I wanted to hit him.

Yell at him.

Hold him.

Fuck him.

Then crush him with affection.

He must have known I didn't want Crisp. Why the hell did he need all the nasty details?

I hurried after him.

Since when do I chase?

Since when did I give someone my heart?

I caught up to him and tapped his hard-muscled arm I loved wrapped around me.

"Can we talk?" I asked, hating how desperate I sounded.

"Unless you're about to tell me you're not marrying Crisp, we have nothing to say."

His voice had a cold bite to it. He didn't even look at me, and when he did for a moment, his eyes resembled an emotionless void.

I knitted my fingers. "How can you have moved on so quickly? I thought you loved me."

"You're the one who moved on." He turned and kept walking.

Pushed along by a desperate need to be near him, I kept going. "But you've got a new girlfriend."

He stopped walking. "None of your fucking business. I owe you nothing. Now fuck off."

His mean words stung like a whip against my arse, only it was my heart that hurt.

Was that the same gentle, sweet Drake whose soft touches were the last thing I felt before falling asleep in his arms?

I didn't recognize this new cold and angry version.

Despite his cruel words, I tried to cling on tighter. Something I was good at. My father used to say horrible things, but I still chased his car whenever he left.

Drake crossed the road, and about to race after him, I came to an abrupt halt when a motorbike sped by. The force made me stumble onto the ground.

On the side of the road, I lay as uncontrollable sobs convulsed through me, like some stranded, unwanted soul who'd just crashed into a wall of apathy.

As I wallowed in self-pity, I felt myself being lifted off the ground.

"Are you okay?" His earlier cold tone had been replaced by gentle-voiced concern.

That same tender tone as when he loved me.

"No. Physically, I'm fine, though."

I sat on the side of the road. He sat next to me and wiped away the dirt on my face.

"Can you stand up to show me you're all right?" he asked.

Rising off the ground, I felt my legs wobble, and I fell into his arms. He held me, and our hearts beat as one. I could smell his bath soap and him, setting off warm ripples through me. Like I'd returned home after being lost and isolated.

I needed his body on mine to remind me I had a life worth living.

I hated how much I needed him. Just that one taste of love, and I'd become pathetically addicted.

Every time we used to watch a movie where everyone hugged a lot, my mother would huff, "Fucking Hollywood fiction. No one behaves like that."

I'd believed her. Until I met Drake. His hugs meant everything to me. It wasn't just the sex and orgasms.

I cried in his arms, and my body shuddered. Unable to let him go, I'd gone from "Fuck him. He's got a new girlfriend, and I hate him" to "No one is going to have him. He's mine."

He pulled away, despite my tight clasp.

"Here. Come away from the curb." His voice was gentle. It was my sweet, darling Drake again.

My mouth trembled as tears soaked my cheeks. I looked up at him as a creature lost in a web of her own spinning.

He led me silently to the other side of the road, and we sat down on a bench on the deserted main street.

From where I sat, the sea resembled a black crinkly sheet with flickering stars that might have fallen from the sky. Something I could relate to because I'd fallen from somewhere myself.

"Manon, this can't continue. You know that. I don't fucking share."

"Do you love her?"

Under the streetlamp, I noticed rings under his eyes. I even sensed sadness, which made me feel less alone. "Misery likes company" as the saying went.

Drake frowned. "What are you talking about?"

"That pretty singer who looks like Cher before she had her face reconstructed."

His chuckle faded quickly. "I don't love anyone other than my mother."

"But you said you loved me."

"You're getting fucking married. How can you not get that?" He went to stand up.

I stopped him. I needed more of him. He could yell abuse at me, call me names. It didn't matter. I just wanted him close.

"Don't go. I'm going out of my fucking mind, Drake. Seeing you with that girl. She's so pretty and talented. Everything I'm not."

"You're beautiful, Manon." He puffed. "Too beautiful." His whisper sounded more like a torment.

"But you're seeing her." Tears prickled my eyes. I'd never cried so much as that past week. "I even went to the vintage market and bought boho clothes, but I hated them on me."

Drake gave me a sad smile. "Just be yourself, Manon."

Having gone from using my body to get ahead to searching for more than just designer handbags and shoes, I didn't know who I was.

"Brooke's gay."

It took me a moment to process his comment. I turned sharply. "She is?"

"Yep. That was her girlfriend in there."

"But you looked so close, so friendly. Your face animated around her."

He laughed. "Animated? Shit, am I that expressive? Here I was thinking I was shy."

I wanted to kiss and hug him. I'd had a scenario playing out all week of him in bed with young Cher, and it had twisted me inside out.

"I wouldn't exactly describe you as shy," I said at last, after bathing in hope.

"I have my moments." He stood and stretched. "Okay. Now that's been established, do you want me to walk you to Merivale?"

Walk me to the other end of the earth. Please.

I nodded.

We walked in silence. It felt nice. No mention of Crisp. It was almost us again. Only it ended at the iron gates of my Disneyland home.

"Thanks." I looked up at him and smiled shyly. I couldn't let him go. So I stared into his eyes, almost begging for a kiss.

He turned, and I turned away. Enough pleading. I was worn out.

I took a few steps, and my heart shrank into a tiny, painful ball. I missed him already.

I stopped and turned to watch him walk away, but he stopped at the same time. Talk about twin flame stuff. I'd read somewhere that an invisible umbilical cord exists between soulmates.

He came towards me, then without another word, he took me roughly into his arms, as though pissed off with me or something. It was an angry kiss.

Of the best kind.

Hot, wet, and hungry.

I couldn't even feel the earth as we devoured each other's lips. Our tongues tangled like we were already fucking. His groans echoed in my mouth as he crushed my tits and his dick grew hard against my stomach.

CHAPTER 22

Drake

MANON ASSURED ME I could come and go undetected. She didn't seem to mind either way. For me, sleeping with Manon at Merivale felt a little uncomfortable, seeing as her grandmother employed me. Before things had gotten complicated, we'd always stayed at my place.

Whichever way, all it took was a taste of her lips, and I would've probably scaled barbed wire to get to her. As it was, we walked up the servants' back-stair entrance.

Once we got to her room, it didn't take long for me to remove her clothes. I almost ripped them as she giggled. Manon loved me destroying her clothes, especially her panties.

The heat cooled somewhat, however, when I noticed more cuts on her upper thighs.

"What the fuck, Manon?"

Her face dipped, reminding me of a child caught doing something shameful.

"Let's not go there. I've had a shit week imagining you fucking young Cher." Her eyes met mine again. "I almost couldn't breathe."

Her mouth trembled into a sad smile, and I took her in my arms and held her.

My heart melted at the sight of her in such a vulnerable state. I knew I couldn't stay away, and if I were being totally honest with myself, I also hadn't been able to breathe thinking of her marrying that vampire.

She looked down at her fingers.

I stroked her soft arm. "You're the only woman I've been thinking about."

Her eyes met mine again, wide and expectant, like I was feeding her important information.

"Tell me what he has on you. I can try to fix it. Even the family would help. They've got the resources."

Picking at her nails, she looked down again. "I'll tell you soon. Not now. Just come to bed." She pulled back the covers.

Those disturbing cuts nauseated me. I was out of my depth. I didn't know how to make things better for her.

I kissed her wounds one at a time, and she winced.

"Sore?"

"No. You're turning me on again."

She sighed. And I was a fucking goner.

My tongue went all the way, and I lapped up her clit like I might have something delicious after being starved, sucking back her juices until she trembled and groaned.

"Please fuck me," she moaned.

I entered her in one deep, desperate thrust, and when she flinched, I stopped.

"No. Hard. Hurt me. Please."

Despite Manon's disturbing thing for pain, I could do that with my dick because, driven by lust and a deeper, indefinable emotion, I didn't want to stop either.

As my dick fought through her wet pussy, my eyes watered from the extreme, indescribable pleasure. I'd never been noisy when fucking before, but no one compared to Manon. The way her tits bounced against me made me want to devour her with everything—my mouth, cock, and hands. I was addicted.

It didn't take long for me to come. But we had all night together, and I didn't plan to do much sleeping.

I RUBBED MY HEAD with a towel. My dick was red raw after a long, hot shower. Rich people's water never seemed to go cold, which worked wonders for blow jobs.

Manon poured a juice and handed it to me. She even had a compact fridge in her bedroom, which was almost the size of my studio apartment.

"Will you promise not to turn your back on me?" She tipped her head, and I saw that same fragile look as the night before.

"I can't watch you marry him," I protested.

"Then kill him."

I studied her, waiting for her lips to curve into a joking smile. "I want us to be together, but fuck, I don't wish to rot in jail, either."

"Then I'll kill him—after I marry him so I can get his money."

My jaw dropped with a fat "What?"

She rolled her eyes and chuckled. "Just joking. Oh my God, you should see your face."

A shaky breath shot out of my mouth as I forced a smile. Manon had made no secret of her ambition to be filthy rich.

She took my hands and gazed directly into my eyes. "There's only you. Please know that. I will do anything to be with you." Her eyes teared.

I believed her. My heart was also in deep. Like it had somehow entwined itself with hers.

That was why I couldn't stay away.

Only I had to keep asking myself if it was my dick guiding me.

But as I fell into those big, dark eyes, I found bits of myself I'd never known before.

Manon had become the only person who I could show all of myself to. Like she knew more about me than I did. Just from being lost in each other's eyes, with me saying little.

Maybe eyes really were the window to the soul.

"Can we catch up later?" she asked, dropping her towel.

I lost myself in those curves again, my dick springing into action. Noticing my erection, she swept her tongue over her lips.

I had to leave to get to work. "Um... I'm at the casino till late."

"Why are you working there again?" She clasped her bra, then slid on her panties.

It took all my power not to push her onto the bed.

While lost in her beauty, an idea suddenly came knocking that I could use the footage to blackmail Crisp into stopping his marriage. That would leave us free to continue exploring each other.

"Your grandmother wants me to stake out the place."

Her smooth white forehead creased. "Oh? And have you seen anything of interest?"

I nodded slowly. "I might have a way out for us. And it won't involve blood."

She hugged me. "I'm already missing you."

We kissed as though it were midnight, then I left, hatching a plan as I ran down the servants' stairs to the back exit.

I WORKED THE DOOR at the casino, as usual, and saw little, only Alec and Goran walking through the back door with Natalia. One didn't have to be a mastermind to know Crisp was screwing her. At least Manon's statement about him only wanting to marry her as a way into the family rang true. It also meant that he didn't have his slippery hands all over Manon. Yet.

I planned to make sure that never happened.

After finishing my shift, I knocked on Crisp's door and took a breath while channeling my inner tough street guy. Having grown up around kids who carried knives instead of schoolbooks, I knew how to flex my muscles when needed.

It was all about survival.

And I wanted Manon all for myself.

She was a fucking mess, and she needed help. Those cuts on her legs disturbed me to no end. If nothing else, I wanted desperately to help her stop self-harming.

My dick rarely went down around her, but it was more than sex. I couldn't abandon her even if I tried. I'd already done that and failed.

"Come in," he said.

I entered, and Natalia sat on the edge of his desk, doing up her buttons.

"Have you got a minute?" I glanced at Natalia. "And can we talk in private?"

He wiggled his fingers for her to leave, and she sashayed off.

He leaned back in his chair. "So, what can I do for you?"

"I'm still seeing Manon, despite your demands."

His eyebrows rose. "She means that much to you?"

I nodded. "She wants to be with me, too."

"I see." He kept staring at me for a long time. "Girls like Manon don't hang around, you realize. She needs lots of money to be happy. The first few months of lust can obscure logic. It doesn't last."

"Thanks for the advice. But I'm sure we'll figure it out," I said.

His piercing stare made it difficult to continue looking at him.

"I must admit, it surprised me when you asked to return. I could only imagine Caroline or one of the Lovechildes put you up to it. Am I right?"

My leg muscles tensed. "No. I thought I could do without Manon, but I've since realized that's not possible. And she doesn't want to marry you."

His thin mouth formed a slow smirk. "I think she should be the one telling me that, don't you?"

"I'm telling you." I sat up, ignoring his smug act. "We're in love."

"Oh, how sweet, young love. Nothing much ever comes from it, however. And what are you going to do when she runs out of that five-million-pound inheritance? Do you think Caroline Lovechilde will keep dishing out cash?"

"That's none of your business."

"Yes, it is. We're talking about my future wife."

"But you're with Natalia," I said.

He shrugged. "So? Manon knows I have certain appetites."

My stomach curled. The man was fucking sick.

"Manon can fuck whoever she likes, only no starry-eyed boyfriends." He sat back with his hands crossed over his belly. "My plans haven't changed. And I will not let some lovesick nobody tell me otherwise. Now, best you leave and not come back. Yes?"

He slanted his evil head, and hell, I wanted to wipe that sneer from his mouth. If the devil had a face, it would look like Reynard Crisp.

And I was about to provoke Satan himself.

"I saw what happened here at the back, early Sunday morning, around 2:30 a.m. to be exact. I filmed it all." I paused, but he remained silent. "Gunshots. The van. An SUV driving off, stuffed with bags that I'm sure weren't heading for charity shops."

"How do you know it had anything to do with me?"

"Because the slain men worked for you. I'll send it to you. I've got other copies."

"You've shown Caroline?" he asked, remaining neutral.

"No one else knows, and it will all go away if you leave Manon alone."

His chuckle was more like fingernails scraping a board. "And there's the clincher. You're blackmailing me." He sniffed. "You wouldn't be the first. And I'm sure you won't be the last."

"Well?"

He nodded slowly. "Okay. Send me the tape, and I'll give you my answer."

I pulled out my phone and sent it to his number.

When his phone vibrated, he picked it up and clicked on the link. His face remained blank as he watched the footage.

"How do I know you'll keep your word?" he asked, putting his phone down.

"I just will."

"She's that important to you that you'll risk your life for her?"

"I'm not risking anything here, just a job that pays well." I went to walk away. "Will you put a stop to this marriage plan?"

His mouth twisted like he was mulling over my demands. After a longish pause—because, I sensed, men like Crisp hated to lose—he nodded. "Can't impede on young love now, can I?"

I left in a hurry, watching my back.

For good reason, I soon discovered.

It had been easy.

Too easy.

First a shadow, then footsteps, and before I could bolt, Goran had me in a hold. I kicked the gun out of his hand and pummelled him like he was the punching bag at Reboot.

Just as he fell to the ground, in my periphery, I sensed another figure—probably Goran's bearlike brother, Alec.

A shot rang, which barely missed me.

Before my next breath, I flew like the wind into the forest. Having run in Chatting Wood often enough, I knew my way through it, even in the dark. My daily sprints had paid off. Alec was more likely to beat me in a burger-eating contest than a race.

Once I was in the middle of the wood, I caught my breath by doubling over and resting my hands on my thighs. My body was covered in scratches and bruises, but adrenaline worked wonders for numbing pain, I'd discovered.

I had two options, Reboot or Merivale, and I opted for the latter since the hall was closer to the wood and there was enough staff around for Alec to think twice about chasing me through the lit-up grounds. I couldn't imagine Crisp would want anyone to know I'd become his latest victim.

When I got there, I found the servants' back entrance locked.

I could either go home and be knocked off or climb up to Manon's room.

Satisfied that he hadn't tailed me, I walked to the front of that sizeable building and studied the façade for ways to climb it.

There were enough embellishments to grip onto, and all I needed to do was get to the top balcony, which sat on the second floor.

Channeling my inner Spider-Man, I jumped up on some lattice, hoping I wouldn't bring it down as I took the deepest lunge I could muster. With my hamstrings threatening to snap, I somehow gripped onto the head of a carved creature jutting from the wall. From there, it was just a matter of swinging onto the balustrade framing the balcony.

All that ninja training with Billy, who was convinced redheads had the edge in that competition, had paid off.

Only I didn't have a pool to fall into.

I finally climbed over the balustrade, and massaging sore muscles, I waited for my heart rate to ease. The thought that I might have mistaken Manon's room sent me into a moment of panic.

Had I landed on Caroline's balcony instead?

It looked familiar to me. Which meant nothing because I imagined all the balconies were alike.

The glass doors were shut, which wasn't surprising. It was a chilly night.

I rapped my knuckles on the damp, cold window as quietly as I could.

CHAPTER 23

Manon

I heard knocking on the balcony, and assuming it was the wind, I ignored it and rolled over. I couldn't sleep. All I could think of was Drake and how things would work with Crisp clawing at me to be his wife. All I had to do was show Drake those horrible images, the thought of which had me carving into my skin again.

Despite the images being fake, I couldn't bring myself to show him because the photos looked like me.

My past had come back to haunt me. Crisp had thrown the mud right back at me. Arsehole.

All along, he'd known I was playing him, but he'd still stuck around, waiting to see if the Lovechildes would take me in like some stray.

The glass door rattled again, even a little louder. Sleeping in that big house, or hall as they called it, spooked me some nights. There were probably ghosts. All those creepy portraits everywhere filled my imagination with all kinds of horror stories at night. I'd even removed one of the late father's great aunt from my bedroom. She had piercing eyes that seemed to follow me around.

A figure appeared on the balcony, and as I went to scream, my vocal cords froze.

Was I asleep and thinking I was awake? I'd had a few of those nightmares before.

The figure gestured for me to open the door.

A shiver ran through me as I clutched onto my arms, digging my nails in deep. The pain confirmed my being awake.

I heard, "Manon, open the door."

Hurrying to the windowed door, I peered through and saw Drake on my balcony. I released all my angst in one happy gasp.

How romantic.

When I opened the door, he almost tumbled in.

"Oh my God, what the hell, Drake?" I laughed. "You've gone all Romeo on me. That's so sweet."

After I snapped out of the sweet fantasy involving me in a tiara and Drake in a cape, I noticed his face covered in sweat and dirt.

He stepped into the lamplight, and his eyes shone with terror.

"What's happened? I guess you didn't climb up here to play Romeo after all."

He fell onto the edge of the bed and held his head in his hands.

I sat next to him and put my arm over his large shoulders. I could smell his tension. "What's happened?"

"I need some water."

I stretched over to the side of the bed and grabbed a bottle of water.

He gulped the lot down in one go, then wiped his mouth with his hand. He puffed out a loud breath. "They chased me through the woods."

My eyebrows rose. "What? Who?"

He wiped his face with his polo top, exposing his abs, and his masculine scent hit me, sending a pulse of heat through me.

Yes, wrong. The poor thing needed my support, not me jumping him. But God, he looked hot.

"I fought Goran off and kicked a gun out of his hand before his brother fired a shot, narrowly missing me. Then I hightailed it into the forest, and Alec chased me." He rubbed his face. "I would've gone to Reboot, but there's no one there, and I don't have a gun."

"A gun?" I frowned.

He told me about how he'd used incriminating footage to blackmail Crisp into backing off me.

I wrapped my arms around him. "You did that for me? Because you wanted us to be together?"

He looked down at his hands. "Well, yeah."

All I could think of was that he nearly died for me, which meant that Drake did really love me.

That was my heart's response. My head, on the other hand, was freaking out because I couldn't lose Drake. I would rather die than lose him.

"Why didn't you come to me first? We could have plotted something," I said at last.

He kept rubbing his head and pushing that sexy dark wave away from his face. "Do you have anything to drink? Like something strong?"

I lifted my finger. "One minute."

I returned holding a bottle of scotch with two glasses. "I didn't get ice or coke. Is that okay, neat?"

"Any way is fine. I just need something." He exhaled.

I poured him half a glass and passed it to him. His shaking hand made me want to cry.

That was my doing. It was because of me that this gorgeous man had nearly died. Reality kicked my butt, and suddenly, I felt like shit for involving him in my train wreck life.

But I wasn't about to push him away, either.

"You're right. I was stupid to expect him to buy it. Now I've put myself in danger. They'll fucking kill me for sure."

The tremor in his voice pained me.

"I won't let anyone harm you. Ever. I'll do everything to make sure of that." Fire bit my belly, as determination to protect him and us took hold. I softened my tone and added, "I think you should show my grandmother in the morning, though." I cuddled him. "Why don't you have a hot shower then come to bed?"

Lost in thought, he rolled his lips and nodded.

As he stripped naked, I wanted to join him in the shower and ravage him, but I knew it wasn't the time to get all sexy.

While he showered, I went over everything in my head, and it all started to sink in—Drake was in serious trouble, and Crisp would stop at nothing to get to him.

I entered the bathroom just as he was drying himself.

"There's only one thing we can do."

He rubbed his head with the towel. "What?"

"We have to go. Like now."

"But where to?"

He dropped the towel, and I had to concentrate on the gravity of the situation and not his dick, which was half erect from the shower.

"Somewhere far, where no one can find us."

His face creased. "We can't just do that. I've got a job. I've got my mother, who needs me."

"Listen, I know Crisp. He's dangerous, and he doesn't like to lose. The sooner he removes you as a threat, the better. He knows judges and cops and has powerful people around him. I saw that when I was working for him."

Drake looked into my eyes, wide and unblinking, as though the shock had only just set in. "I fucked up. Didn't I?"

I smiled sadly. That he'd risked his life for me kept circulating in my mind. Seeing him falling apart, I felt guilty for thinking like that.

"Look, it was brilliant that you filmed it, but you should have spoken to my grandmother first." I touched his arm. "It's happened. Can't you see we have no other option?"

"We? He won't hurt you," Drake said.

"No. But I would die for you, Drake." Tears pricked my eyes.

He looked dazed, as though I'd confessed to murder. Drake was out of his depth with me gushing undying love. I was sure all he could think of were those maniacs coming for him.

I sucked back my sudden flood of emotion because we needed a plan. Like fast. "Desperate situations call for crazy shit actions like us running away. I can take one of the SUVs in the garage. I've got money." Adrenaline surged through me. "Let's do it. Then I'll contact Grandmother when we're in France or somewhere far."

"France?" His eyes widened in fear, as though I'd suggested we visit a shithole.

"Maybe Ireland. I don't know. We just have to get away. Like now. Can't you see that?" I was suddenly finding it hard to breathe.

As the minutes passed, my anxiety worsened. The danger was real, and we had to run.

He released a shaky breath and nodded before burying his face in his hands. "Fuck."

While he was cupping his face, I had my suitcase out, tossing clothes into it.

"I've only got these clothes." His eyes were wide and lost. I wanted to cuddle him and offer support, but we didn't have time. My heart raced, telling me to hurry along instead.

That was fine. I had the strength of a tiger at that moment because the energy that flowed through me was like nothing I'd ever experienced.

"Back in a minute. Ethan's room was open the last time I looked." I gave him a guilty smile. "I know, I'm nosey."

I crept into the neighboring room and, from the wardrobe, removed a hoody, sweatpants, jeans, and a pair of Nikes. In the drawers, I found briefs and T-shirts, and even a beanie.

Carrying an armful of stuff, I snuck back to my room. Luckily, my grandmother's room was down at the other end of the hall.

I dumped the stuff on my bed and placed the trainers on the ground.

"These look like they'll fit, luckily. I can see you made a mess of your shoes."

"I ran like the fucking devil, and I hit a few rocks along the way."

"I'm sorry." I slanted my head. "I forgot to ask if you're injured."

"I'm fine." He changed into the jeans and shrugged into a blue polo. "It's tight." He pulled down the top, which showed off that buff physique.

"You look hot."

He must have noticed my starry eyes because he rolled his eyes, and for the first time since arriving, his mouth curved slightly.

"At least the shoes fit." He tied the shoelaces, then looked up at me again. "We're really doing this?"

I nodded. "We have little choice."

I went into the bathroom and filled a small suitcase with makeup and toiletries, then changed into black sweats, sneakers, and a hoodie.

He sniffed. "You look like you're about to pull a job."

It was nice to see him a little more relaxed, and though I would never admit it, I was more excited than I'd ever been.

It was an adventure. And I loved adventures. With a hot, sexy guy in tow.

Two large suitcases and one small one later, I was ready.

Drake didn't look so excited, however, as he stared in wonder at my suitcases, scratching his neck, wearing a hesitant expression.

CHAPTER 24

Drake

MANON SUGGESTED WE DRIVE to Dover for the channel crossing to France. While her enthusiasm wasn't lost on me, it was the opposite for me. I hated the unknown, especially with all my responsibilities. Namely, my mother and a job that I liked.

I wanted to keep hitting my head in frustration at how stupid I'd been. Manon was right. I should have spoken to Caroline before confronting Crisp.

"I haven't got a passport, Manon," I said, steering the car towards Liverpool instead.

"Really?" She frowned.

"I haven't gotten around to it. I've never left the UK."

"Oh." She looked at me strangely, like everyone had a passport.

"I didn't think I'd be heading to France on such short notice."

She giggled, which at least eased some tension. I hadn't realized my shoulders were so tight until that moment.

"I've never traveled either." She looked sad. Like that was something to be ashamed of.

"We're both young, Manon. There's time."

I didn't feel young. At that moment, I felt like an old man. Stressed over the crazy decision to take off. However, I valued my life, and Manon was right. They would have come for me had I stayed in Bridesmere.

We'd been driving for two hours when a petrol station with a café came into view.

"Can we stop here and get a coffee?" she asked.

A caffeine hit was just what I needed, so I pulled up.

"Can we stay at the next hotel we spot?" she asked as we hopped out of the car.

"Yeah, good thinking. I'm totally exhausted."

She touched my hand and pulled a sad face. "You've been through so much, and now look at us bandits running away in the middle of the night. It's kind of exciting."

I lifted my chin for her to keep moving.

Her smile faded. "Are you pissed off with me?"

I shook my head. Pissed off with me, more like it.

We used the toilets first, where I splashed water on my face. The basin was filthy, and a cold sinking feeling swept through me. The adrenaline had gone, and all I felt was dread, like Mondays after a big weekend. Only far worse.

Manon brought doughnuts, and though I wasn't hungry, I took a bite if only for the sugar hit, then sipped on awful coffee. I preferred tea, but I needed that shot of caffeine badly.

When we were back on the road, I said, "We should have waited and spoken to your grandmother."

"But she may not have been able to do anything."

"Really? A crime took place close to her land. I've got the evidence, and I should go to the cops." That corrupt detective came to mind, and I realized that wasn't such a great idea after all.

"Crisp has something over her. We're trying to find out what. She has little control over him."

"But you posted that video to her, didn't you?"

She nodded. "I did."

We stopped at the next hotel.

"This looks awful," Manon said.

"I can't drive anymore. I'm exhausted."

"Then I'll drive. That way, we can go somewhere nicer."

"How long have you been driving?" I asked.

She scowled. "Long enough. God, Drake, you don't half trust me with anything."

I was too tired to argue.

She turned to face me. "We can go back if you're going to be like this."

I puffed. "No. I'm just rattled."

Her face softened, and she stroked my cheek. "You did it for me. Didn't you?"

"Well, yeah. I didn't want you to marry him. You know that. I just wish you would've told me why, then maybe this could've been avoided."

"See. There. You are shitty with me." She opened the door and walked around to my side, and I stepped out.

I took her in my arms. "Manon. I wouldn't be here if I didn't want to be with you. You just owe me some kind of explanation why he's forcing you into this. You get that, don't you?"

She nodded, looking lost suddenly, and though I should have said something, I wasn't in the conversing mood, so I forced a smile instead.

We'd been driving for twenty minutes when Manon looked into the rear-view mirror and said, "I think we're being followed."

Having dozed off, I took a moment to process her comment. I sat up and picked up her bag. "Shit. Your phone."

She kept looking into the rear-view mirror, then me.

"Watch out!" I yelled, as she nearly rear-ended a car.

"You can't destroy my phone," she appealed.

"He's obviously tracking us. I have to."

She sped up, and my heart raced the faster we drove, considering Manon had only just gotten her license. That kind of driving required experience.

She kept speeding up, narrowly missing a car coming from the other direction while overtaking one in front.

"Careful!" I yelled.

"Don't fucking yell!" Her screech scraped at my nerves.

I peered at the dashboard, and the needle sat on a hundred miles per hour.

My knuckles turned white as she overtook cars. Horns sounded everywhere.

"Hey, I want to live to see my next birthday."

An irate driver was close to ramming our arse.

"Where are all these fucking people going to at this hour?" she asked.

"We should take the next turnoff towards Liverpool. If only to get off the motorway."

I kept looking behind me and saw that the black SUV was only a few cars behind. We turned off the motorway and headed down an open road when a side road came into view.

"Drive in there quick. There's a forest." I smashed her phone under my foot and tossed it out the window.

"Was that completely necessary?"

"Yep."

"But what about your phone?"

Good fucking point.

I took it out of my pocket, crushed it, then flung it out the window.

"We're now without phones." Her voice had gone up in pitch.

That seemed to worry her more than us being pursued.

"We'll buy new ones as soon as we hit Liverpool," I said, taking a deep, steadying breath after having almost hyperventilated over Manon's drag racing.

We came to a cottage that looked abandoned, buried in weeds with a gate hanging on its hinges.

"Pull up here. I think we've lost them. They didn't see us turning, and I destroyed the phones before we deviated."

She turned off the ignition.

I faced her and forced a smile. "Hey, that was outstanding driving."

As tears poured down her face, I leaned over and cradled her in my arms.

"Hey. I'm sure we're going to be safe."

I grabbed a bottle of Coke from the plastic bag, screwed off the top, and passed it to her.

Just as I gulped Red Bull, we heard an engine, and both turned at the same time.

"Fuck. They've found us." I mustn't have crushed the phones properly.

"Do you think they can see us?" she asked with a tremor in her voice. "We can't even call for help. You shouldn't have destroyed our phones."

"I had little choice."

"But they've found us," she cried.

She reached into her bag and brought out a flick knife. I took it from her shaking hands.

"I think we should drive off," she said.

They couldn't see us because they were driving in the opposite direction. But then, just our luck, a light went on in the cottage.

The car drove up to it, and with us parked behind a bush close by, it wouldn't take them long to find us.

"Here, quick, swap with me. We have to go. Like now."

Manon climbed over to my side, and I almost flew into the driver's seat, turned on the ignition, and drove off without lights.

It was dangerous because the track wasn't easy to spot, but we found the road, and I breathed again. Switching on the lights, I drove like fury.

Manon kept looking over her shoulder. "They're coming again."

I put my foot down, and seeing another turnoff, I took it.

"This is our only option," I said. "They could easily catch up and shoot at our tires on that open stretch of road, especially since it's deserted."

I entered a thick forest and parked the car somewhere hidden from sight. "Come on, let's get out. We'll hide in the bushes."

We locked the car and raced into the thick scrub, which scratched and scraped at us, while I did my best to clear the way for Manon.

We heard an engine.

"Fuck, I bet it's them," she said.

It might have been around five, and with dawn arriving, we would soon be exposed.

It felt like nature assaulting us as we pushed through the scratchy scrub.

"Let's wait. We're hidden," I said.

"I wish we had a gun," she said.

Despite my dislike of weapons, I had to agree. A gun would have come in handy. It was us or them. And I planned to protect Manon with my life.

CHAPTER 25

Manon

As I CLUTCHED MY scratched and bruised arms, I felt things crawling on me, and I kept brushing my face and hair with my hands.

"Shh. Don't move," Drake whispered as he held on to me.

My ankles and muscles ached from the awkward squatted position. I couldn't believe what was happening. I'd seen that kind of thing in films but could never have imagined living it.

My teeth chattered in terror. "Are we going to die?"

"I'll kill them before anything happens to you." He turned to look at me. His eyes were shining with fearless determination.

I imagined that was how soldiers in battle might have looked when surrounded by gunfire and bombs.

I stroked his cheek to remind myself he was real, and for a second, the tightness in my chest released. That moment of basking in the glow of his moving—if dark—words was sadly short-lived when we heard steps.

Treads grew louder, and Drake clutched a log as his weapon.

I could barely breathe.

Should we have stayed at Merivale and brought in the cops?

Crisp would have wiggled out of it somehow, and that footage had put Drake in direct danger. They would have knocked him off for sure.

I couldn't risk losing him.

I would go down fighting to save him, just like he was doing for me. After all, he'd blackmailed Crisp to be with me.

We were a team. Together in life and death. And I planned to make sure we made it out alive.

No one was going to take Drake from me.

As that thought surged through me, my fingernails turned into claws, but then something bit me, and I had to shift my weight.

Drake gestured for me to stay down, then leaped out of the bush. As I buried my head, I heard a gun go off.

I gasped.

I peeked over the bush. Dawn had just broken, and Drake was wrestling a man on the ground.

He pushed his attacker's arm away just as the man fired another bullet, which barely missed me.

After he kicked the gun out of the man's hand, Drake punched him, causing the man to stumble back.

We had the winning edge, and though my heart was in my mouth, I went to grab a rock in readiness to help bring the man down.

After he kicked the gun away, Drake had his back turned when the guy grabbed him by the ankle and dragged him onto the ground again.

They rolled around, struggling in each other's arms. Drake kneed the guy in the groin and somehow grabbed the log and slammed it into the man's skull. Blood poured out.

He'd knocked the guy out cold.

Drake rubbed his neck and arms and looked stunned.

"Hurry, let's get out of here," I said, taking him by the hand.

As I picked up the gun, the bushes rustled.

"There's another one of them," Drake said.

He took the gun from my hand, then went to the man on the ground and placed his finger on the guy's neck.

"What are you doing? We should go," I whispered.

Drake gazed up at me with a troubled frown, which suggested the man was dead.

"It was you or him," I said. "Now let's go."

We spotted the other man with a gun heading towards us.

Drake hid with me behind a large tree and whispered, "Let's run. Through there." He pointed towards the car.

I looked behind me, and the man was on his knees, checking on his dead colleague.

"Quick. Run." Drake led me by the hand, and I nearly flew as he pushed me along.

We jumped into the car and drove off. I kept looking behind me. The gun was by our side, within reach, but the man hadn't even tried to pursue us.

"Maybe he's given up on us." I released the breath trapped in my lungs.

Drake didn't answer.

I touched his arm. "Are you okay?"

His slight nod told me otherwise.

A CITY HAD NEVER looked so good as we attached ourselves to crowds, despite not being followed during that last leg of our journey.

We checked into a hotel, looking a sight, going on the receptionist's stunned expression, where we crashed onto the bed in our clothes and fell asleep within a second.

I woke up first and stripped out of my torn jeans, which for once, hadn't been bought that way but were proof of the heart-pounding danger we'd experienced.

The hot water from my shower made my bruises and scratches sting. At least they weren't self-inflicted. Nevertheless, I sighed as the water washed away the dust and stress generated from that white-knuckle journey.

After putting on a pair of jeans and a shirt that took a while to choose, given I'd brought half my wardrobe, I stood at the mirror for my daily makeup routine. Empty of thoughts, like someone had knocked me on the head and my memory had been wiped, I dabbed makeup on my cheeks to cover the scratches.

Standing on the balcony, I studied the street, and with it still being light, I could only assume it was late afternoon.

While Drake slept, I called room service. I was too scared to face the world alone because I half expected to see the gun-wielding man waiting for me.

I ordered enough for both of us, but I didn't have the heart to wake Drake. He looked so peacefully asleep like nothing had happened.

While waiting for the coffee to arrive, I went to the balcony and watched the parade of strangers on the busy strip.

I already missed Merivale and the new life I'd made for myself, but that meant marrying Crisp, and he was to be avoided like the plague. A criminal husband was not what I wanted for my future. Maybe I could have stomached a rich, older man during my hungry days, but never a killer.

A knock at the door woke Drake, who sprang up, appearing disoriented as he scanned the room. "Don't answer that."

"It's room service. I ordered some food." I smiled, more at how he looked—like he'd been in the wars—but his astonishing good looks still made my heart skip a beat.

A sleepy blue-eyed, messy-haired hunk who'd saved us.

My hero. He did this for me. For us.

With that sweet thought swishing through me, obscuring the actual drama we faced, I opened the door, and the server pushed in the trolley. My mouth watered as the aroma of roast beef and chips hit me.

HAVING GONE TO BUY phones, Drake was taking longer than I would have liked, and I paced about impatiently.

When a knock came, I jumped, then opened it. "Shit, Drake, that took forever. I started to panic."

He placed a plastic shopping bag on the bed. "We lost that guy. Don't worry."

"But won't they expect us to be here? I mean, this is the closest city."

He shrugged. "There are a ton of hotels. In any case, I'm about to go to the cops. At least then we can head back home in the morning."

"Do you think that's a good idea?"

What if the police didn't believe him and charged him with murder?

I couldn't stand losing him. Not now. Not ever. "Let me call my grandmother. She needs to know what's happening."

He held my eyes, and for a moment, I forgot about everything. We hadn't even touched. Our only tender moment was while hidden in those scratchy bushes with him holding me tight.

"What?" A glimmer of a smile touched his lips.

"I was just thinking that you haven't touched me yet."

He rubbed his neck. "Well, it hasn't exactly been a romantic getaway. Has it?"

His edgy tone scraped at me, and tears burned in my eyes. I'd never cried as much as I had since being with Drake.

Toughness had once been my middle name. My mother always said that emotions weakened us. But Drake had penetrated so deeply into me, he'd smashed that hard shell that had once hidden my heart and soul. Even from me.

My lowered guard had turned me into an emotional mess, though.

Everything affected me. Before Drake, I had been a virgin to love, and I'd become so sensitive that it was like scorching sun on pale skin.

Perhaps my unaffectionate mother had a point when she said that love turned us into weaklings.

But then, love had also helped me bloom into the person I could become.

Drake kept staring at me with those deep-blue eyes, making me forget myself again. He must have read my insecurity, because he took me into his arms and held me close to his chest, almost crushing me. His heart beat against my ear.

"I'm sorry. I've been so messed up I haven't exactly thought about how you're going with all this crazy shit. We nearly fucking died."

He kissed my hair, and suddenly, life felt good again. I could handle anything with him close to me.

"I love you, Drake. I hope you realize how much."

His silence bit hard, and instead of a smile or even that warm look he often wore whenever I expressed affection, Drake stepped away and fiddled with the shopping bag.

"Here." He passed me a new phone. "It was one of the cheaper ones."

I took the phone from his hand. "I'll upgrade when life goes back to normal."

Normal? What does that look like?

Sudden insecurity filled the space. Like I could almost touch the air between us. Where were those sparks that ignited that invisible force of attraction?

I passed him the phone. "Do you mind setting it up?" I scribbled my details on a pad by the hotel phone.

He tinkered with my phone for a while, then I noticed a deep line grow between his eyebrows.

"What?" I opened my hands.

"Fuck, Manon." He tossed my new phone on the bed like it was on fire.

I picked it up, and glaring back at me were the images that Rey had threatened to show to the world in all their brutal, slutty shades.

The food I'd just eaten made its way up my throat.

"What were you doing going through my messages?" I snapped.

"They were impossible to miss. I read 'Deadline or else' with Crisp's name against it. I thought he was about to threaten us with more of his heavies. But then I saw that." He pointed at the phone like it might be a bomb.

He shook his head. Disgust and hatred shone from his eyes, and my chest ached like a knife stabbing my heart.

When I saw him going for the door, I went into a spin. "Where are you going?"

He didn't respond and just left.

Though I hadn't left that hotel room since we arrived, I chased him. "Come back. Where are you going?"

He turned. "I'm going for a fucking drink. Alone."

"But you can't leave me here." I hated how desperate I sounded.

"I can do whatever the fuck I like."

I caught up to him and grabbed his arm. "Hey. Let me explain."

"There's nothing to explain. You're fucking sick. It was because of you I blackmailed Crisp with that footage. It's because of you I killed a guy, and now my life's in danger." He pointed in my face. "All because of you."

"That photo isn't me," I cried as I chased him down the hallway. The former me would have told him to shove it up his arse, but I was no longer her. I was weak and helplessly in love, despite hating him for blaming me.

I hated myself more.

"That's your face."

I stopped him again. "Come back and let me explain. It's not me. He photoshopped it."

And didn't I know it? I'd created the photo in the first place, but I couldn't fess up to the fact that I'd once tried to coax Crisp into marrying me.

First Peyton, then Crisp. Instigated by my mother so she could dip her fingers into a deep bag of cash since Peyton had paid her a truckload of money to have me for those three years.

I could have and should have reported her and Peyton. Instead, I'd walked away, cut myself, and shoplifted.

Drake rolled his eyes. "Pull the other one." He shrugged out of my clasp and walked off.

Tears poured down my face as I lumbered back to my room, where I raided the bar fridge, then called my grandmother.

"Oh, Manon. I've been worried." Her motherly concern comforted me like a cup of tea on a wet, miserable day.

"Did you get that footage from Drake?" I could hardly speak his name without my voice trembling.

"You don't sound well."

You think?

"It's been horrible, and we're in danger. We were chased, and Drake had to knock a guy out. We don't know if he's alive or dead. He wants to go to the police."

Her sharp, emphatic "No" made me wince.

"You need to come back straight away. No police without a lawyer present. Our lawyer." She took a breath. "What were you thinking, running off like that?"

"Drake was chased through the woods. Crisp has set his heavies on him. They are out to kill him. We had to run away. Don't you see?"

She let out a breath. "I spoke to Rey after I received that footage. Whatever you do, please don't send it to the police."

That brought up a ton of questions.

"Rey reassured me he had nothing to do with that murder at the casino."

"That's crap, Grandmother."

"Just get back here, then we'll talk it through. Don't involve any police. Don't talk to anyone. Okay?"

I sighed. "Okay. But we're still being pursued."

"Let me talk to Rey."

"So, you're basically going to tell him to not murder us? I mean, Grandmother, what the…?" I stopped there knowing how much she hated swearing.

"Where are you?"

"Liverpool."

"Try to come back tonight, then. The sooner the better."

"Tomorrow. We're exhausted." And my boyfriend hates me. "We've been through the wars. It was terrifying."

"Don't talk to anyone." The tremor in her voice wasn't lost on me.

Is she worried about my wellbeing or something else?

"And tell Drake, not a word to anyone—his mother, Carson, or Declan. Promise me."

"I promise." I sighed. "Bye, Grandmother."

I closed the call and buried my head in a pillow, screamed, then cried my eyes out.

I needed Drake to hold me, not to hate me.

The pain was so intense I grabbed my flick knife from my bag and headed to the bathroom.

I cut into my inner thigh, where recent wounds had almost healed. I hadn't cut myself for weeks, thanks to Drake and how happy he'd made me.

Sitting on the bathroom floor, I kept sobbing. The sting in my leg failed to mask the pain in my heart.

CHAPTER 26

Drake

A BLACK-AND-WHITE PHOTO OF the Beatles crossing the road with a shoe-less Paul McCartney caught my eyes as I sat in the old pub, which might have doubled as a museum to that famous band.

Despite some interest, since my mother was a keen fan, I couldn't get that gut-twisting image of Manon naked with her legs wide apart out of my head. It made me want to throw up. Add to that the fact that I'd killed someone, and I just wanted to hide somewhere dark and alone.

I drained my glass in three gulps. The barman filled it up without me even asking. I guessed he'd seen his share of troubled people clinging to glasses like their lives had fallen into a ditch.

A few days ago, life had been smiling at me. My account looked healthier than ever. I was about to put down a deposit on an apartment for my mother when I'd stupidly agreed to spy on that piece of slime. Then everything had descended into a dangerous game of cat and mouse.

After two pints, I rose and returned to the room to face Manon square on. The images had made me sick, but I also couldn't leave her there alone.

My instincts were to run, to break loose, to get as far away as I could, but something tugged at my heart. I couldn't abandon her, twisted as she was.

My legs felt like concrete as I made my way back to the hotel.

What would I say?

When I returned, I found her on the bathroom floor, her leg bleeding and blood dripping on the white tiles.

I took the knife from her hand, then grabbed a towel.

She looked up at me, stunned like she didn't know what had just happened.

"What the fuck?" I rubbed my head.

She just kept staring, as if blinded by a light.

I felt like a first-rate shithead. That was my fucking doing. I shouldn't have yelled at her over those images.

Women did that shit all the time with their boyfriends. She'd sent me an image or two, which I'd loved, of course.

But Crisp?

I sat on the floor and placed my arm around her as a friend would.

"I'm sorry. I'm pretty fucked up." Her voice cracked.

"So am I," I responded without thinking. I had done things I wasn't exactly proud of. After my father died in that car accident, I'd gone crazy there for a while, picking fights with anyone and everyone.

"Come on." I helped her up.

I dampened a face wash and washed her leg as she leaned against the wall.

I passed her the cloth. "Here, press that onto the wound, and I'll look for the first aid kit."

After bandaging her cut, I wiped the bathroom floor, then poured her a drink from the bar fridge, and helped myself to a beer.

"I'm sorry for blowing up at you," I said at last.

She drank in silence, staring into space.

"You need to see someone about—"

"Why do you care, anyway? You hate me. You think I'm a fucking slut."

"I didn't say that." I rose.

"So, you're going to storm off again, are you?" Looking haunted, her eyes were wide and almost black.

"Let's not do this." Hypervigilant, I went to the balcony, which had become a habit since arriving.

All I saw were people going about their normal lives.

I wanted to be one of them. I wanted normal—away from drug deals gone bad or sleazy billionaires with filthy images of the woman I thought I loved. A woman I suddenly found I couldn't trust, even though leaving her seemed just as difficult.

Her eyes burned into me, and we had one of those staring contests we were good at. Funny, before Manon, I didn't do that, but she had a magnetic pull on me.

The more dramatic her life, the more beautiful she looked, as though the dark shit inside of her brought out an alluring quality.

Or was that me signing up for a dose of masochism?

Why some men were drawn to women struggling with issues was something that used to puzzle me. I'd seen it often enough with my mates. Though complex and still difficult to understand, I suddenly found myself sympathizing because of my own inexplicable and over-whelming need to protect Manon, like I was driven by some primal urge, which went beyond the sexual. Even after seeing those sickening images, a part of me screamed to run, but I couldn't help but return. And there I found her in a pool of blood, crying to be saved.

But how could I when she kept pressing buttons that triggered all kinds of fiery responses in me?

We were on a rollercoaster, for sure.

One minute, she looked like she wanted to devour me, then she would switch into that lost child in need of rescuing. I also wanted her more than I'd ever wanted any woman. And though I hated her choices, I also wanted to hold her, fuck her, make love to her, and everything in between.

Was there a dictionary for feelings? Because to make sense of my emotions, I needed to learn a whole new language.

"Do you want to get a meal?" I asked.

"I don't feel like eating. But knock yourself out."

"I'll pop out and get a burger then." I went to the door.

Just as I started to leave, she rushed over. "No. Don't leave me here alone. Order room service."

"I can't afford room service."

"I'm rich. Or have you forgotten?"

I took a step away from the door. "I haven't forgotten, but I don't like to take."

"Please let me." Her mouth curled slightly.

Is that a peace offering smile?

"Okay then, if that's what you want. Then sure, thanks. I'm still hungry."

"So am I." She was almost like her old self like nothing had happened. If only.

While we waited for our orders, I said, "After I've eaten, I think I'll go to the cops and tell them everything."

"No. You can't. I spoke to Grandmother. She asked that we return, like ASAP, and work it out with her. She doesn't want the police involved at all."

"But it hasn't anything to do with her, has it?" The urgency in Manon's tone suddenly had me questioning Caroline Lovechilde's involvement with Crisp again, given that she'd sent me to spy there.

"You just should have spoken to her before showing Crisp that video." Her voice softened.

"Yeah. Stupid. I know. I'll never forgive myself." I puffed.

"Will you ever forgive me?"

There it was, that lost little girl who I couldn't resist. Her hair had fallen over her face like it did whenever we fucked.

I shrugged. "I'm trying. That image was pretty out there. Pure smut."

"I know." She sighed, staring down at her fingers. "That's why I couldn't tell you. That vagina is not mine. Surely, you'd recognize it by now."

I almost laughed. Were we about to compare notes? "Um... well, to be honest, I didn't study it."

Her mouth tugged at one end. "Did it make you hard?"

I rolled my eyes. "Oh, for fuck's sake, Manon. It's not always about my dick, you know."

"I'm sorry. You're right. I would hate it if I found a dick pic you'd sent to Kylie."

"I'd never send her or anyone a dick pic," I said.

"You sent me one." She pulled a cute little grin.

"Well, that's because we had that session." I had to smile a little too.

She undid her buttons and spread her legs. Her teasing eyes had that come-and-touch-me look.

I shifted in my seat, having to adjust my growing dick. "Manon, you don't have to prove anything. I am attracted to you."

"I know that. I can see your dick getting hard."

She rolled her tongue over her lips, and helpless to resist, I joined her on the bed and kissed her like she was that girl I'd been dying to kiss forever.

Her lips tasted sweet and bitter, too, like a complex cocktail of desire and tension.

I ran my hands roughly over her big tits, and my dick dripped pre-cum down my leg. The need to fuck was so overwhelming I knew that if I didn't enter her, I would come.

I went down on her and licked her clit until she pulled at my hair and cried out for me to stop.

We were both hot and hungry and desperate for each other.

Impatiently, I thrust into her. The sudden fiery need between us was intense. Like I would combust if I didn't enter her.

Her nails dug into me, and I went in hard for the buildup. Her orgasm clasped my cock tightly, which moved like a piston, and unable to hold it back, an orgasm rushed through me like rocket fuel.

I'd never come that hard before. I even growled as I exploded. It was like I was emptying all the angst and stress of those past hours.

Each time we fucked or made love, it became even more intense for me. Like I was building up to an enormous head-blasting climax. Regardless of the drama in our lives. Manon took me somewhere I just couldn't have imagined existed.

"I hate how fucking addicted I am to you," I said while trying to catch my breath.

"Me too. I can't live without you, Drake."

I pulled away and stared into her eyes. They had that film of tears, which almost made me cry.

AFTER DINNER, I SAT back to watch the football with a cup of tea. I almost felt normal. Especially after that steamy session with Manon. But then she started sulking again. Which might have had something to do with me telling her I couldn't promise anything about us together in the future.

I just said, "I can't think beyond tomorrow, to be honest."

Manon went quiet and just kept packing and unpacking her suitcase.

After thirty minutes of doing that, she stopped and gazed at me.

"What?" I asked.

"When we return to Merivale, will you see Kylie?"

I nearly laughed at that ridiculous question. "That's the furthest thing from my thoughts."

"Am I in your thoughts?"

"Well, right now, I am wondering why Eriksen's not getting a red card." I pointed at the television.

"I hate you!" she yelled, then went into the bathroom and slammed the door.

I got up and released a loud frustrated breath, unsure of what to say to make it better. I knocked on the bathroom door. Mainly because I didn't want her to do something stupid.

I'd removed her knife, but she might have stashed another somewhere.

"Hey. Come out. Let's talk about it."

About what? I wondered. What did she want me to say? I was in so much conflict over everything, I hardly knew my fucking name, let alone where we were going as a couple.

She walked out naked. "Do you still hate me?"

"I never said I hated you."

Her tits bounced slightly as she came towards me. "Then why are you being like this?" she croaked.

"Like fucking what? I was just watching the game, minding my own business."

"That's what I mean. You're treating me like I'm invisible."

"Oh, for fuck's sake, Manon."

"You can't even look at me naked? You hate me that much?"

"I don't hate you. It's just that those images were pretty extreme. Anyone would have reacted as I did."

"So, you're only here because you think I'm going to cut myself again?"

"Maybe." I rubbed my neck.

She stared at me with wild eyes, like I'd told her something disgusting, then she started to hit me. "I hate you. I hate you."

I held up my hands to defend myself. "Hey. Chill. What the fuck?"

She kept hitting me like I was a punching bag.

"If I hadn't fallen for you, my life would be different. Better!" she screamed.

"Well, I'm sorry for being here." I tried to hold back on sarcasm, but the situation was becoming intense. "Do you want me to go?"

"No!" she yelled. "I want you to fuck me. To love me. To forgive me. To forget how fucked up my life was before you came along." She fell on the bed, buried her head in a pillow, and sobbed.

My jaw dropped. I was speechless.

I sat next to her on the bed and placed my arms around her, then rocked her in my arms. Her body was soft and pliant as she sobbed uncontrollably.

I allowed her to let it all out because that was what a breakdown looked like I imagined.

After her sobs stopped, I said, "What happened to you?" I asked that under my breath, given that I already knew her history.

She sniffled. "My mother happened to me."

That was the quietest she'd been and probably the most honest. At that moment, I saw her for the first time. Away from all that astonishing beauty, Manon reminded me of a young, helpless girl.

I rocked her in my arms, trying to absorb her pain. I got it. For a twenty-one-year-old, she'd been through more shit than most. I'd met Bethany, and she had rotten sewn into her soul.

It was some time before she unwound from my arms. Her smile was slight and uncertain. "Sorry if I said awful things to you."

"You didn't. This has been a traumatic experience." I sighed. "For me too. And seeing you cutting yourself, Manon, I want to help."

"Do you?" She gazed at me with eyes full of hope and longing, as if she had never felt love before.

I could see she needed someone she could depend on, hold on to.

We stopped talking at that point, and I made love to her like I was fucking for the first time. Exploring all of her. Taking care of her, while too aware of the wounds on her legs.

Raw and real, it was one of those moments I would never forget. Manon wasn't trying to play a game with me. She gave me all of herself, and it became more than just fucking.

She fell asleep in my arms, and her soft breath on my neck sent me off into a deep, restful sleep.

The following morning, I found her up and about, and by the bed, a trolley with a big breakfast stared at me.

I combed back my mess of hair in desperate need of a cut. "Hey, you've been busy, I see."

Her giggle was as good as the morning sunshine. I almost forgot about us having to get back to Merivale and all the drama.

Then anxiety kicked in again, and it had nothing to do with Manon going all temperamental on me.

I walked to the balcony and spotted Jim Reilly, the chubby detective connected to Salon Soir.

What the fuck?

I raced over to my bag and started stuffing everything into it.

"What's wrong?" Manon walked out of the bathroom with a full face of makeup.

"We've got to go. Like now."

Her face scrunched. "Why?"

"Just pack. We're leaving."

We paid the bill. Or I should say, Manon paid the bill, which made me feel uncomfortable about having maxed out my card. But it was hardly the time to discuss money.

Once we were in the car, she asked, "Will you tell me what's happening?"

As we made our way onto the highway, I explained how I'd just spotted the same detective I'd seen hanging out at Salon Soir.

"Oh, you've met Jim?"

"You know him?" I turned sharply.

She nodded. "I met him when I was working at the Cherry bar."

"I suppose he's another sleazebag into young girls."

"Don't know. He was there for the free drinks and to have a perv, I think," she said. "So, you think Crisp has sent him here to get us?"

"Pretty sure of it. What else would he be doing here?"

Manon kept looking over her shoulder as we drove onto the motorway.

"How the fuck did he find us?" I asked.

Manon's silence stirred suspicion.

"Do you know something? Because if you do, you better fucking tell me." With that car virtually up my arse, I was back to adrenaline mode.

She remained tight-lipped.

"Have you been in touch with Crisp?"

She turned away.

"You have, haven't you? Tell me."

"I contacted him to tell him to stop chasing us. I even promised..."

I turned to look at her. "You promised what?"

"Watch out!" she yelled.

I nearly ran into a truck. Taking a deep breath, I focused on the job of driving and not losing my mind over what was becoming a fucking shitshow.

"I promised to marry him if he called off his men."

"That won't do anything. He'll still try to wipe me out. I've got that footage, remember?"

"That was dumb, and you know it. And stop blaming me for everything."

Gripping the steering wheel, I puffed out a nervous breath and peered into the rear-view mirror. I saw the same blue BMW.

"That's him for sure. How does a detective afford a nice car like that, I wonder?" I spoke to myself because Manon was back to sulking.

I put my foot down, and the pin pushed up to a hundred. Speeding ticket or not, I needed to lose the prick.

Manon gripped on to her arms. "You're scaring me. I want to get to Merivale in one piece."

She was right. He was probably trying to get us to crash.

"There's nothing he can do while we're on the road, is there?"

I slowed down to seventy and sat on that. Of course, he came up close behind us. "Yep. There he is up our arse again."

Manon took out her phone and crushed it, then tossed it out. She then turned and gave him the finger.

"There." She looked at me, and I touched her leg.

"Sorry for yelling at you."

"You're forgiven. Now lose the arsehole."

I stepped on the accelerator, and seeing an exit, took it.

"At least it's just one person this time, and I've got this." She waved a gun at me.

"Put that away. Have you got the lock on it?"

"Don't know. I've never held a gun before."

CHAPTER 27

Manon

I COULDN'T BELIEVE WE were in another car chase. Despite hating myself for sending Crisp that message, I hated him more for trying to kill us. "I'll marry you. Now lay off Drake," I'd told him.

"Get back here, and we'll talk about it. Drake's in danger while he waves his dick around."

I'd almost laughed at the mention of Drake's dick, which if I was being honest, I'd fallen in love with. Even with all that was happening, with Drake hating me and making me feel like shit for all my fuckups, I wanted him more. It was like all the drama had made him sexier.

The shock on Drake's gorgeous face when I'd asked him to fuck me till I bled. Poor thing. He was right out of his comfort zone.

Maybe the therapist I'd seen that once had been right when she'd suggested my father's physical abuse had turned me into a pain junkie because his slaps had been our only physical contact since he'd never hugged me.

Physical pain I could do, but not the heartache at the thought of Drake leaving.

As we sped along, I gazed out the window at the open fields.

"If I weren't so freaked out, I might even enjoy the scenery out here," I said. "Look at all those cows and sheep oblivious to us silly humans out to hurt each other. I'm sure animals only hurt each other for survival."

"Isn't that what we're doing?" Drake asked.

"I thought it was to avoid me marrying Crisp. That's why we're doing this, isn't it?"

"When you put it like that, it seems rather excessive."

"Are you having regrets?" I asked.

He kept looking at his rear-view mirror. I turned, and sure enough, the blue car was on our tail.

I kept looking at Drake, waiting for a response.

"It was dumb of me to approach Crisp."

"Are you pissed off with me? Can we survive?"

"Let's see if we get through this in one piece, then we can start the therapy sessions."

His cutting tone hurt. "Fuck, Drake, you don't have to be so sarcastic."

"At the moment, all I can think of is making sure we make it out alive."

As he swerved abruptly, I was thrown forward and had to grip the dashboard. And the next minute, we heard a crash.

"Shit, he missed the turnoff and ran into a fucking tree." Drake stopped the car.

"What are you doing?" I frowned.

"He could need help."

"What? Hello. He's been chasing us. He's probably got a gun. And if he's still alive, he'll kill us."

Looking like he'd just run over a cat, poor Drake rubbed his head and face, puffed loudly, then restarted the engine and drove off.

MERIVALE DURING TWILIGHT HAD a fairy-tale look about it, and as we drove through those swirly iron gates, I sighed with relief.

"We're home."

"You're home."

I turned to look at Drake, who hadn't said a word since that accident.

"Hey"—I touched his arm—"it's not your fault that he crashed. And it's not mine."

He pulled up at the parking lot, among SUVs, electric cars, and my favorites—the vintage collection of sports cars, which Cary had taken to driving around.

He stepped out of the car, and normally, he would open my door, but I let myself out. He looked pale.

I took his hand. "Drake."

I noticed tears in his eyes and held him, not wishing to let him go. I wanted to absorb his pain. "I'm so sorry."

After a while, I separated. "I can't lose you." It was the rawest and most honest I'd ever been. Because, as I held those dark-blue eyes pooling with tears, I became something more than just a love-struck girl. I wanted to cradle that beautiful man in my arms like a mother might her son.

He wiped his eyes. "I'm not going anywhere."

My heart bloomed. "Does that mean you forgive me?"

Brushing his hair off his forehead, he smiled sadly. "I never blamed you. I was the one who blackmailed him. Remember?"

I took his hand. "Come on. Let's go inside, then."

I rang the bell, and when Janet opened the door, I gave her a big smile and almost hugged her.

"Is Grandmother here?"

She nodded.

My grandmother was in her office with Crisp when we arrived. I gave him the dirtiest look I'd ever given anyone.

I pointed at him. "He had us nearly killed."

"Don't be so melodramatic. Nothing to do with me." His signature devil's smirk was painted on his face. "Drake, it seems, has some enemies."

I turned to my grandmother. "You cannot believe that. It's bullshit. He tried to have both of us killed. Not just Drake. It's because of that footage."

My grandmother turned to Drake. "Can you give us a moment? There's food in the kitchen."

"I think I'll go back to mine."

He left the room, and I followed him out. "Stay."

He shook his head. "No. I can't handle this right now."

He left, and it felt like I'd lost him as I watched him walk away.

Anger bubbled over, like a looming volcanic eruption, and I stormed back into my grandmother's office. "You're both in on this."

My grandmother pointed at a seat. "Calm down."

Crisp poured himself a whisky and one for me too. He handed it to me, wearing his patronizing don't-act-like-a-child expression.

After I gulped down the burning liquid, I looked expectantly at my grandmother.

"Rey has agreed to call off the marriage."

He held up his finger. "On the proviso that the footage is destroyed."

"Well, we could have had this discussion without your men trying to kill us, couldn't we? One of them is lying in a forest somewhere, probably dead for all I know."

"Goran's alive. They weren't out to hurt you. It was because Drake wouldn't return my messages for us to talk and arrange something."

"What about the detective chasing us?" I asked. "He crashed his car just as we were coming back. Now, he might be dead."

"Detective?" My grandmother questioned Crisp, who failed to respond.

"You know, Jim, who hangs out at Salon Soir."

Crisp gulped back his whisky and remained silent.

I turned to my grandmother. "The one you sent Drake to spy on."

Her brow creased slightly, and I saw what looked like a hint of alarm in her eyes. "I think you've got your wires crossed, Manon."

I sighed. "I need a shower." I turned to Crisp. "So, you'll lay off? You won't continue to try and kill Drake or me?"

"You've got a vivid imagination, Manon. Let's not forget it was you who tried to entice my hand in marriage with all those lurid images."

Blood drained from my face. I couldn't stand the idea of my grandmother seeing those.

"Well, they were fakes, and you know it."

I couldn't stand it anymore and left them.

Crisp had my grandmother wrapped around his finger, and there was nothing I could do. At least he'd released me from marrying him. That was something.

But what of Drake? Could we survive this?

THE NEXT DAY, I was about to go in search of Drake, after he hadn't answered my calls or texts, when a couple of men in suits, flashing their badges, were let in.

No one saw me, so I hid. I needed to know why they were there.

Savvie had just arrived carrying a basket of fruit, and I gestured for her to come with me into a private space.

"You're on a fruit diet?"

"No. I bought some organic stuff for the kitchen. I've decided to eat nothing but organic." She frowned. "What's up?"

"A couple of detectives have just arrived. You heard about our ordeal?"

"Not much. I know that Drake's left for a break."

My heart sank. "Where?"

"I think he's gone back to London. Do you know what those detectives wanted?" she asked.

I had almost forgotten about the detectives. "No. But after everything that's happened, I'd love to know."

She curled her finger. "Come with me."

We stood close by the door of the office. I'd since learned that the door had needed repairing for a while, which worked well for eavesdroppers like us.

"Alice Ponting," we heard as we snuck to the side.

Just our luck, Ethan came bouncing in, and Savvie placed her finger on her mouth.

He got it. That family and their secrets.

"There's a DNA match to Alice Ponting's recently excavated place of burial."

Ethan frowned deeply as he turned to Savvie.

"I believe you were visited a month ago about the bones found at a building site owned by Reynard Crisp—bones belonging to Alice Ponting, who was not only affiliated with you through university but was also your late husband's fiancée."

Suddenly, I understood why both Savvie's and Ethan's jaws had dropped.

"DNA from a recent crash victim is linked to the remains found at the said building site. The DNA belongs to Detective Chief Inspector Jim Reilly, who we've been watching for a while because of his connection to Reynard Crisp, a business partner of yours we believe."

Still no response. I would have donated a kidney to see my grandmother's expression at that moment.

"And you're telling me this because?" Her voice remained steady.

"We need to know exactly what happened the night of Alice's disappearance."

"But I have already given you a statement."

"We'd like to hear about it again. Sometimes, vital details are left out due to heightened emotions and whatnot. And your husband, her fiancé, is no longer alive. Perhaps he said something."

"I refuse to comment without my lawyer present."

We heard chairs shifting, and all three of us escaped quickly, ending up outside. I followed both brother and sister, who looked like they'd seen a ghost.

"What the fuck?" Ethan said at last.

We made it to the labyrinth, which I'd discovered was where they had gone as kids to get up to no good—like kiss, smoke, or later, as adults, take drugs.

I would have loved to have been in that family growing up because, from where I stood, that family's story was more exciting than some bingey Netflix series.

"We need to speak to Dec," Savvie said. "Maybe he knows more about Alice Ponting. Remember how Dad said it had broken his heart when she disappeared?"

He nodded, looking pensive before turning to me. "And your interest?"

I told them all about being chased and how the detective that their mother had sent Drake to spy on had crashed while pursuing us.

They both shook their heads in disbelief.

"Poor Drake will be gutted to hear that the detective died. We left the scene," I said.

"That's major. I wouldn't go around telling anyone that," Ethan said.

"I was terrified that if we approached the car, he'd shoot us."

Savvie nodded. "It's not a normal situation. Don't worry. It's safe with us."

Ethan nodded in agreement, and the tension in my shoulders loosened. In many ways, it was therapeutic sharing the drama of those past few days with someone.

But with Drake not taking my calls and now a murder investigation implicating my grandmother, could things get any crazier?

CHAPTER 28

Drake

"ARE YOU SURE YOU'RE okay?" I'd lost count of how many times my mother had asked that.

"I'm fine, really."

She popped down her crossword, which had become a daily habit since she'd been couch ridden. "Have you heard what happened to that detective?"

I shook my head.

"From what you told me, sweetheart, it was probably wise not to stop. He might have killed you."

Having forgotten my recent buzz cut, I went to sweep my hair from my face—an action that had become a nervous tic.

"And you cut your beautiful hair, which looked just like that handsome Harry Styles's." She turned down her mouth.

I had to smile at my mother and her fixation on pop stars and their lives. Too many hours spent reading magazines.

"I look tougher this way, and I've got a gig this weekend at some political event. A bunch of world leaders getting together."

"That sounds so exciting. Maybe you can get a photo of someone famous." Her eyes shone with sincerity.

"I'm afraid that's not the done thing in this game."

"I hope they're paying you well, at least." She balanced her cup and saucer in her palm.

"More than generous. Carson's agency runs on fair terms."

"And you're staying here in London for a while?" Her face brightened.

"I'm not sure how long, Mum." I played with my fingers.

That question came as a reminder of how confused I was about my future. I missed Bridesmere already. The relaxed lifestyle suited me better than the frantic city, but for the time being, distance from all the crazy shit going on around Manon more than suited me, if only to regain some sanity.

Declan had understood when I'd asked for time out. No doubt he'd heard about our adventure. He'd reassured me that there would always be a job for me at the farm, which was thriving since the market had opened.

Carson had more than enough work to keep me in London permanently, and that beat moping around, which wasn't me. I liked to stay busy. I also needed to keep saving to get my mother into a place that was wheelchair friendly, should she ever need one.

At least with me there, I could get her moving and doing rehab stretches.

"Your phone keeps beeping, love. Maybe you should see who that is." Her eyes shone with concern.

I hadn't spoken about Manon, but my mother read me like a book. After I'd lost it as a teenager, I had seen that almost-permanent worried look on her face. Just like she wore now.

This time, it wasn't the aftermath of a regrettable street fight. It was worse. I'd killed a man, left one to die, and in among that constant, grim merry-go-round, I couldn't stop thinking about Manon.

We should have been having the time of our lives at our age.

There were a ton of messages from her. All begging me to call her. Telling me she was losing her mind with worry.

The trouble was I missed her, too. I would wake up and see her before falling asleep. It was like she was there, holding me. Like I felt her spirit or something just as flaky but still profound.

"Is it serious?" my mother asked.

I poured her some fresh tea. Sally, her carer, would be over soon. Then I was off to Billy's for some game time.

"It's just a girl I've been dating."

"Does she know you're here?" She leaned over for a biscuit.

"I haven't told her." I rubbed my spiky scalp.

"Then you must. The poor girl must be worried sick."

That was my mother, always thinking about other people.

I smiled at her. "I'll let her know I'm staying here for a while."

"You like this girl?" She kept staring at me, trying to get me to open up. "You sound so sad, love. Why don't you have a chat with someone?"

"A shrink, you mean?" I pulled a face. "No. I just need some space to process everything."

"Of course you do, love. I'm always here for you. You know that."

I kissed her on the cheek. "I know that, Mum. Just going for a run."

I grabbed my phone and headed over to the park opposite the flats, where we'd lived since my dad had passed. We'd had to downsize because my mother couldn't work, and it was tough trying to make ends meet. After school every day, I'd worked, cleaning at the gym where I'd learned how to box. With that money and my mum's pension, we had just managed. That was why I was dead set on making things better for her.

I RAN LIKE A man possessed, working up quite a sweat, after which I plonked myself down on a bench, gulped back water from my bottle, then called Manon.

I'd been gone for a week, and I owed her a call.

"Drake." She sounded puffed out.

"Have I caught you in the middle of something?"

"I'm driving to London."

"Oh."

"So why the silent treatment?"

I puffed. "I just needed some space, so I've moved to London for a while."

"For a while?"

"I'm not sure how long. I'm not sure about anything, to be honest."

"And you've left me without telling me?" Her voice cracked. "Would you have told me if I hadn't kept calling and texting you?"

"Sorry. I've..." I took a breath.

"You no longer like me?"

She sounded like a lost child, and I froze, worried she would cut herself again.

"It's not that. I just need some space." What words could I find to explain how being around her reminded me of all the crap we'd just experienced? Even if my body craved her like a junkie does heroin. "Have you heard what happened to the detective?"

"He's dead."

I puffed loudly. "Fuck."

"Don't give yourself a hard time over it."

"And it doesn't worry you?"

"Of course it does. I haven't stopped crying. I'm a mess."

"Please tell me you're not self-harming."

"What do you care? You hate me, and you're blaming me for what happened. Aren't you?"

"No. I'm not." That was a bit of a lie because, if I hadn't been so hot for her, I wouldn't have resorted to blackmailing Crisp.

"Detectives are circling Merivale. There's all this shit going down. Crisp's name has come up regarding some bones found, and the DNA of that detective's all over the crime scene."

"Really?"

"Yeah. He was scum, Drake."

"Still, I killed him."

"You did not kill him. Oh my God, Drake. Speeding drivers often crash their cars."

"But I should have stopped to render help."

"Oh. My. God. The guy would have shot you. And you weren't to know that—"

I interrupted before she said that word responsible for my fucking nightmares. "And you were going to tell me when?"

"You haven't exactly been taking my calls, have you?"

I sighed. "No. Sorry. I've been with my mum. She needs my help." That was bullshit because, if anything, it was the other way around.

"Do you still think about me?"

"All the fucking time."

"Do you get hard thinking about me?"

"All the fucking time." That wasn't a lie. My dick thickened at just hearing her soft, breathy voice.

"Then why won't you see me? I'm coming to London. We can hang out there for a while. I've got a new apartment, which means I don't have to stay at my horrible mum's."

"Let's see. Give me some time."

"That's you dumping me."

"I have to go," I said.

"Go to hell!" Her scream pierced my eardrum like a knife.

I buried my head in my hands and shook my head. All kinds of nightmarish thoughts did the rounds. Dead detective—a potential murderer who probably would have executed us.

Manon was right. I needed to let go.

I needed to let go of her.

But how? She was all over me.

My fucking heart. My dick. My head.

Chapter 29

Manon

THE WOODEN FLOOR ECHOED loudly as I walked around my new Soho apartment, which was empty and in need of furniture. The thought of shopping for new things should have excited me, but all those zeros attached to a number in my account seemed meaningless given the dark cloud following me.

What had happened to my inner shopaholic?

The only activity that roused the slightest interest was shoplifting.

Along with cutting myself, stealing was my only coping mechanism. The thrill of doing something wicked. Sex used to be that, but since Drake, sex was no longer a game. My vagina was in direct dialogue with my heart. Weird to think body parts even talked. I was weird, though. Fucked up. Especially now.

How could I do life without Drake?

I'd been so absorbed in him and escaping Rey that I'd forgotten about everything else, including my English course with all those assignments sitting on the computer I'd barely switched on.

I was rich. Free to be and do as I wished.

Then why did I feel trapped?

How could Drake have put a wedge between us?

Especially after everything we'd been through.

If anything, all that death-defying shit should have brought us closer. Like in the movies. I tried scanning my thoughts for a similar movie, but all I could find were small-town romances where some tired executive chick meets a hot shirtless baker.

Nothing like us. Small town, check. Hot, wish he was always shirtless, despite him not being a baker, check. And me? A tired exec? Hardly. Tired new adult more like it. Exhausted. Like I was about fifty years old or something.

Though I wasn't in the mood to see her, I had to visit my mother to grab some clothes I'd left behind and other little trinkets of sentimental value, like my only photo of my dad holding me as a baby with love in his eyes. A photo I'd often stared at to remind myself that I was wanted. If only for a moment.

Yes. Feeling sorry for myself again. Been there too many times. That dark feeling where everything had gone dull and gray like someone had turned the color down on the television.

I drove to my mum's, and despite owning a key, I knocked just in case she had George's dick in her mouth. It wouldn't have been the first time I'd barged in on a sickening scene involving my mother.

My heart felt like a heavy rock, making my chest sag. I couldn't even move my facial muscles to fake a smile when she opened the door. A waste of time anyway, given that my mother only smiled when she wanted something.

"So, no Lord Bourgeois?" I kicked off my shoes and lounged back on the leather sofa, radiating that new furniture smell.

"It's Lord Burgoyne." My mother didn't realize how ugly she looked when she scowled.

Nice people with good hearts never seemed ugly, I'd noticed. Even plain people. But black-hearted people, no matter how good-looking they were, grew uglier the longer I stared. Especially the eyes. And my mother's had a cold, hard edge to them when she wasn't sugaring herself up to someone.

Crisp was the only other person I'd met whose smile never quite made it to his eyes.

What a shame he could only do it with teenagers. He and my mother would have made a great match.

"Why are you here? You've got a new apartment, haven't you?"

"Mm... good to see you, too, Mum." I smirked. "Don't get your knickers in a knot. I'm not staying. I've just come to get my gear, then I'm moving into my new apartment."

She went to the decanter and poured herself a drink.

"So, where's Georgie Porgie?"

"George is away on business."

Her biting tone wasn't lost on me. I knew my mother well. Unfortunately. Maybe if I hadn't, I might have thought better of humans. I believed Cary called it "misanthrope."

When he'd described that word's meaning, I'd put my hand up. "Guilty."

He'd smiled at me as though it was cool to admit to hating humans.

"Why do I get the feeling things are not going well?" I asked.

She gulped back her liquor. "He's left me."

"So, will you lose this house?"

She shook her head. "No. I've got him over a barrel."

"Oh, good."

My sarcasm had her heavily Botoxed face straining a frown.

"What's he done?" I asked.

She opened the drawer of an antique sideboard, brought out a pack of cigarettes, and lit one. I gestured, and she tossed the pack to me, then the lighter.

My mother had never cared if I smoked. I guessed that was one small blessing. I hated being preached to, even when it was meant for my own good.

"He's got a wife that he refuses to leave."

I lit my cigarette. "But I thought you were married."

She shrugged. "It kept Will off my back. He still wants to marry me. Imagine that?"

"Yes, imagine that? He went to jail for you. Mm... strange."

"Hey, cut the fucking sarcasm." She puffed out smoke and downed a shot.

"So, Georgie Porgie's married. What have you got on him?"

"I've got him visiting prostitutes."

"Really? Even while you were his... what's the name again?" I thought about the books I'd read with those nice chunky words. "Ah... concubine."

"He likes variety."

I shrugged, wondering if all men did. Would Drake have fucked other women had we done the mileage as a couple? The thought of that made my blood boil, despite the pointlessness of that hypothetical since he'd dumped me.

"Let me guess. You had him followed and photographed, and you've kept that as your insurance."

She nodded with the makings of a crooked but proud smile.

"Then him being married shouldn't bother you, should it?"

"It bothers his wife. She found out and threatened to march. He stands to lose too much, so he left me. He even asked me to move, but then I threatened him."

"Then if she knows about you, why would she worry about him going off with the odd prostitute?"

"In that scene, a mistress is one thing, almost acceptable, in some marriages, but being caught with street-walkers is another."

"He didn't even use high-class escorts?"

She shook her head. "He liked to walk on the wild side, so to speak."

"Oh?" I frowned and thought about this for a moment. "You mean trannies?"

She nodded slowly. "Uh-huh. Now if anything would put a lady off her scones and tea, it would be her husband bum-fucking a man in a frock."

I had to giggle at her dry delivery of what sounded like another story of a rich lord behaving badly. And here I was thinking that my little world was screwy.

I puffed away on my cigarette, and from the large bay window, I watched an elderly couple walking a poodle wearing a cute, checked sweater.

"Oh well, I guess you'll have to attract some new rich guy."

She shrugged. "I've got money."

"Oh, that's right, two billion pounds."

"Less than that. Will owns half."

"Oh, gee, one billion pounds. You're virtually destitute."

"Enough of that." She stubbed her cigarette abruptly into a crystal ashtray.

"Wouldn't they confiscate it if he's in prison?"

"It's tucked away in a foreign account."

"Did he kill their father?" Savvie spoke often about the loss of her dad, and for her sake, I wanted to know.

"He had nothing to do with it. It was some hitman-come-hacker who was meant to get Lovechilde's thumbprint for his Swiss account, not kill him. But apparently, he woke up, and that was when he was strangled."

"But Will arranged it," I said.

"He arranged the robbery but had no intention of murdering Harry Lovechilde. That weighed heavily on him. He liked Harry."

She poured another drink, then held up the decanter, which I declined.

"You can stay, you know. I didn't mean what I said earlier."

I studied my mother for a moment and noticed tiredness. Or was that loneliness? I'd never seen her like that before.

Was she finally showing vulnerability?

"I might for tonight. I'm exhausted."

"Then why don't we go out somewhere for a meal?" she asked.

I got the feeling that she'd been alone for a while. Using people didn't lend itself to collecting friends.

That was me, too, before my grandmother had accepted me into the Lovechilde world. If I were her, I would have rejected me after I'd stolen from her, treated everyone like shit, and flirted with Crisp.

I'd dodged a bullet there. Only the price was enormous. I'd lost Drake. Had I?

He needed space, he'd told me. Mm... more like a nice way of dumping me.

The thought of sharing a meal with my mother suddenly appealed. I brightened a little. "Just give me half an hour."

WE ENDED UP AT an Italian restaurant near Piccadilly, where we shared a bottle of wine, and I ate everything put in front of me. I'd forgotten how hungry I was. It was the first time in a while that I'd even had an appetite.

My mother drank too much, which wasn't unusual. She had a tendency to overdo alcohol.

"So, what now? A new lord?" I asked, taking a spoonful of Italian ice cream.

"It's getting harder to compete with the young ones." She gave me one of her loaded stares.

"Hey, I'm not interested in older men. Been there. Done that."

"Peyton wasn't that much older, and he was hot," she said.

I rolled my eyes. "I was only fifteen, Mum. Don't you feel bad about that? It kind of fucked me up, you know?"

We sat outside so she could smoke. And as she blew a smoke ring, my mother became that Cockney, council flat single mum again. No amount of designer wear would ever remove that.

"I could have sold you for a higher price to someone much older and uglier. At least I dropped the price for Peyton."

I shook my head. "You're fucking kidding me. You didn't feel bad?"

"Nope. We were hungry."

"Um... no. I was hungry. You were too busy going out with every dick that came along and bought you a meal. Until you tracked down Will, that is. I guess life got a little more stable for me, despite your lack of interest. I mean, you only dragged me along to Merivale so you could try to sell me to Crisp."

"Well, it's all worked out well for you. Caroline, through some guilty conscience, I imagine, has attached herself to you. I didn't expect that. There's something going on between her and Crisp. They're fucking thick, those two. I noticed that much when I worked there." She studied me for a moment. "Do you know anything about that?"

I thought about the detectives and how a body had been found connected to both my grandmother's past and Crisp.

Out of respect for my new family, I remained silent. "Nothing much."

She kept staring at me. My mother missed little, and I did flinch. "You do, don't you?"

"Only that he owns her. That's all."

"I know that." She sounded frustrated.

She stood and ran her hands down her skin-tight skirt, and after paying the bill, we left.

We rode the taxi in silence, despite a ton of questions bubbling away inside of me. It was the most we'd ever spoken about things from our past.

When we got back to her Edwardian house, I poured her a drink and even made myself one.

I settled on the sofa and lit a cigarette. So much for kicking the habit. Drake had even had me drinking those yucky green juices, but with him turning his back to me, I'd returned to not giving a shit about what I did to my body.

"You shouldn't hate Caroline, you know. She's super intelligent and classy. We could do worse than take a leaf out of her book. I want to."

She laughed dismissively, as a mother might to a child aspiring to be a fairy princess or something equally fanciful and unachievable.

"One thing about Mummy dearest is that she's smart. Highly educated. Something you're not."

Fire bit my belly. "That's because you kept moving us around so you could be with some dickhead or other."

She knocked back her drink and refilled her glass. "Get over it. Look at you. You're richer than most at your age. You've got everything going for you. I could've fucking aborted you."

My spine stiffened. "Why didn't you?"

She shrugged.

My eyes burned into hers. I couldn't let that loaded comment slide.

She turned her back and stared at the window. "Do you think it might rain?"

"Why didn't you abort me, Mother?"

She turned. "Because I'm not a fucking murderer. I couldn't bring myself to do that. And I thought about my mother. Despite her throwing me away, she still gave me life. And that's all I could think of. So, I went ahead with it, and here you are—a stunning, foul-mouthed, unappreciative daughter who hates her mother and cuts herself."

How the hell does she know that?

Peyton must have told her.

He'd discovered me once on the bathroom floor after I'd seen that young girl on his computer screen. I should have reported him to the police.

That was when he'd asked me to leave.

Nice as I'd thought he was, one couldn't expect anything good to come from a pedo.

I'd already decided to report him, after that difficult conversation with Drake. Anonymously. I wasn't about to expose myself to trials, however. I would just type out a letter giving the police all the details, then they could follow up by cracking into his computer.

Better late than never. I could sleep knowing that dirty detective was dead, but I couldn't sleep knowing that some poor girl had fallen victim to Peyton.

"Did Peyton tell you?" I asked at last.

She shook her head. "I saw you cutting yourself."

I frowned so hard my brow ached. "Why didn't you say something to stop me?"

"Because I was shocked. Because it reminded me of what a mess I'd made of not just my life but yours. I couldn't deal with it."

Her eyes went glassy.

Were those tears?

Impossible. She was the toughest person I'd ever known.

I couldn't recall if anyone had ever shown her kindness. Having spent my life hating her for chasing away my dad and for all the men that had

CORRUPTED BY A BILLIONAIRE

come and gone, I'd never felt the urge to hug her. Only for show. Then her body would go all rigid in my arms.

"Did you love my father?" I asked, despite emotion choking my speech.

"I did."

She hid again by turning her back. Something my grandmother often did. If hiding feelings ran in the family, I'd missed out because, when it came to emotions, I cried at the drop of a fake eyelash. Especially since Drake had come into my life and stripped away at me, leaving a ton of raw emotions on display for anyone who came close to see.

Even with her back to me, I sensed something wanting to burst out from my mother.

"Then why cheat on him?"

She opened her palms, as though the answer were too obvious. "We were starving."

"Didn't he work?"

She turned and faced me. "He gambled. He drank. And when he drank, he became a monster. He'd attack me. Nearly killed me one night."

The haunted look in her eyes stole my breath.

I backtracked to those yelling matches I'd heard as a child. I'd always assumed she was the provoker. Mainly because I had been on my father's side. He was the one who had swung me around and brought me lollies and hugged me. How could he be the bad guy?

There were all those bruises that she had covered with makeup. Whenever I asked, she would blame an accident. I guessed she was protecting me, or was that my father?

As I navigated my turbulent upbringing, I wouldn't stop until I understood how we arrived at this point in our lives, largely constructed by her questionable choices.

She lit a cigarette, and her hand trembled lighting it. She puffed out smoke and continued, "I met this guy one day while shopping. He offered to pay for my groceries after my credit card was declined. I went back to his and let him have his way. It became the easiest option."

"But you could have worked."

She rolled her eyes. "I did work. Shop assistant. Waitress. You name it. That is before you came along, but your father kept gambling everything. We were consistently poor."

"Then why was he so upset about you being with other men?"

She shrugged. "Because he didn't want to share, I suppose. I don't know. Life's full of contradictions."

We stared at each other in silence for a moment.

"And about Peyton. Yes, it pained me that I made money out of my daughter, but I had little choice in the matter. It was either that or starve, and I'm weak like that. I was sick of the hard life. I wanted more. And Peyton promised to marry you. To stay with you. Only he let me down. Don't worry, he got what was coming to him."

Wrestling with a barrage of emotion, I tried to process her words, looking for bullshit as I always did with my mother, but her haunted expression told me otherwise. She meant every damn word.

Her last comment had only just sunk in, and scrunching my brow, I asked, "What do you mean he got what was coming to him?"

"I set the cops on him. I hate fucking pedophiles."

"But you played into his slimy hands by giving me to him."

"Yes. I know." She puffed loudly. "As I said, life's full of fucking contradictions."

"Did he get locked up?"

She nodded. "Last time I heard, he's still in prison."

"Did you tell them about me?"

She shook her head. "No way. I'm not so stupid to incriminate myself. I hired someone to hack his computer, and the idiot had images of young girls. Fucking sick cunt."

I paced about, shaking my head. It was too much. "He promised you he'd marry me?"

Looking into the distance, as though reliving the moment she'd signed my childhood away, she nodded. "If it was good enough for Elvis and Priscilla, it was good enough for my daughter."

That jarred. Why bring up that famous couple? "What?"

"Don't worry." She half smiled. "He was meant to marry you. That's what's important here. And... at least you weren't thirteen."

My eyebrows crashed. "That happened to you?"

"All kinds of things happened to me that you don't want to know about. I've wiped them out. I don't dwell. I move forward. Like I'm doing now."

Our eyes locked.

Who is this woman?

What has she done with my cold-hearted mother?

I went to her and wrapped my arms around her slim frame. Her emotional response swept me away as our bodies shuddered violently together.

In my arms, and for the first time, my mother cried.

CHAPTER 30

Drake

The ceiling of my childhood bedroom resembled the universe. When I was little, my father had meticulously arranged a moon amongst the stars to reflect the cosmos. At night, it glowed, and as a kid, I was dazzled by the sparkly display when tucked away in bed, like I was looking up at the actual galaxy. My dad, an amateur astronomer, had taught me all about the planets, introducing me to supernovas and black holes. At the time, I hadn't quite gotten those, but he'd planted a deep fascination for all things cosmic. On occasion, I still flicked through his cosmology books. It kept me close to him.

Why did I have to fuck around in maths? Figures had always come easily to me when I was at school, and my parents were so proud of my high marks. Then, after that accident, life had come tumbling down. I'd lost focus, and chronic sadness had meant I couldn't even handle my own company.

My mother knocked on my door. "I've made you a cup of tea, love."

"Sure. One minute."

I forced myself out of bed. Sleep didn't seem to stop the tiredness. If anything, the more I slept, the more lethargic I felt.

I joined my mother in the kitchen. Despite wearing a worried frown, she gave me an encouraging smile. "Are you going for a run today? Or perhaps you could ring Billy."

About to push away hair that was no longer there, I rubbed my forehead instead. Strange, it was like those stories I'd heard about people losing limbs and still feeling them. That was how it was with my nonexistent hair.

Was that how it was with Manon, seeing as I often woke thinking she was lying next to me?

"I made scones." My mother laid the tray on the kitchen bench.

"Maybe later."

She tilted her head. "But they're nicer warm."

I sat on the couch with my tea and stared blankly at the game show on television.

My mother sat next to me and placed a plate with scones and jam on the table. "Have you heard from Manon?"

I shook my head. It had been a week since her last text.

Maybe she'd moved on. She had intense needs that, before the dark cloud had swallowed me, I'd been more than happy to serve.

"Do you miss her?" Her tentative tone wasn't lost on me. My mother knew me. I wasn't one to talk about feelings. Even after Dad had died, I'd chosen silence over tears.

"I heard you yelling in your sleep again, sweetheart." My mother slanted her head. "Perhaps you should speak to someone."

"I'm speaking to you."

Wearing a sympathetic smile, she patted my leg. "I'm here for you. This will always be your home, darling. No matter what. You can be yourself here. If you want to yell, cry, scream, or whatever, I won't mind."

My mouth trembled into a smile. "Thanks, Mum." I sipped my tea. "I'm fine. Just needed some time out."

She passed me a plate with a buttered scone. "I know, son."

"WE'RE SO UNDERSTAFFED. I can't tell you how happy I am to have you here," Carson said.

I scanned the façade of the ornate historic mansion. "This reminds me of Merivale."

He chuckled. "They all do, these old places."

Noticing his black suit, I asked, "So, you're working too?"

He nodded. "I had to. I just don't have the men."

I thought of Billy, who I was meeting after my shift for a drink. "I can see if Billy's interested."

"He looks tough enough, but he needs training. I can't have him chatting up women or winking at them."

I laughed. Billy was a bit of a flirt, for sure. "Let me have a word with him. He could probably use the extra money."

A call came, and when Carson peered at the screen, he held up his finger. "One minute, got to take this." As he listened, his face lit up. "Really? Oh my God, that's amazing. See you tomorrow. I love you."

I guessed it was Savvie.

Though brimming with joy, Carson looked like he might cry.

"You look like you won a lottery," I said.

"Better than that. Savvie's pregnant."

I hugged him. "That's so good. Congrats."

Looking starry-eyed, he nodded. "We're over the moon."

Carson must have transmitted some of his bliss because seeing that glint of joy in his eyes made me realize how lucky I was just to be alive and healthy. I had money. I had a loving mother. What more could I want?

Manon?

"How's Manon?" he asked.

Mm... mind reader.

"Don't know."

His forehead creased. "I saw her at Merivale the other day."

"How is she?"

"Well, she seemed okay. She had her mother with her—who could have been a vampire going on Savvie and her brothers' reaction like they wanted to run to the kitchen for garlic."

I laughed. "That's a little extreme."

"You haven't met Bethany."

I thought of that brief encounter in London. Despite my quick exit, I hadn't exactly gotten a welcoming vibe from Manon's mum. At that stage, I hadn't heard about how she'd once sold her daughter to that rich dickhead. Had I known, Bethany would have gotten my middle finger instead of an uneasy smile.

"She certainly freaked everyone out by being there." He chuckled. "But she was civil. She spent some private time with my mother-in-law. It seemed to make Manon happy to have her there."

I frowned. "Right."

That piqued my curiosity. Manon hated her mother.

AFTER WHAT HAD BEEN a long night standing at doors with crossed arms and nodding at all the dignitaries, I went off to meet Billy.

I couldn't get over Manon taking her mother to Merivale. What had happened? Why the forgiveness?

Had she gotten over me too? Had she met someone? The thought punched me in the guts.

Billy was waiting for me with Sapphire when I arrived.

We hugged, then found a table away from the crowd. It was a Thursday night at our favorite Irish pub. We loved our stout, and that pub had its own brewery.

Billy ran his hand over my buzz cut. "Holy shit, you look like a soldier."

"You cut your hair." Sapphire looked shocked. "You had such nice hair."

I shrugged. "I'm sure it will grow back."

She kept looking at me as though trying to figure something out.

We drank pints and talked about football, which was something we always did when catching up. I even apologized to Sapphire for talking about nothing but the game.

"I don't mind. It's nice just being here." She looked at Billy, and he returned a sweet smile.

"So, what's the plan now?" he asked. "Are you going to stay in London or return to Downton Abbey?"

"Downton Abbey?" Sapphire asked.

"Merivale."

"Oh, that's where Manon lives. I'm going to a party there next weekend."

"Oh?" I asked. Carson hadn't mentioned a party.

"Manon invited me. I'm not sure what it's for, though."

That made sense. They always had parties.

"You aren't going?" she asked.

"I haven't been invited." I clutched my glass.

"I'm sure Manon would like to see you," she said.

"I haven't heard from her for a while."

"You should call her then." She slanted her head.

Changing the subject, I turned to Billy. "Hey, do you want to do some security work? Carson's hiring. The money's good. You just need to get some black gear and not flirt with the girls."

Giving Sapphire one of those he-doesn't-mean-it looks, Billy said, "I wouldn't dream of it. Why would I flirt when I've got this gorgeous girl?"

A smile grew on Sapphire as she blushed.

They suited each other, in that I could imagine them being together forever. Even if Sapphire was still young, she was clearly devoted to Billy. They were also opposites—he was a loudmouth, and she was a giggler who hung off his every word. After a few drinks, he'd admitted to how much he loved and respected her and how she was the one for him.

Seeing his eyes shining with sincerity, I felt both happy and a little envious.

Was Manon the one for me?

I knew, deep down, that I couldn't imagine any girl making me feel like Manon did.

It was just that I needed to sort out my head.

Would I lose her if I stayed away too long?

Or was I trying to wean myself off her, like she was some kind of harmful drug?

Despite those questions keeping me awake at night, I still couldn't find an answer.

All I knew was that I missed her.

Badly.

"Well, what you do think? You just have to stand around looking tough. Second nature for you. All those misspent years on the streets trained you well enough."

Billy nodded slowly. "Yeah. Could be good for some extra cash. Count me in. Though I don't have a ton of time. I'm doing that computer degree. You know about that."

I certainly did. Go Billy.

"How's it going?"

"Great. Love it. I'm a geek at heart."

"A big muscular one who fires up at the slightest insult."

He laughed. "Nuh. Anger management. Remember? I had to do that."

I'd done one of those after that fight that saw me locked up for a night.

"What about you, Drake?" Sapphire asked.

My insides recoiled at that "What are your plans?" question.

"Um... well." I knitted my fingers. I wasn't thinking on the run for a change, because after Billy had spoken of his computer programming course, I'd gone and enrolled myself in a mathematics degree.

"I'm also doing a course."

"What are you studying?" she asked.

"Complex mathematics."

Her brow creased. "Oh, you wish to teach?"

"Not sure. I just want to understand how everything works. I'll see where that takes me."

"He's actually brainy. He just looks dumb." Billy pulled a face.

That was the friend I loved—the one that poked shit at me so I could poke shit right back.

Sapphire rolled her eyes and giggled.

CHAPTER 31

Manon

THERE I WAS SHOPPING with my mother, and I didn't even have the urge to shoplift.

As we walked through Harrods, she went through racks of designer dresses.

"What did you talk about with Grandmother?" I asked.

She shrugged. "Just lots of apologizing. Mainly about Will on my part, and on hers, for ghosting me. Not that she referred to her avoiding me as that. You know Caroline and her big words." She rolled her eyes. "I'm so used to being a bitch. Being nice isn't easy, and all this smiling is hurting my face."

I had to laugh. "I know what you mean. The same thing happened to me the first time Grandmother sealed my acceptance into that family with a hug. I'd grown so used to walking around like a stuck-up princess."

She sniffed. "Then you're more like me than you care to admit."

Was I like her? I studied her face for her usual smirk, but she maintained an even expression. If anything, I'd learned from her selfish, manipulative actions how not to be, but I kept that from her.

"One can change. And at least Grandmother gave me a second chance. That's big of her. Don't you think?"

She nodded abstractedly. "She owes us. We're blood, and she's making amends, I'd say."

"If you were Caroline, would you have accepted us?" And so the questions continued because I was still trying to process our new happy-family arrangement. Suspicion had been woven into my heart where my mother was concerned, so I couldn't help but wonder if she had a hidden agenda that may erupt into a shitstorm at any minute.

She moved her head from side to side to stretch her neck. "Not sure. I'm not her, so I can't answer that. It's all about what life throws at us. That's how we're made. It's all very well to have nice intentions, but after a life of nothing but crap, you harden. You have to. The soft ones are the first to fall in this wild push of life."

I nodded slowly, processing her response. "But would you have forgiven us?"

She exhaled loudly. "Maybe. As I just said, I haven't had the privilege of sitting in that swish office with all those smelly old books and priceless antiques. Had I, maybe I would've been in the pardoning mood."

I couldn't expect my mother's hard-edged views of the world to suddenly turn all churchy and nice. So, I stopped there and got back to what we did best—shop.

She pulled out a red dress with a scooping neckline.

"That might be a bit too sexy," I said.

"Hello, I'm single. And there'll be rich men at that party, won't there?"

I studied her. "You won't try to hook up with Cary or do something gross like that?"

"Are you kidding?" Her frown melted away. "He's broke, anyway."

It was like a role reversal. She was the unruly daughter, and I was the mother. I even regretted brokering the truce between my mother and her family, which hadn't been easy.

My grandmother was the one who had invited her to the party. My uncles and Savvie had been predictably cold towards her. I was pretty sure they had been in their mother's ear as soon as we'd left.

"I'm pulling your leg," she said, putting the dress back and selecting a pink dress with a tight bodice and a full skirt.

"That's nice," I said, despite it being the last thing I would expect my mother to wear.

She was skin-tight jeans and low-cut blouses or bodycon minis and skyscraper stilettos. Streetwalker chic, I called it. I'd worn the same until I met Savvie and decided to copy her stylish approach to clothes.

She held it away from her. "Mm... too Sunday school for me."

I laughed. "What's Sunday school?"

"Religious studies."

My eyes widened. "You attended?"

"Once or twice. Hated it. Ran away into the forest and looked for mushrooms to poison my super-religious foster family instead."

Was that her doing her dark humor act, or was she for real?

My mother hated talking about her life growing up. Whenever I asked about her homes, she would sidestep the question by saying that we "only had ourselves and that was all. So, get used to it."

"You really did that?" I asked.

She returned one of her hard-to-read grins, which meant she may have tried poisoning them or that it was a joke.

Baby steps with us.

I still couldn't believe that the Lovechildes had allowed her through that impressive front door.

"You never know. Savvie might just do that—go out and find some poisonous mushrooms for your dinner."

She laughed as we walked through the aisles of dresses. "I've noticed we share some similar traits."

I couldn't disagree. Savvie could be rather blunt and loved to poke fun at people and life, but where my mother took herself seriously, Savvie made fun of herself too.

As strange as it was to get on after despising her for so long, keeping it friendly beat taunts and jeers any day.

Hate was so exhausting.

As a self-confessed hater of hugs, my mother was a work in progress when it came to affection. I did, however, feel her body soften when I hugged her, which was a step up from those stiff hugs done mainly for show.

"But really, Mum, how do you feel about all of this? You know, socializing with the Lovechildes."

"It's surreal. They have every reason to hate me." She took a moment to think. "But I've had to turn myself inside out, too. It's easier being despised than pitied. At least for me. I've grown so used to people sneering at me that when they smile, it feels fake."

"You think that they're only letting you in because of pity?"

She shrugged. "Maybe. Who knows? Though Caroline tried to act cool, I sensed guilt, pity, and all those hard-to-define emotions."

"Did she cry?" I wished I'd been a fly on the wall.

The whole family had been at Merivale the day I'd arrived with my mother, and one could have cut the air with a knife.

Savvie had been ready to punch my mother in the nose and had to be held back by Declan, while Ethan had looked like he might froth at the mouth. I really couldn't blame them, seeing her involvement in the death of their dad.

She'd then followed my grandmother to somewhere private behind a closed door.

Looking distant, my mother shook her head.

Intuition told me that her conversation with Grandmother had shaken her. But stoical to a fault, my mother's walls were up—a trait passed down by her mother because I'd seen that same cool, hard-to-read expression on my grandmother's face often enough.

Not like me. I was falling to pieces. My heart was shattered over Drake.

"Grandmother's going through a lot. There's that crap with Reynard Crisp. And now the cops are poking around. Something to do with the remains of a close friend of hers being discovered."

My mother responded with a faint but worrying smile. "I get this feeling Caroline's covering up a lot of stuff."

I frowned. "You better not try to mess up her life again. I hope this isn't another vendetta."

"Big words, darling." She slanted her head. "No. I'm too tired for re-venge. I've had my moment of glory." She sniffed. "I'm just fascinated. Aren't you?"

"Maybe." I sighed. "I love my grandmother, and I don't want any harm coming to her."

Frowning, my mother studied me closely, like I'd admitted to taking acid before an exam. "You love her?"

"Well…" Was she jealous? Her shocked expression showed a lot more than it normally did. "She's taken me in, Mother. After everything. And she treats me like an equal. She's taken a personal interest in my stud-ies. She was genuinely worried about me during this latest shitshow with Rey. Yeah, I love her. And she's helped me become an independent woman who no longer goes around hating the world."

Looking pensive, she nodded slowly, as though seeing the real me for the first time.

"Why? Does that freak you out?" I had to ask.

"It makes sense."

Was that the makings of a sad smile I spotted on my mother's face? Was she regretting something?

There we were, in Harrods, lost in a deep and meaningful when Savvie came bounding along. She wrapped her arm around me and nearly swung me around.

Nice to see you too.

She wasn't so upbeat with my mother. But all in good time.

"Fancy seeing you here." She looked from me to my mother. "Why don't we grab a juice or something just as boring and healthy?"

I laughed. She was chipper. Pregnant and full of life.

My mother looked a little lost. Another new expression. She'd never shown that kind of weakness. Or was she, at last, becoming human?

"You, too, Bethany." Savvie wore the makings of a smile, which was the warmest she'd been so far towards my mother.

I could only assume my grandmother had smoothed the air between them.

It was a big step, though. Stealing her mother's boyfriend and then plotting to rob their father, which had ended in his accidental murder, was not a small thing, despite Will attesting to being the sole perpetrator.

Whichever way, it was still mega-forgiveness in my book.

My mother looked a little thrown by Savvie's invitation. "Oh. Okay then. I guess I can come back for that dress."

"Which one were you thinking?" Savvie asked.

"Well, I kind of liked that one." She pulled out the sexy red number with the low-cut neckline. "But... Manon thought I might run away with the new man of the house."

Savvie's mouth fell open, and she turned her eyes on me and then laughed. "For what it's worth, I like it, and it's a Donatella. Can't go wrong with Versace. Her shapes are always so flattering."

I pulled out the pink Sunday school dress. "What about this?"

Savvie's mouth curved downwards like she'd tasted something bitter. "Oh no. It's too 'look at me, I'm an eight-year-old again.' Very Alice in Wonderland."

"That's kind of what Mum said. Only she called it Sunday schoolish."

Savvie chuckled. "Good one." She slanted her head towards the red dress in my mother's hand. "I'd get that one. And by the way, Cary's broke."

Instead of shock, my mother laughed, as did Savvie.

And there we were—a few months ago, enemies—suddenly working at something close to resembling a family.

ANOTHER PARTY AT MERIVALE, and spoilt for choice, I had to change four times before settling for a black Prada silk gown that Savvie had so generously tossed my way after I'd gushed about it. She'd told me she'd worn it once during her Gothic period and had passed the shimmery dress to me, adding, "You'd look great as Morticia."

Despite being amused, I kind of liked the idea of slinking around in a fishtail gown.

I didn't normally wear black to those events, since most women favored color, but I was in mourning over Drake.

My mother stood at the mirror in her red dress with the scoop neckline that hung seductively low, and with a slit to the thigh, the gown showed off her curves. For someone who didn't use gyms, she was still in great shape. Something she put down to regular, vigorous sex.

"Sex in at least five different positions beats boring yoga any day," she'd once told me in the same way a normal mum might rave about the virtues of eating greens.

"Black suits you. Even if it's a little somber, wouldn't you say?"

I slanted my head while studying myself in the mirror. "Mm... I like it. And I'm not exactly in a cheery mood these days."

"Don't worry about him. There are plenty more to come. And you need to aim higher."

I turned to face her. "I don't want plenty more, Mother. Unlike you, I have no desire to fuck half of London's elite. And I don't need to, anyhow. I've got my own money. Besides, give me yoga and running any day over boring sex."

I was half expecting her to call me naïve and stupid, as she used to whenever I would roll my eyes at her, suggesting that I use my body to move up the social ladder. But she just stared at me in the mirror and nodded slowly.

"I need a cigarette," she said, looking nervous.

I'd never seen her all jittery before. Her normal fearlessness didn't extend to having to mince with a bunch of rich snobs.

"Let's go out to the labyrinth," I suggested. "That's where everyone goes for a smoke or to do drugs."

"Show the way," she said.

I suggested we use the path as opposed to the grounds, having learned the hard way after my Louboutin heels sank so deep into the ground, I thought I was about to be swallowed up in a bog, and despite wearing chunky heels, I wasn't about to risk it.

"Are you okay?" I asked, brushing off a leaf from her dress as we stood in the labyrinth and lit our cigarettes.

"I'm just prepping myself for the starring role in a gossip fest." She puffed smoke. "I'm surprised they're letting me stay, let alone inviting me to this party."

"Grandmother's good like that. She's rather forgiving."

"Mm... or just guilt-ridden."

"Well, if she is, then it shows she's got a heart. We all make poor decisions. Don't we?"

"Please, let's not talk about Peyton again. Okay? He's locked away, so that's all you need to know—and that I'm sorry."

My neck cracked as I turned to stare into her eyes. "What was that?"

"I'm sorry." Her eyes glistened, and I even thought she might cry. "Now, can we move on?"

Another big first. She'd never apologized to me about anything, ever.

She was right, though. Enough talk. It was phase two of our lives.

If only Drake could find his way in there somehow. With all the forgiveness in the air, could he find it in his heart to do that?

I took her hand. "Come on, let's get some bubbly."

She smiled and let me hold her hand, which felt incredibly awkward but nice too.

We headed inside when Drake came around the corner, and I squeezed her hand.

"What's wrong?" She frowned.

"That's Drake."

She took a glance. "He's gorgeous, but I prefer him with hair. He had nice hair, from memory."

I'd almost forgotten about my mother's chilling reception towards Drake that morning they'd met after he'd stayed with me at her house.

His gorgeous hair was gone, but he still looked hot.

As we were on the same path, it was going to be difficult to ignore each other. He hadn't even tried to call me.

Sapphire had told me they'd met for a drink and that he hadn't smiled much.

"Hey," I said as our eyes locked.

He stopped in front of us.

"You've met my mother."

His mouth barely moved.

"Okay. I'm off inside for a drink," she said, no doubt catching his chilly vibe.

As he watched her go, he frowned. "What's she doing here?"

"It's a long story. And I feel like you hate me."

He scratched his jaw. "It's not that."

"Then why haven't you returned my calls?"

He shrugged. "I needed a break from everything."

"From us, you mean?"

No answer, just those big blue eyes swallowing me up and making me want to run off somewhere and howl.

I missed him. I hated how much.

"Are you better now?" I really wanted to ask if he missed me. But I wasn't prepared for a negative response.

We lingered nevertheless. He seemed to want to say something but seemed lost for words again. I'd experienced that often with Drake. When we first met, he'd gawk at me as though he'd lost his tongue.

I sighed. "Oh well, best get inside and get a drink, since you've decided to give me the cold shoulder."

I went to walk off when he grabbed my wrist.

"No. Let's go for a walk to the cliffs and talk."

I stared down at my chunky heeled shoes.

"Take them off."

A little smirk grew on my face. "That's what you said to me the last time we met, but it wasn't my shoes."

Finally, he cracked a smile, and my heart unwound like a flower about to bloom.

"Here"—he held out his hand—"I'll hold on to you." Like the sunlight bursting through a bleak, cloudy day, his smile grew.

As he linked his arm to mine, his familiar male scent hit me, and a surge of arousal turned my legs to jelly.

Underused facial muscles ached as I smiled brightly. "Where are you taking me?"

"Somewhere private."

"Mm... that sounds dangerous."

Yes, please.

He stopped walking and turned to me. "I wouldn't describe it as that... more like me trying to unravel a puzzle."

"Oh, now you've got me completely fascinated."

We headed for the cliffs.

"I won't be able to walk up there in these for sure." I bent and took off my shoes. "Luckily, I didn't wear stockings. I just coated my legs in fake tan instead."

He helped take off my shoes, then his hand stroked my calf, and who would have thought the calf could be an erogenous zone?

"You're already naturally olive-skinned without that stuff on you," he said.

"My tan's fading since my one and only beach holiday."

I had to walk lightly as pebbles dug into the soles of my feet.

He stopped walking and, noticing my discomfort because Drake always noticed things like that, suggested, "Let's sit here."

We found a bench with a perfect view of the sea thumping against the cliff's edge.

"I often come here to think," he said.

"You're deep, aren't you?" I smiled weakly. "The opposite of me."

"I wouldn't exactly call you shallow."

"What would you call me?" I tilted my head.

"Mm... messed up, confused, troubled."

I pulled a face. "Shit. I sound horrible."

He smiled sadly. "I didn't mean it like that, but you asked."

"How did you mean it?"

"I'm not a doctor, but you could do with some help to deal with issues."

"And you couldn't? After what happened to your dad, you admitted to losing the plot. Which I can understand." I knitted my fingers. "I would have too. But it helps to talk about it."

"I know that. You're the only person I've ever told those things to." His lids lifted slowly for his eyes to meet mine. Sometimes, when he was inside of me, he wore that same vulnerable expression.

"That's a compliment of sorts, I guess," I answered.

We sat in awkward silence, watching the waves tumbling along, all frothy and turbulent, just like my emotions.

"I've missed you so much. You know more about me than anyone has ever known. It's like I gave you the only key I owned to my heart and soul, which means I can't let anyone else in. Not that I want someone else." My voice cracked, and I had to choke back tears.

"You make us sound like torture."

"Us?" I smiled weakly. "There's still an us?"

"Why have you forgiven your mother?"

That sudden shift in subject jarred. "We had a long talk, and she explained everything to me."

"And what about her selling you to that pedophile? How can you forgive her?"

"Peyton promised her he'd marry me," I said.

"At fifteen?"

I almost laughed at how preposterous he made that seem.

"Well, they do in the Middle East. And Elvis Presley met Priscilla when she was thirteen or something."

"What?"

He looked so stunned, I had to control the urge to laugh. More out of nerves than humor.

"That's fucking nuts," he said. "And you're talking about last century when rape was seen as a Saturday-night sport."

"I was nearly sixteen, and she thought I was better off with a billionaire who'd promised to marry me than other men."

"Other men?" He shook his head. "I get that she's your mum, but her actions were fucking inexcusable."

"It's complicated. We had nothing. She gave me life, for God's sake."

"There are tons of single mothers who don't resort to selling their children to creeps. Billionaires or not."

"I know." I puffed out in frustration.

I wanted to talk about us, not my crappy past. All the discussion about morality was muddying my perspective on things again.

"She apologized. Something she's never done before. Resentment weighed down on me. I felt fucking trapped. Forgiveness is liberating, you know." I released a breath. "Can you ever forgive me?"

I turned to him, but he kept staring ahead like he couldn't face me.

Silence grew like crippling punishment, placing a wedge between us.

My heart sank. His wordless response answered that question.

I rose. "Good luck finding that squeaky-clean girl brought up on nice Christmas dinners and lots of family cuddles."

I charged off, carrying my shoes. The pain from sticks and stones digging into my heels took my attention away from the ache in my heart.

I could never be that girl to make him proud. And what hurt more—he didn't even come after me and take me into his arms and kiss me.

That only happens in movies.

I returned to the party and drank like it was my last day on earth.

My grandmother tinkled her glass. "I'd like to announce my engagement."

Cary stood next to her, love pouring out of his gaze.

A smile grew on my face. Tears of joy for my grandmother, who looked seriously in love, mixed with sadness at having lost the love of my life.

I couldn't imagine ever loving someone like I loved Drake.

I emptied my glass in one gulp and watched my mother chatting to some older man in a tweed jacket. Maybe that was all women like us could expect—men who laughed at our jokes, paid for our drinks, and hung around like puppy dogs.

The thought of that had me lunging for another champagne.

I would rather go on some brainless reality show set on a turquoise island, flirt with dumb, tattooed muscle heads, and bitch with a bunch of girls sporting terrible lip and boob jobs than end up with a man I didn't love.

Forever was too long to spend with someone I hated the smell of.

Drake had raised that bar so high it reached the heavens.

I couldn't imagine meeting anyone like him again.

But I would seek help before I hurt myself again, too, because I was going to do better with myself and discover things about myself I liked, other than boobs or hair. Something real for a change.

CHAPTER 32

Drake

MANON SWAYED HER HIPS, and men surrounded her as she danced like a goddess.

Carson passed me a bottle of beer. "Manon's letting her hair down, I see." He studied me for a minute. "You're no longer an item?"

"Not sure. She's really messed up. I mean, she's reached out, but it's my fucked-up head that's asking too many questions."

"Oh, don't I know it. But take it from a man who married someone who was pretty messed up—people change. Love changes people for the better."

I frowned. "That's right. Savvie was pretty wild, wasn't she?"

"That she was. She still is a bit." He wore a wicked smile.

Manon was a tiger for sure, and I loved how wild she was with me in the bedroom. "I'm with you, a hundred percent. I don't know if I can ever do 'normal' again."

"No. I had the same issue. Once you've had a taste of something exotic and potentially dangerous, everything else becomes a little insipid."

He had that right. During my night out with Sapphire and Billy, I'd stayed on for a few more drinks after they'd left, and I met a girl. She was pretty and someone I wouldn't have thought twice about fucking in the past.

"This girl in London the other night invited me back to hers. But I just didn't feel turned on at all."

"Hey, I've been there. It's just that certain women are the ones. You know? You dream about them. They follow your thoughts. And I'm happier than ever. Savvie still has her moments, but then, so do I." He laughed.

"Are you trying to encourage me to make it work with Manon? You didn't seem too keen on her once. Remember you told me to stay away?"

"That was before I got with Savvie, and people change. I've noticed Manon has matured somewhat. She's more respectful of others. Not as pissed off with the world. She's not the same girl I met when she worked for Crisp."

At the mention of that devil, I had to ask. "Any news on him?"

"I know the cops are sniffing around over bones exhumed at a building site he owns."

"Are they going to lock him up?"

"He's still at the casino last time I looked. We were there the other night with a bunch of friends for a poker game. Doing a little spying for Caroline." He chuckled.

"There are drugs there, man, for fucking sure."

"We all know that. But they can't pin anything on him."

"At least he's not here tonight." I wondered about that video. "You know he tried to kill us?"

He nodded. "Don't worry. The cops know everything. He'd be crazy to try anything."

"I guess so." I sighed.

He tapped my shoulder. "Hey. I think you should muscle in on that dance. That good-looking guy's getting frisky with Manon."

I'd been watching and had even noticed my veins tightening.

I stepped onto the dance floor just as the music changed, and a slow number came on for a waltz. The guy in the designer suit went to hold her when I cut in.

"She promised me this dance, mate." I flicked my head and gave him one of my fuck-off glares, and off he went.

"Hey." She pouted. "I never promised you anything."

I took her by the waist and drew her in very close, so close my dick sprang to life for the first time in weeks. "I think you did promise me."

"Are we talking about dancing?" Her chin tipped towards me, and her eyes shone with a suggestive smile, and I knew deep inside that I could no more deny myself that sexy, albeit troubled girl than I could air.

Breathing her in as I would a perfumed flower, I allowed all the angst to melt away.

It was that moment and nothing else.

The past could just stay there.

And the future? Well... no one could tell what that might bring.

But one thing was for sure. I was going to be the one unzipping that pretty dress tonight.

"Does this mean you've forgiven me?" Her eyes were wide and searching.

"I forgave you ages ago, Manon. It's me I've needed to forgive."

Her brow creased. "What have you got to be angry with yourself about?"

"Lots of shit. Let's not think about it. Just let me enjoy this moment."

She clutched me tighter and buried her head in my shoulder, and suddenly, all I could see were possibilities.

EPILOGUE

Caroline Lovechilde

ENGAGED TO THE LOVE of my life, I should have been on top of the world. Instead, I found myself distracted by the ghost of Alice Ponting, who'd come back to haunt me. No amount of champagne could help me forget those intrusive detectives and their endless questions. I just had to keep up the charade. Something I should have been good at after thirty years of playing my role.

Pushing those niggling thoughts aside, I had another ghost from my past to deal with in the shape of my first daughter.

Bethany circled the room as though facing me would hurt. Even when she'd played that fake maid role, I recalled how she couldn't stare me in the eyes, as though she'd had something to hide.

Funny about that.

I still hadn't forgiven myself for failing to read the signs where Bethany and Will were concerned. However, dealing with the humiliation of Ethan marrying a folk singer, my mind had been otherwise preoccupied.

It had hit me hard learning of Will's involvement in Harry's murder.

Despite the popular belief that my husband's death had served me well, I'd grieved deeply for Harry's loss. Only the world never saw that.

I'd made a promise to myself long ago never to cry in public.

Discussing business on the day of his funeral was in poor taste, but it was my way of dealing with the war being waged in my heart.

I still missed my husband. He was my best friend, and his ability to navigate the machinations of London's elite had been unparalleled. That was why I'd attached myself to Harry Lovechilde.

Everyone just assumed we hated each other, but that was far from the truth.

It was Rey, and only Rey, who had forced me into building Elysium.

It hadn't taken me long to realize that the luxurious, high-end resort I'd fought for was merely a façade for his criminal activity. The thought of which had me lying sleepless at nights, pondering ways to extricate myself from the poisonous, tangled web he'd ensnared me in.

Owned by a billionaire, I'd done a deal with the devil to attain my current position—a woman in love, blessed with unimaginable prosperity, and holding the reins of a long-established wealthy dynasty.

But at what cost? Unsavory and illegal activities at our doorstep and the law circling like hungry wolves.

My engagement to Cary should have lifted me high, given he was the love of my life. My soulmate. The one I harmonized with in that celestial orchestra as described by Plato. However, as a pragmatist, I had little room in my heart for the poetic musings of ancient philosophers.

Before Cary, I'd viewed the whole soulmate, twin flames concept as New Age nonsense that clouded people's minds into idealizing the institution of marriage.

I'd always viewed marriage as a practical business arrangement that ensured my survival, and even more importantly, that my children had everything their hearts desired, thus enabling them to reach their full potential.

That hadn't exactly gone to plan. No peerage to speak of. Yet. All married to commoners. But that was another matter.

Never in my wildest dreams would I have ever imagined falling madly in love.

My affair with Will had been purely expedient in that he was good in bed and we both shared high libidos, thus sparing me the need to seek other sexual partners, which had gotten exhausting and messy after the odd lover became attached. During my earlier days of marriage,

I had gone a little rogue and fallen for men from the darker side of London.

There had been one in particular... but that was another story.

Harry didn't mind. If anything, he encouraged my little adventurous trysts outside the marital bedroom.

Strange marriage, that one. But I loved him as one would a brother.

Now there I was in that rarely visited green room with the daughter I had given away.

Of course, I'd often wondered about her, but I hadn't dwelled on it.

Looking back summoned up too many ghosts.

In that red dress with a cleavage to kill, she had men drooling.

"What plot are you hatching, Bethany?"

She fiddled with a ballerina figurine, then her eyes slowly lifted to meet mine. A smirk took shape on her glossy red, collagen-plumped pout. "Why would you think that?"

I took a breath to process an explosion of thoughts. "Need I explain?"

"Oh, the Will incident?" She shrugged. "I did you a favor, didn't I? Your fiancé is a step up. You look seriously in love."

Our eyes locked, and my pulse picked up. "I ask again, what are you plotting?"

She chuckled. "I'm not interested in Cary if that's what you're asking. He hasn't even noticed me. He can't take his eyes off you, it would seem."

She stroked her long red nails. A habit of mine. Other than our physical resemblance, was that our only similarity?

If anything, her sardonic smirk reminded me of my rapist foster father. Her father.

Why had I allowed her into my home? Particularly after everything she'd done to me and my family.

It was Manon who'd brokered that truce, and I loved my granddaughter. In Manon, I saw myself at her age. Only I had been less outspoken and coarse. Which I put down to growing up during the eighties.

I had been more inspired by the poised and steadfast Queen Elizabeth rather than firebrands such as Germaine Greer.

While at college, I had shunned those students clutching copies of the Female Eunuch while proselytizing in matching punchy prose, preferring high tea at Claridge's instead. I'd soon learned that the pampered wives of powerful men carried more clout than the braless brigade, campaigning raucously for a sexual coup.

Not that I didn't believe in equality.

The queens of England were a clear example of how women could master the push and pull of power by using razor-sharp observation and juggling tasks as effortlessly as a trained dancer while reserving their hearts for those trusted few.

My daughter reclined on the chaise longue, looking like the wealthy woman she'd clawed her way to become. Especially in that Versace sheath and blood-red Louboutins. She just had to keep her mouth shut.

At least Manon was working at removing that gutter accent. I'd gotten rid of mine after Reynard had recommended clipped articulation if I wished to become a woman of substance.

I'd even read the book with that same title after seeing it lying around somewhere. Despite finding it an inspiring read, I wasn't about to traipse through the moors and work as a maid, only to get impregnated by the lord's son.

I went about it the easier way, by affiliating myself with a slippery character possessing all the right contacts and answers for me—a naïve eighteen-year-old who thought she'd met the man of her dreams.

Yes, I had been head over heels in love with Reynard.

However, looking back, it wasn't love that I'd felt, given that the sex was ordinary. It was his ticket into a glamorous world that I could only dream of inhabiting. A rich world, where intelligent minds mingled, dressed fabulously in designer, smelt like a heavenly garden, and spoke in clipped Queens English, uttering long, esoteric words. Back then, being that starry-eyed social climber, I had found a large word more of an aphrodisiac than the size of a man's penis.

Cary had it all—brains, beauty, and a nice, big, overactive penis to match.

Considering my considerable carnal appetites, it was ironic that I should marry a homosexual who, at the time, had been bisexual.

We had three lovely children to prove Harry's sexual fluidity, and paternity tests had confirmed his patrilineage. Something I'd done on the sly.

"Must I have a motive for being here? Can't I just want to bond with the family?" Bethany asked.

I studied her closely for a hint of sarcasm, but she returned a straight face. Something else she might have inherited from me.

"I need to know I can trust you, Bethany."

"Then tell me about my father, and I promise to stay away."

That winded me.

Though unexpected, her request shouldn't have surprised me. It was only natural.

But how could I tell her?

The truth meant exposing my heart.

And showing one's heart made one weak.

Something I'd learned the hard way... early in life.

OWNED BY A BILLIONAIRE is the fifth and final installment of
Lovechilde Saga.

ALSO BY J. J. SOREL

THORNHILL TRILOGY
   Book One Entrance
   Book Two Enlighten
   Book Three Enfold
SIZZLING STEAMY NIGHTS SERIES
   A Taste of Peace
   Devoured by Peace
   It Started in Venice
LOVECHILDE SAGA
   Awakened by a Billionaire
   Tamed by a Billionaire
   Chased by a Billionaire
   Corrupted by a Billionaire

   The Importance of Being Wild
   The Importance of Being Bella
   In League with Ivy
   Take My Heart
   Dark Descent into Desire
   Uncovering Love
BEAUTIFUL BUT STRANGE SERIES
   Flooded
   Flirted
   Flourished

jjsorel.com

Printed in Great Britain
by Amazon